Lycentia: Harrak's Scrolls

The Land of Betrovia
Book Two

Dave King

Copyright © 2012 Dave King

ISBN: 1479109290
ISBN-13: 978-1479109296

All rights reserved. No part of this publication may be reproduced, stored in a retrieval system or transmitted in any form by any means, electronic, mechanical, photocopy, recording or otherwise, without the prior permission of the publisher, except as provided by USA copyright law.

About the author

Dave King, retired high school English teacher, husband to Diana Frances King, and father of three was born in Topeka KS about the time JFK was thinking about running for President. He currently resides in the fine City of Jefferson MO with his beautiful bride. Since being delivered into this world, he has resided in four states and on two continents. It is hoped that the entirety of his experiences in those places has positively influenced his writing.

ACKNOWLEDGMENTS

To Diane
my dearest and ever-loving wife
of many wonderful years, who continues to be
both my greatest source of inspiration as well as
my most-exacting critic

To Lycentia's beta-readers
who offered not only wonderful insights into how
to improve the quality of the novel but who also
blessed me immensely with their sincere
excitement and encouragement

To T. J. Shreffler
of The Runaway Pen (runawaypen.com) for
finalizing Lycentia's cover

To Jesus Christ
Lord of all
who because of His great love
and faithfulness continues
to make all of this possible

CONTENTS

CHAPTER ONE 1
CHAPTER TWO 11
CHAPTER THREE 26
CHAPTER FOUR 46
CHAPTER FIVE 66
CHAPTER SIX 88
CHAPTER SEVEN 98
CHAPTER EIGHT 116
CHAPTER NINE 128
CHAPTER TEN 143
CHAPTER ELEVEN 164
CHAPTER TWELVE 180
CHAPTER THIRTEEN 194
CHAPTER FOURTEEN 215
CHAPTER FIFTEEN 232
CHAPTER SIXTEEN 251

INTRODUCTION

Lycentia ... the City of Light ... the city where finance, fellowship and faith are being blended together to produce a rosy future for all Betrovians.

Patrik, the recalcitrant innkeeper and Galena, his younger daughter, load up the wagon, lock up The Lonely Fox Inn and head east for Lycentia. The goal? To hand-deliver Harrak's scrolls, the ones Patrik discovered in a musty cave, to Oliver III, the Netherene High Priest. The problem? The scrolls are not what Patrik thinks they are! But how, if at all, can Patrik discover the truth before it's too late?

Who was this Harrak, the supposed author of these infamous scrolls? And why are the Lycentian Netherenes striving to eradicate Harrak's writings? Even to the point of killing those who express faith in those writings? Teophelus, the neophyte priest, is in love with both his calling and Patrik's daughter Galena: what are his motives for helping Patrik understand the eternal, life-giving secrets hidden within those scrolls?

Edelin, the conniving, self-serving and desperate thief who contemplated stealing the scrolls when he worked for Patrik, is nearly caught up in a battle between Betrovian militiamen and Haarigoian raiders. He escapes by finding refuge in a village on the edge of the untamed Plains of Dreut. Not long after arriving there, he disappears into the night after stealing what may be the most-valuable piece of jewelry he has ever possessed. How might this bauble lead Edelin into a future that no one would ever wish for?

Tamara is no longer the elder daughter of an innkeeper: she is now the wife of the King of Betrovia with the entire city of Lycentia at her beck and call. But why isn't she happy? Isn't this what she has always dreamed of? What, if anything, can bring her the happiness she desperately desires?

CHAPTER ONE

"Even when the corn does not tassel, the grapes do not ripen before insects destroy them, or even when the cattle conceive but do not deliver, Othleis is still to be praised. For he is The Creator; it is all according to His Plan."

"How much further can you travel today?" Dalten shouted over his shoulder. His head remained cocked at a slight angle as he listened for a response. As his horse continued moving east, he turned around to see how far his traveling companion was behind him. Even though his horse was traveling on the shady and narrow woodcutters' path at a fairly-moderate pace, Kristof's mount continued to lag. "Kristof! Can you hear me? Where are you? Tell me that you are still back there!" There was still no response. "The things I am forced to endure!" Dalten said as he pulled on the reins, bringing the dapple-gray mare to a complete stop. He then jerked hard on the reins, turning the horse around and stared down the road in the direction from which they came. Expelling a deep sigh, he crossed his arms and waited. About the time he was prepared to shout again, a blond-haired, slightly-younger man riding a white-speckled chestnut pony came around the bend.

"Why are you lagging so far behind me?" Dalten asked as Kristof guided his mount up along side him.

"I am going as fast as this tiny beast will allow," Kristof replied curtly. "If you want me to go any faster, then maybe we should trade?"

"Oh no you don't," Dalten chuckled. "Before we left Noran, I gave you the choice of horses." He reached over and patted the pony between his ears. "And you selected this fine specimen."

"I picked the pony because it is the smaller of the two horses and I – "

"Because I weigh a bit more than you? Because the mare is better-suited for a man as rotund as me?" Dalten interrupted. He then scowled and threw up his hands. "If you really want to trade horses, it matters not to me."

"No, no it is fine," Kristof replied. "There's no reason to get angry. I will try to make do. I will try to make this pony move faster. Let's just keep going." Dalten shook his head and again jerked the reins to turn his horse back in the direction in which they were headed. Before he gave the order for the mare to continue on down the path, he spun around again.

"If you think you can force yourself to go for at least another hour, we will have ridden just far enough for one day," he said. "Then we can stop and make camp," Dalten then added.

"Camp? In this part of the forest? Surely you are not implying that we sleep here tonight? In the forest?" Kristof whined.

"And what alternate plans might you be thinking of?" Dalten quipped. "There's no hostel here … and no one has built a residence of any kind on this nearly-abandoned woodcutters' path. And even if someone had, do you think I would venture the chance of us revealing our identity? Have you forgotten that just two days ago we abruptly ended our stint with the Noran militia? We are deserters, Kristof!" Dalten emphasized as he smacked Kristof hard on the arm. "You do not want to discover what Leitser would do to us if he ever found us!"

The two former Noran militiamen then continued to ride for a little more than an hour. Kristof successfully kept the chestnut-colored pony closer to Dalten's mare than before, but by the time Dalten had dismounted and was taking his things off the horse, Kristof and his pony arrived.

"This may be as good a spot as any," Dalten said as he looked up through the trees. "And clouds are moving in above us," he then added."Let's hope it doesn't start raining."

"Actually, a cool shower would feel quite nice right now," Kristof replied as his feet hit the ground. Before the sky became completely dark, they agreed to make camp in a small clearing not too far from the path.

"You gather some wood for starting a fire," Dalten said. "But don't make too large of a fire, though … no need to draw any unneeded attention to ourselves," he added as he again hit Kristof on the arm. "While you do that, I will go find us some water."

"But didn't you say," Kristof blurted out. "Didn't you tell me earlier that no one ever comes along this path?" Kristof countered. "So … if no one is around, how could we possibly be noticed?" Dalten stared at Kristof for a moment then took a deep breath.

"Why take a chance, Kristof!" he replied, pausing slightly after each word. "Why take a chance?" He then shook his head, grabbed a skin for collecting water and melted into the dense forest.

"*Why take a chance, Kristof?*" Kristof mocked. "Just how did I get myself into this mess? How did I allow myself to join up with that idiot? The more I think about Molic, the more I utterly detest him," Kristof muttered. "I know! I simply will not think about him anymore! Ha! From this moment on, Molic simply does not exist! Ha! Now that should work!" he chuckled as he began to gather the things needed to build a fire.

In the near-darkness, Kristof had no trouble in finding a half-dozen fairly flat stones and with them assembled a small fire-ring. He then grabbed some dried leaves and twigs and was about to lay a handful of larger sticks on top of them when a gust of wind suddenly blew nearly all of the leaves out of the ring. "Argh! I will have to gather them all over again!" he complained. As the much-cooler wind continued to flow out of the northwest, he finally positioned enough dried forest material into place and lit it.

The wind promptly extinguished his first attempt. So he tried again. The second was a success, but he had to position himself between the blustery breeze and the infant embers to keep them alive. As he crouched at the edge of the fire-ring, the sound of something moving through the dead leaves on the forest floor came from the other side of the woodcutters' path.

"Dalten! Have you found any water yet?" Kristof hollered in the direction of the disturbance. There was no response, but the noise continued. Kristof then stood up and began to squint to somehow see who – or what – was crunching that forest debris. "Dalten? Is that you?" Before he could say another word, two dark figures immediately crossed the path and entered the flickering circle of the campfire's orange-yellow light.

"Well, well, well, look at what we have here! It appears we have stumbled upon a young woodsman ... a truly-fine specimen! What think you, Truk?" The man was covered in darkly-tanned animal skins and pointed a jagged-edge short sword at Kristof.

"Might we have found what we have been searchin' for, Zut?" The second interloper wore a similarly-rustic outfit but instead of wielding a short sword, he displayed a spiked wooden mace which he menacingly twirled like a band-leader's baton.

"What be that, Truk?" The voice was dark, deep, and raspy.

"He be a hostage, that's what! This boy must be worth somethin' to somebody! All we gotta do is find out who wants him!" Both of the intruders then laughed menacingly. "And how much they would pay for him!"

"What ... what do you want with me?" Kristof interrupted as he slowly backed away from the fire. His left hand caressed the sword that was sheathed on his left hip but did nothing else with it. "I ... I have no money ... nothing worth stealing ... nothing at all and – "

"Wrong answer, boy! Wrong answer!" the first intruder shouted as he pointed the sword at Kristof's throat. "Now you've done it! What think you of us, boy? We are no common robbers? Did you hear, Truk? He's offended us! The boy thinks we be robbers!"

"Sad ... so very, very sad, my good friend," the second man replied. "After all we have suffered today ... and this is what we earn for our troubles! Labeled as *robbers*!" Both men then stepped closer towards Kristof and closer to the fire. The light from the flames revealed that the first intruder's face was covered with a thick, salt-

and-pepper beard while his friend's sported a dark but overgrown and unkempt mustache. "Zut, my dear brother, we must help this lad better understand – " Before he could express the thought, an arrow suddenly came whistling out of the darkness and buried itself deep into the middle of his chest, its iron head exposing itself on the other side. As if he had been clubbed with a ten-pound sledgehammer, the brute's body crumpled in a heap at the edge of the fire.

"Truk! Truk!" was all the second man could say before another missile found good lodging in his breadbasket. He screamed but then fell to his knees. Kristof looked around to see where the arrows may have come from. Then, from out of the darkness behind him, Dalten came out of the forest, and in his right hand was a longbow.

"Dalten! It … it was you!" Kristof exclaimed.

"Now who else would it be?" the dark-haired young man replied as he walked up to the fire.

"I … I thought you said that no one but us would be in this part of – "

"Kristof! Stop jabbering!" Dalten interrupted. "Take out your sword and finish them off!"

"What? Finish? Finish them off?!" Dalten then grabbed the hilt of Kristof's sword that had remained in its sheath the entire time and yanked it out.

"Take it and finish them! Now! Do it now!" he commanded. "Do you think these Haarigoians are going to lay there all night!"

"Haarigoians!" Kristof gasped. "Are you certain?" he asked just as the second interloper moaned and then started to stand up.

"Argh!" Dalten exclaimed as he let his bow fall to the ground. With Kristof's sword, he then ensured that the

Haarigoian would never stand up again. "There! Now it is your turn! Take the blasted sword!" He grabbed Kristof's right hand and forced the blood-stained weapon into it. "Finish off the other one! Do it now!" Kristof backed away.

"But … but I have never … I have never killed … anyone," he stammered.

"You are a militiaman! You have been trained! You know what to do! Now do it!" Dalten commanded as he pointed at the Haarigoian laying aside the campfire.

"Maybe … maybe he's … maybe he is already dead?" Kristof continued to mumble.

"Now, Kristof, now!" Dalten persisted. Kristof passively shuffled over to the first robber and grimaced as he pushed the sword slowly into his midsection.

"There! I did it!" he announced as he then quickly pulled it back out.

"Again! Do it again!" Dalten ordered. Kristof merely stared at the gory weapon that he now grasped with both hands. "Again! Make completely sure!" Kristof didn't move. "Bah! Give me the blasted thing then!" Dalten shouted as he yanked the blade away from the former stable-hand. The sole recipient of the Molic family fortune then rammed the shiny blade not once but twice into the highwayman's abdomen.

"There," he announced perfunctorily as he wiped the sword on Kristof's shirt before returning it to the sheath. "It is done. You have now officially killed someone."

=======================

After resigning from his position as stable-hand at The Lonely Fox Inn, Kristof returned to Noran, his hometown, to once again work at his father's haberdashery. But he soon tired of mending shirts, stitching pants and repairing leather goods. He soon began to wonder what else there was to do with his life. At the same time he contemplated the possibility of yet another career-change, he was coerced by Dalten Molic, along with a few other boisterous young men, into joining the local militia. Surprisingly enough, his father gave him his blessing, and that same day, that handful of Noran roustabouts men marched down the street and directly into Commander Leitser's office.

However, before too long that as well didn't turn out how he had hoped. Barely a month after signing up, a raucous band of ruffians – consisting primarily of Haarigoians but containing more than a few rebellious Rigarians as well – attacked Noran. The marauders killed and wounded close to a dozen townspeople and torched the northern half of the village in the process. They then retreated as quickly as they arrived but not without depositing within Kristof's psyche enough horrific images to fuel a lifetime of nightmares.

Because of the events of that day, Kristof retired from the Noran militia in much the same way he vacated his position at The Lonely Fox Inn. In the dead of night, as he was about to leave Noran before the Commander could discover that he was missing, Dalten ran up to him and announced that he, too, was leaving the militia. He also convinced Kristof to go with him to meet with one of the most-unusual residents of the small mining town. Because of that pre-dawn meeting, the two young deserters found themselves bound for Lycentia.

The afternoon after the excursion with the two Haarigoian highwaymen, Kristof and Dalten arrived at a hamlet five miles north of the capital city. Dalten assured his partner that staying at a hostel in this out-of-the-way woodcutters' hamlet would be better than seeking lodging in Lycentia. "We are, after all, deserters," Dalten emphasized again. "From this hamlet, we can safely travel to the city to learn the remaining details of our mission."

Late that night, primarily because of imbibing too much of a bottle of cheap Knaesin wine, Kristof finally fell asleep. But his time in bed was not uneventful. He was soon dreaming of his short but horrendous tenure in the Noran militia. The caustic images of the horrible encounter from the day before became intertwined with his memories of the battle in Noran. As his body rolled back and forth on the straw mattress, his subconscious mind picked one warrior in particular to focus on, one brutish Harrigoian officer that led the attack on Noran …

A man attired in blackened goatskin climbed down off his bone-gray steed and shuffled into the small and dingy cabin. In this cabin built amidst dark and mossy rocks near a shallow bay of brackish water, the leathery-skinned warrior tended to a wound to his right thigh.

Once the bandage was in place, he exited the cabin and re-entered quickly, carrying this time a Knaesin-steel sword, a large saber of valor and distinction; it graciously reflected the light of the cabin's solitary candle throughout the cramped hovel. The warrior then placed the sword next to other swords, axes and mauls that had already been meticulously placed on the wall …

"No! No!" Kristof screamed as he sprang out of bed. "No! It cannot be!"

"Kristof! What?" Dalten asked groggily. "What are you bellowing about?!" he added as he sat up and glared at the former stable-hand.

"That sword! A Lycentian sword! That cabin ... *his* cabin ... it ... it ... it is full of Lycentian weapons!"

CHAPTER TWO

"Those who wait for Othleis, who wait at his doorstep, who wait on the path for Him to pass by, they will be blessed with life abundant; they will attain His favor."

It was another muggy morning, another sultry example of what was sure to be an unusually warm autumn. That morning, the same morning in which Kristof and Dalten left Noran, Patrik's eyes opened late, much later than he had planned. The sunlight coming through the porthole window of his bedroom on the second floor of The Lonely Fox Inn. At first, the sudden brightness startled him, but then he became aggravated by it.

"Bah! Last night I told Galena that we had to leave early today for Lycentia. And what did *I* do? Oversleep! Bah!" With more frustration than consternation, he threw off his bedclothes and, as quickly as his fifty-five year-old body would allow, located the traveling clothes he had set out the night before. This outfit included the dark green shirt that Tamara, his oldest daughter, had ordered especially for him from the king's personal tailor. It was an amazing blend of silk and wool that he never would have purchased on his own. But his oldest daughter, who was also the young queen of Betrovia, insisted that he be fitted for it.

"Strange ... this feels looser than it did when I tried it on last Spring," he whispered. As he continued to dress, his stomach rumbled, notifying him that he had forgotten to eat dinner the evening before. Once he was attired for the day, he pulled open the door to his room, expecting to see Galena's door which was directly across the hall to be opened. But it wasn't.

"Galena!" he said gruffly as he knocked on the door to her room. "Galena! Are you still in bed?" He thought he heard a muffled groan from behind the pine-wood door. "I overslept. Come downstairs quickly and make us something to eat!" He knocked again, this time slightly harder than before. "Could you please tell me that you're going to get up?" Before he finished the sentence, his reddish-blond-haired younger daughter's head appeared through the slight opening in the door.

"Father, I … I do not feel well … my … my stomach hurts," she mumbled. "Can I go back to bed?" Because her hair nearly covered her face, Patrik couldn't see her eyes to detect any falsehood in her words.

"Stomach problems, eh? You had no complaints when…." The door closed abruptly before he could finish his sentence. "Now listen here, young lady! We were supposed to be on the road to Lycentia about right now!" From behind the door came the words: "I don't care." Instead of arguing with her, the innkeeper headed down the stairs, his stomach rumbling again.

Before he reached the bottom of the stairs, Patrik's left knee made a noise akin to someone stepping on a very dry pecan. "Hurmph! Not again!" he grunted, limping down from the last few steps onto the dusty hardwood floor. He rubbed the joint with his right hand, walked a few feet through the dining area, but stopped short of the pantry door. "This is just perfect … the knee has been fine for over a month ... now it chooses to act up! What a day this has already been!" He limped out of the dining room and into the pantry and subsequently felt a sudden coldness shoot up the leg that wasn't already in pain.

"What? Water! Of course ... last night's storm ... the roof leaked ... again!" Rainwater from the previous night's storm had created a large puddle that covered the pantry floor. Instead of getting angry, which he might have done any other morning, he simply pulled off the wet sock and plopped it on the butcher-block table in the middle of the room. Then he removed the dry one, placing it next to its wet sibling. With both feet fully exposed to the cold water, he moved from cabinet to cabinet looking for something to stop the noise emanating from his midsection. The fifth cabinet revealed a small loaf of dark rye bread, and next to it was a charcoal-sized chunk of cheese wrapped in brown paper. "Ah, breakfast at last," he sighed in relief.

Choosing to not endure the torture of standing in the cold water, the innkeeper took his first meal of the day into the dining room and sat down at the table closest to the pantry door. Holding the whitish-colored dairy product in one hand and the dark bread in the other, he thought about going back to the pantry to get something to drink. "Barefoot ... I can wait." The sun's morning rays mingled with the wind-blown treetops, and the interspersing of bright light and shadow entered the dining room through the four windows on the east side of the inn. Patrik stared at the sunlight as it bounced off the shiny dining room floor but then turned to see Galena, clothed in a heavy robe, coming down the stairs.

"Good morning," she mumbled softly, her strawberry-blond hair still covering most of her face.

"Well! And a fine 'Good Morning' to you, too! Look! There actually was something to eat!" he responded, holding up the small bit of cheese that remained.

"Give me a few minutes. I will put together something else," he heard her say as she sauntered through the pantry door. That "something else" could have been fresh eggs and ham and even some fried onions and potatoes. But it wasn't. It couldn't have been since every last one of the chickens had been taken to Noran and sold for barely what they were worth, and the potatoes and onions had been dug up and eaten or sold at the market as well.

"Father! The floor is covered with water!" she yelled from behind the pantry door

"Yes, don't you remember that the roof leaks now whenever it storms?" he responded. What he heard next was the slamming of cabinet doors.

"Ham. It's all I could find," she said a few minutes later, setting a plate covered with three slices of ham on the table. "Once the water is hot, I can brew some tea … if you would like some."

"Tea? Yes, a cup of hot tea would be very nice," her father said as he picked up the largest piece and began to nibble on it. It was not more than five minutes until she returned with two cups. She put one in front of her father and began to sip from the other.

"Aren't you going to sit down and eat your breakfast?"

"Stomach still hurts," she responded, blowing on the hot liquid before taking another sip. She pushed back her bangs that were laying over her forehead and, for the first time that morning, Patrik saw her eyes.

"What could be done make yourself feel better?" he asked, trying to smile.

"I suppose I could go back to bed," she said, moving towards the stairway. "If that would be fine with you?" She turned towards him and again pulled back the unkempt hair. She stood, transfixed, appearing to be waiting for an answer.

"Ah ... since we appear to be already behind schedule..." was all he could think to say. And with that, she quickly headed back up the stairs. The innkeeper picked up another slice of ham but this time, instead of taking one small bite, he shoved the entire piece into his mouth. The cup of tea came in handy for washing down the dried and much-too-salty pork. But it was not to be enough; his stomach growled once again while one more slice of ham remained on the plate.

Once the last piece was consumed, Patrik trudged back into the pantry and saw something that he hadn't noticed before. By the back door that opened out into the yard between the house and the barn was a rag mop and a the oaken bucket used for bringing in water from the well. Still shoe-less and with his stomach barely satisfied, he began to mop up the rainwater. As he cleaned up the mess, he thought about how to motivate Galena to come back downstairs and to help him finish packing the wagon for the trip to the capital city.

"Wait!" he exclaimed as he blotted up the last bit of cloudy and cold water. "Where are the scrolls? The barn? Are they still in the barn?" He quickly opened the back door and, while still shoe-less, scurried the thirty-or-so feet to the dilapidated structure that was used primarily as a shelter for his two horses. The barn also served as a makeshift workshop where he would create and repair small animal traps. But his life as a trapper seemed to have abruptly come to an end.

He pulled open the large and heavy door, and it creaked loudly. Once inside, he first patted the gray mare on the head and then scratched the muzzle of the younger, reddish-brown bay.

"Good morning, you two. Hope you're ready for a long journey today." They whinnied in unison which he translated as their request for fresh grain and water. "Yes, yes, I've not forgotten you," he said, grabbing their feed bucket that was on the workbench close to one of the two barn windows. He scooped up a mixture of a few pounds of corn, barley and oats and meticulously poured it into their feeder; Patrik took pride in never allowing a bit of grain to fall on the dust of the barn floor.

"In a few minutes, I'll be back to refresh your water. There's something I need to take care of first." Before he could even finish the sentence, both horses ceased looking at him and had begun crunching up their breakfast. Patrik set the bucket back on the bench, right next to one of the small animal traps that he had been repairing, and crouched down on the right side of it. From there he then pull opened a trapdoor covered by a thin layer of wheat-straw.

"Ah yes, they are still here. And thank you, Othleis, for reminding me about getting these before leaving for Lycentia," he said, looking upwards and out of the barn window. He then lifted a dark leathery pouch out of the shallow hole that had been dug in the hard reddish-orange clay. He tucked the pouch under his left arm and was about to leave the barn when he remembered that he promised to do one more thing for the horses. "I'll be right back with fresh well-water. Need to take these into the house first. I'm sure you both understand," he said as he pushed the barn door back into its original position.

"Father! What are you doing outside barefoot? Are you trying to catch cold?" Galena scolded as he walked back into the pantry, closing the door behind him. "Sometimes you make me wonder."

"You're up ... again! Might you be staying out of bed for awhile this time? I surely hope so since we are scheduled to head for Lycentia *sometime* today." Her furrowed forehead revealed displeasure with the sarcasm.

"I came back downstairs to find some honey ... you know ... to add to my tea. It might even make my stomach feel better," she answered with both hands planted squarely on her hips.

"The honey ... it's over there. See it? After I got a bit for my cup, I put it on top of the hearth," the white-haired, white-bearded innkeeper said.

"On top of the hearth? Father, why would you set the honey pot on the cooking hearth?"

"I didn't give it much thought ... I just put it there ... seemed like a logical spot at the time. By the way, didn't you notice that the floor was dry? Performing that task seemed more important than worrying about where to place the honey pot."

"Never mind ... it's not worth getting in an argument about," Galena said meekly. "Oh ... and thank you ... for taking care of the mess on the floor." Patrik's only response was to smile as he gently set the camel-brown leathery pouch on the table next to the socks. He then re-opened the back door, picked up the bucket that was placed right outside the door, and headed for the well, the inn's only source of palatable water. Galena, after adding a small spoonful of honey to her fresh cup of tea, swallowed the remaining tea from the cup. Then she picked up the pouch that her father had laid on the table.

"The scrolls ... so *that's* what he's all excited about," she grumbled. "Why does he still think Othleis has appointed *him* to take them to the priests in Lycentia? Teophelus ... he is much-more qualified than Father to deliver the scrolls to the high priest." She untied the pouch strings and pulled out a few sheets of the yellowish paper. "Oh, how I wish I could make sense out these things," she whispered as she was then distracted by an itchy spot in the middle of her back. She returned the papers to the table and went to find something to help her soothe the skin irritation.

"Galena! What are you doing here?!"

"What? What are you yelling about now?" She rushed back into the pantry, armed with a long wooden spoon in her right hand.

"My pouch! You opened the pouch! If you would but ask, I would gladly share these parchments with you! But you cannot be allowed to get into the pouch without my assistance!" She slammed the spoon that she had planned to use as a back-scratcher on the table very close to the pouch in question.

"I was only curious, that's all. I didn't think you'd mind. Even though they seem so *very* important, they cannot be *that* important for you to get so angry about me just *looking* at them!" She glared fiercely at him. "And wouldn't it be better if you allowed Teophelus to take them to Lycentia?" With that, she stomped out of the pantry and went back upstairs. As Patrik proceeded to count the pages to ensure that none were missing, the tea cup and spoon on the table rattled when the door to his daughter's room slammed shut.

"Good, they are all here. Everything … is here," he whispered.

Taking the empty pouch in one hand and the papers in the other, he went into the dining room and sat down at the table closest to the inn's front door. This was his favorite place to sit and sort out his plans for the day because the morning sunlight illuminated quite well whatever was placed on that table. Once all of the sheets were back in their proper order, Patrik first thought about returning them to the pouch. "Wait … I should review those passages that Teophelus helped me with the last time he was here." So, instead of shoving them back in, he leafed through the first few sheets until he found one particular page.

"Ah yes, this is it. Let's see if I can still make sense out of what's written here." With his right index finger, he pointed at a few lines in the middle of the hand-written document, furrowing his brow as he struggled to decipher what was before him. "*Time and time again*," he began to read aloud. "*The Creator has revealed* … no that's not it…. *The Creator has given* … yes, that's it … the word must be 'given' not 'revealed'. Now I'm remembering…" As he continued to first read aloud but then silently, he scratched his head that was, for a man of his age, still thick with an ample supply of long, white hair. Like his father before him, his haired lost most of its pigment before he turned forty.

The innkeeper grunted as the passages either reminded him of their meaning or persisted in hiding it from him. "Now then, here's the part the young priest got so excited about! '*The Central Lands are the home of all that the*

Creator will one day make pure; the green forests have…' concealed? Yes … it is concealed … *'have concealed for too long the path to purity. Soon they will not only reveal the path, but will also show the way to the source of life eternal'.*"

"Life eternal…" Patrik said, this time a bit louder than before. "But what to make of this 'eternal life' business? Bah! And why can't I remember if any of the Noran priests have talked with me about it? If this life … my life in this miserable patch of forest … is supposed to be eternal, wouldn't that mean that Dalneia could … might she … someday…" He leaned back in the chair, laid the page that he had been reading back on the table, and put his hands behind his head. He then allowed his mind to begin to drift off. He thought about a journey he and his wife had taken into the Rigar Mountains: that journey was their little adventure to Lutea Reast.

"We don't need to go to the temple," Dalneia said. "We can just turn around and go back home. I feel fine. Really I do."

"How can you say that you 'feel fine'? You have lost so much weight that you're as skinny as that red oak sapling I transplanted last fall," Patrik responded. "You haven't been able to eat anything substantial in nearly a week. The longer we wait, the weaker and thinner you get." He stood up and moved away from the bed to look out the window. "And there seems to be a break in the snowy weather right now. Surely it is a good time to head further up the mountain ... to head for Lutea Reast. It is as good as can be expected for it being so close to winter."

Even though the air in the dining room was warm and humid, he shivered as he remembered how the snow came down thick and heavy that day, the wind blowing as hard as he had ever experienced it. But, the morning in which they left the hostel, the sun appeared to make its way high into the sky quicker than usual. Patrik took that sign as a blessing of ample light and even some warmth for the journey. But much to his chagrin, not much heat at all accompanied its bright rays.

On both sides of the trail, the drifts were six feet or higher. As the wind's power persisted, however not as hard as the previous night, powder from the peaks of those drifts flew off and sparkled light-blue in the cold light as they settled on the path around the two travelers from the Great Forest. Patrik then smiled; as he walked slowly in front of the horse, he was somewhat entertained by the light show fabricated by the dancing flakes and the cool rays of the winter sun.

But, more often than not, he was forced to shade his eyes from the white rays, particularly when he glanced back at Dalneia who was huddled uncomfortably on the saddle. The blankets loaned by the Rigarian who ran the hostel were wrapped tightly around her to help provide insulation her frail frame needed against the frigid air. The image of those ornately-decorated blankets reminded Patrik of that old hostler: the innkeeper was surprised at learning that the crusty tradesman had been acquainted with his grandfather, Jespar Vellein. The elder Vellein's propensity for exaggeration, especially when sharing hunting stories, produced a another grin on the innkeeper's face. But that grin quickly returned to a frown as his thoughts careened back to the plight of his ailing wife pathetically clutching to the neck of that packhorse.

The day before they left the hostel for the last leg of the journey up the mountain to the temple at Lutea Reast, both of them rode on the back of the sturdy mount. But that was when the slope of the mountain wasn't as severe. And the snow at the lower elevations was only a dusting in comparison which also made it simpler for both husband and wife to ride. That day, however, presented much more of the white stuff and too steep of an incline for Patrik to sit in front of his wife to shield her from the wintry gusts.

"Do you know where we can stay, Patrik? I'm very tired and could use a drink."

"Our host told me that we need to ask any of the temple monks. They will know, he said, where we can find lodging."

The innkeeper then thought about the first monk they talked to upon reaching Lutea Reast. He was a younger man, probably at that time not much older than the innkeeper. That monk introduced them to not only the man who was to provide their lodging but to also arrange for Dalneia's much-needed lung treatments. This second monk's eyes were large but dark and his face, except for black and bushy eyebrows, was void of any facial hair – no mustache, sideburns or beard. And from what Patrik could recall, so it was with all the men of Lutea Reast. The monk, upon determining their reason for being there, led them to the cabin where they were to stay while Dalneia underwent the treatments.

Those irritating lung treatments began at dawn the very next day. The mountain village of Lutea Reast was known for its medicinal hot spring waters and people like

Dalneia, people who had contracted the mysterious and too-often deadly Noran mine lung illness, would venture to the temple to breathe in its moist vapors and bathe in its curative waters.

"Patrik, do you remember that time during that one winter ... when we were just children ... I don't know ... I suppose we were only five at the time ... and the snow was so deep that we had to wait for the adults to clear away paths so all of us could go outside? It was so much fun to run from the door of the house to the end of the path and see nothing but a wall of snow on both sides! Do you remember that?"

"Not sure I do. How am I supposed to remember things that occurred when I was only five years old? Wait, now maybe I can ... a heavy snow when we were growing up..."

"And do you also remember how we would sing? Especially when we played outside? Especially this song? Do you remember this one?

'Come along, dearest one, come along to the river's edge; Come along, dearest one, and drink from the cool waters.
Come, beloved one, and refresh your parched soul With the waters from the Rigars' whitest snows'?"

"Dalneia, you really shouldn't sing ... it can only be hard on your lungs. I think you should just breathe in and breathe out ... don't need to sing..."

"Why don't you sing with me? It really cannot hurt anything if you'd just sing with me?"

"No, for these treatments to have any effect, I think you should remain as quiet as possible and just breathe."

With the leathery pouch gripped tightly by his right hand, Patrik's thoughts turned to another time when he preferred quiet over singing. He had taken their girls, Tamara and Galena, with him to check traps; it may have even been the first time he allowed them to accompany him. He gave Tamara the larger of the two burlap sacks that were used to carry back the rabbits, etc. that would be found in the traps while Galena's task was to carry any back any traps needing repairs. She was also to carry an extra trap or two just in case any of them that had already been set had somehow become damaged. It wasn't like the girls singing their childish songs was going to disturb anything, but he grimaced as he remembered yelling at them that it was not proper to make so much noise when checking traps. It was his routine, his tradition, his *modus operandi*, to move silently through the trees, even though remaining silent had nothing to do with the effectiveness of setting and checking traps.

Patrik suddenly stood up as his thoughts inadvertently returned to Dalneia's treatments, and he slammed the pouch onto the table.

"But she never got better!" he yelled to himself. "Six days of sitting … immersed up to her neck in that putrid-smelling hot water … sucking into her lungs those noxious gases! And she just didn't get any better!"

"Father, what are you upset about now?" Galena had re-entered the dining room. She was fully-dressed in preparation for the proposed long ride to Lycentia and consequently her long hair that was entirely unkempt earlier that morning was now formally tied back into a single ponytail.

"Galena? You think I am upset? Me? Upset?"

"Of course you are! You were yelling about 'putrid gases' or something like that. Now don't tell me you are getting all riled up again about the trip to that temple? That time you and Mother traveled up into the Rigars?" She stood at the edge of the table, waiting patiently for a response. But she didn't look directly at him; her attention was drawn to a doe and a young fawn that had scampered across the road and had moved near the stand of scraggly cedar trees not far outside the dining room windows.

"And do you know those monks had the audacity to ask for … to demand … twenty gold pieces for those treatments? For treatments that didn't even work?" He slammed a fist on the side of the table that contained the scrolls, nearly ripping one of the pages in two.

"Yes, I know. You have fumed about this before," Galena responded as if she had been asked what she had just eaten for breakfast. "Too many times, in fact."

"I surely was not about to pay that much gold," he murmured as he sat down, wincing as the left knee responded again with a the crack of a dried pecan. "*Twenty* gold pieces…"

"How much did you give them?" She asked, her attention placed squarely again on his white-bearded face since the doe and her spotted fawn had merged with the cedars.

"Ten," was his answer, "I only gave that monk ten gold pieces … even though he said he wanted twice as many."

CHAPTER THREE

"Why do the people complain that their plans fail? It is because they rob Othleis; they steal from Him with their falsehoods and lies. Their money is offal; it is used for the wrong reasons. In order to please the Creator, gain His wisdom; riches may come soon after."

"Let's leave now, Father," Galena said, with more than a hint of irritation in her voice. "And you win. I can't think of anything else to say to convince you that we must remain here." She then climbed up into the wagon and positioned herself as far away from the innkeeper as she could: she then plopped down at the very back of the wagon and hung her bare feet over its end. The air was still as moist and as thick as it was earlier in the day, and the sun was beginning to peer out from behind the thick, cauliflower clouds.

"Good!" was all Patrik could muster as he then climbed onto the wagon, patting the coffee-brown mare on the rear. "We should be able to make decent time since the road may not as muddy as I first thought," he added as he grabbed the reins and urged the horses to head east. With the rays of the sun behind them, and the wagon stocked with – conceivably – all but their least-essential belongings, Patrik looked ahead and sighed. "Yes, it appears that we are finally making our way to Lycentia," he whispered.

The trip from The Lonely Fox Inn to the capital city usually would take most of three days; since they were leaving a half-day later than planned, they wouldn't be entering the city gates until the end of the week. Patrik then smiled. "And this weather is nearly perfect for the trip!" he exclaimed. Consequently, he shook the reins to urge the horses to pick up their pace.

Close to hour after leaving the inn, Galena repositioned her body so she could lay down and stare up at the azure-blue sky spread out above her. The clouds had all but misted away, and the rays of the late-afternoon sun forced her to squint. She then took a deep breath and began to sing at the top of her lungs:

> "Red bird! Blue bird! Fine yellow bird!
> Can you sing, sing, sing for me?
> Might you sing your wonderful songs for me?
> The air is crisp and clean;
> The rain, the rain, has come and gone,
> Has come and gone to make it clean;
> The air is so very crisp and clean!
> So won't you sing, sing, sing for me?"

"Aha, you're awake! And that song! It's one I haven't heard in ages! What cajoled you into selecting that tune at this particular moment?" Patrik asked, looking back momentarily to see Galena prostrate on her back, waving both hands back and forth.

"No reason. Must things always have a reason with you?" She released a deep sigh. "Maybe it was a lark … the one that flew over my head a minute ago. Or maybe not.

Must I have a reason to sing that song?" she responded without looking at him.

"*Must* you always get so snippy with me, young lady?" The innkeeper teased. "It … it is just that you haven't said a thing since we left home and now … completely out of the blue … you start singing a song that the two of you, you and Tamara, sang when you were little children!" He almost turned around to look back at her again, but this time the wagon was quickly approaching a sharp curve, so he chose instead to focus on what was ahead.

"My, my! Look at who's getting *snippy*. It is such a beautiful afternoon, and I want to sing. Can't you *just* leave it at that?" Galena then sat up, tossing back her long bangs and glaring at him to make her point.

"Fine. Sing all you want … whatever you like. I am not at all concerned," he concluded with a slight smile detectable on his face. And with that, she laid back down, again waving her hands in the air and singing the same song, but a few decibels louder than before.

"If my memory serves me correctly, you two would sing that song over and over again," Patrik muttered to himself. "While your mother and I…" he then added with more volume than before. But no response came, even though none was anticipated. Before long, the singing ceased because the innkeeper's younger daughter had fallen asleep. And so, the monotony of the humming of the wagon wheels against the moist ground caused both the end of the spontaneous serenade as well as her father's thoughts to move on to more important concerns.

His stomach had been quiet since he climbed up onto the wagon, but the rhythm of the wagon wheels on the bumpy road caused it to become unsettled again. Frowning from the sudden discomfort, he began to think of a time when, as a teenager, he had gotten ill. It was unusual for him to get sick, but when he did, he ended up being stuck in bed for an entire day if not more. He remembered being in bed and being so drowsy from the stomach pains – as well as the fever – that he lost track of how long he had been there. But he had no problem remembering one detail from this particular bout. His mother had told him that he when he was in that foggy place between sentience and unconsciousness, he would sporadically cry out, fearing that he was about to die.

It was right after he had awakened from one of these crying spells that he remembered seeing Dalneia come into the small room that he shared with his younger brother Pieter. Dalneia came into the room, softly asked how he was feeling, then placed a small basket at the foot of the bed. Embarrassed, his only response was to quickly pull the blanket up over his head and say: "Thank you." Before leaving the room, she added that the basket contained a pot of freshly-made soup and a loaf of bread. But it wasn't just any bread: it was her first attempt at baking black-bean bread – fashioned after his own mother's recipe. All he could again muster was another "Thank you" and with that she backed out of the room, closing the door behind her.

He remembered that his mother then came into the room and asked him if he felt strong enough to sample what was in the basket. Since he hadn't eaten anything for more than a day, he relished the idea of trying to put down something. The soup was chicken, and it was still warm while the bread was definitely black-bean. But it was not warm; it had almost no flavor at all, he chuckled at the memory. "And it was so dry that I had to dunk it in the soup to make it palatable!" he said out loud.

Still directing their two horses down the muddy road, Patrik could not help but grin from ear to ear as he thought about that day. As far as he could remember, that was the first time Dalneia had prepared any food for him. At that moment, as he allowed the horses to continue their methodical pace, he reviewed – even evaluated – the entirety of her culinary skills. But, as he tried to categorize certain dishes she would routinely make, even pies and such, he soon began to create quite an appetite. So, instead of thinking more about his wife's cooking, he chose to just let his mind move on to something less "hunger-inspiring."

After helping the horses to negotiate a few more curves down this highway that connected Lycentia to the Haarigoian territory known as the Plains of Dreut, the innkeeper planned who he would need to talk to once they arrived in Lycentia. The sun was beginning to set behind him, but, because of a few natural landmarks on both sides of the road, he determined that they were still at least ten miles from the place where they could safely stop for the night. He looked back over his left shoulder to see if Galena was still sleeping, and she was. In the dimmer light of dusk, the expression on her face caused him to think of both her older sister and her mother. And for some reason, he began to get teary-eyed. He then turned back around just in time to miss hitting a deer that had decided to search for something to nibble on in the middle of the road. Before he could pull back on the reins to signal a warning, the horses kept moving forward, as if to make their intentions clearly known. But the young buck quickly bounded back into the dark forest, and what might have been a serious accident was thankfully averted.

The innkeeper took a deep breath. "Now that was much too close. Thank You, Othleis, for keeping us from hitting that deer," he whispered. "And no thanks to you two for seemingly wanting to ram into the beast!" he yelled. He had never collided with any creature before and categorized the near-collision as a once-in-a-lifetime occurrence. "Yes, Othleis, you have protected me once again," he said prayerfully as he then contemplated other times that the Creator had protected him from physical harm.

"What? What was that?" Galena asked, interrupting his thoughts.

"Oh, you're awake again," her father replied.

"Awake? Why, I was never asleep," was her quick response. "Why did the horses suddenly speed up?"

"Is that what woke you up? There was a large buck in the middle of the road ... and we almost hit him! Before I could do anything, the horses appeared determined to run right into him! It's funny, though. I don't remember ever being that close to a deer in the middle of the road before. And as I think about it, that buck was sporting a very unusually-shaped rack! Why, if I were to label it, I would say that one side was much wider than the other!"

"A deer? You mean there are still deer in this part of the forest?" she asked as she laid back down.

"Why wouldn't deer be in this part of the forest? And when did you become so opinionated about the deer population of central Betrovia?"

"Oh, I don't know ... I guess I overheard Kristof talking about them with someone ...."

"Aha," Patrik said, scratching his head. "What could cause you to believe anything our former stable-hand had to say?"

"Father! Now you're getting angry about Kristof again!" she yelled. "I'm sorry I even brought him into the conversation."

Kristof, former employee of The Lonely Fox Inn, had tenured his resignation a few months before the innkeeper and his budding naturalist of a daughter loaded up the wagon to venture forth to Lycentia. He had worked for Patrik for over four years before leaving the inn to return to Noran to work again for his father. This wasn't what Patrik had desired, and he surely did not appreciate the youngster's method of quitting: packing up before dawn one morning and leaving a hastily-scribbled note in the barn to inform his employer of his plans. But might the innkeeper still harbor some ill-will towards his former stable-hand? Patrik sighed loudly, shook his head, and then pulled back on the reins, bringing the wagon to an abrupt stop.

"Now what are you doing? Why are we stopping?" Galena asked.

"I need to explain something ... to clarify once and for all. And right now appears to be as good a time as any," Patrik declared. "Even though Kristof and I did not see eye-to-eye on many things, I fully appreciate the young man's efforts as well as his congenial attitude. I might even go as far to say that he was a considerate and polite young man. Furthermore, I cannot say that I remember him complaining much about anything."

"Oh, Father, you cannot be serious! A day did not go by without you saying to either me or Tamara that you wished Kristof would either grow up, take life more seriously or ... basically ... be more responsible. Surely you do not expect me to believe that you are changing your opinion about him now?"

"I ... I don't know. Am I really altering my attitude towards him? Why yes, I suppose there were times when I was a little ... disenchanted ... with his behavior ... but overall, I – "

"Oh, now I know what this is about! You *miss* Kristof!" Galena shook a taut finger at the innkeeper.

"Miss him? Why not in the least! That is entirely preposterous! Far too many times, I was the one to fix something that he broke ... or to find something that he had lost. Or even complete the chores that he had forgotten or chosen to not even complete!"

"Confess, you silly man, confess! You miss him! You most assuredly do," she said with haughty confidence and laid back down. Of course, Patrik knew that he was not wishing that Kristof was still his employee. But he didn't want to continue arguing with Galena about such a preposterous supposition. So after a few minutes of silence, it appeared that the conversation had ended as abruptly as it began. The silence then allowed Patrik to return to thinking about something that he wanted to think about: the reason for going to Lycentia in the first place. "It is my duty ... my calling to present the scrolls to the Netherenes and hopefully to Oliver III, the high priest of the Netherenes personally. And that is what I am going to do," he whispered confidently.

But was it going to be impossible to merely walk into the Lycentian temple and request an audience? His experiences with the Netherenes in Noran proved this point rather well. The only way he was granted an audience with the elder Noran priests to discuss the scrolls in the first place was with the help of Teophelus, a young priest who had formulated a somewhat curious – if not casually frustrating – relationship with Galena. Earlier that year, the neophyte had gained the status of a full-fledged Netherene due to determined studying and dedicated servitude in the Noran temple. And because of his enthusiasm about the scrolls, he agreed to instigate an opportunity for Patrik to meet with the head priest in Noran to discuss the veracity of Harrak's prophecies contained in those parchments.

Patrik's grasp on the reins became even tighter as he wished that Teophelus had accompanied them on this trip. However, the innkeeper believed that it was the Creator's will for him to deliver the scrolls to Oliver III personally – without any outside assistance. "After all," Patrik whispered, "it was Othleis who allowed me, and me alone, to discover the scrolls that were hidden in Felegian."

Teophelus periodically visited the inn to not only spend time with Galena but to also help Patrik better understand the intricacies of Harrak's writings. And it was during one of those sessions when the young priest offered to accompany him in delivering the scrolls to the Netherene authorities in Lycentia. The innkeeper graciously refused, believing that the more Teophelus pressed this issue with his Netherene superiors, the less chance he would have to be promoted out of Noran and into the more-influential temple in Lycentia. During another visit, Teophelus then brought up an interesting point: someone else, someone other than Oliver himself, may want to be familiarized with the scrolls. This someone, Teophelus emphasized, would be Viktor the Prophet.

Viktor, Oliver III's chief spokesman and – more often than not – his most-adamant critic, had reached a high level of notoriety since taking up residence in Lycentia. He was not much older than the Netherene high priest and, like Oliver, believed that he too was destined for a life of celibacy, the path that only the most-serious Netherenes would take to prove to the Creator their desire for purity. Viktor was a tall man, nearly a foot taller than Oliver, but drastically thin. His skin was deathly pale – a pallid tone like that of someone who purposely shunned exposure to the melanin-inducing rays of the sun.

Even though the experiences at the twilight of their careers were intertwined and even quite similar, those at the dawning were distant and very dissimilar.

Oliver, the eldest of three children, grew up in a small village east of Lycentia, a quiet hamlet nestled in the foothills of the Knaesin Mountains. As he matured, he quickly mastered many of the most-important rudiments of Netherene teachings. Like a veteran chef who methodically commits to memory the ingredients and step-by-step routines of his most-cherished recipes – even to the exact amount of salt or sugar to add at just the right moment – he would assault the priestly podium wherever it was to be found. From that spiritual precipice, he would then attempt to impress his audience with his eloquent interpretations of Netherene doctrine.

Besides being an expert in the priestly edicts, he, ironically, had also attained notoriety as a caring and benevolent spiritual leader. His greatest spiritual achievement, according to those who monitored this meteoric advance through the ranks of the Lycentian Netherenes, was his success in brokering a truce between two obstreperous clans of Knaesin foresters. It was believed that until Oliver determined to journey east into the mountains to craft that treaty that the ill-will between the heads of those two clans would too soon boil over into a bloody feud.

    Viktor, on the other hand, appeared one cold winter's day seemingly out of near-obscurity. The rumor was that he had grown up in the Plains of Dreut, but all that was actually known of him was what the lanky shaman himself determined to disclose. Nearly all that Patrik would discover about this mysterious man, Viktor The Prophet, came to him via his conversations with Teophelus as the young priest helped him with the scrolls…

    "Yes, Viktor comes from the Plains of Dreut … from one of the small fishing villages that dot the coast of the Great Sea. At least that is what everyone in Lycentia has been led to believe."

    "But is there no one who can confirm his heritage? I mean … shouldn't the history of someone so powerful … someone with as much influence in all the temples throughout Betrovia … especially with such influence over the high priest himself…"

    "It is possible that someone still alive on the coast knows about Viktor's heritage. But there appears to be no way of knowing exactly the specifics of his lineage."

    "So what do you think is his family's history?"

    "From what Viktor himself has aloud to be known, his father was Haarigoian while his mother was a Muad."

    "Muad … and Haarigoian?! How is it possible? I cannot believe that a man working so closely with Oliver, the Lycentian high priest, could be both a Muad and a Haarigoian!"

"It is hard to believe, but might it be possible that Othleis' intends for someone with the blood of our enemies flowing through his veins to be in a position of such influence in Betrovia?"

"Othleis? How could? Teophelus, I must say that I will always have a difficult time accepting anything of value from a Haarigoian – even if he is the second most-powerful man in Lycentia!!"

However, Teophelus knew one thing about this supposedly half-breed prophet but did not divulge to Patrik during these conversations about the parchments: Viktor, through the Haarigoian side of the family, could be a descendant of Harrak – the author of the scrolls that Patrik intended to deliver to Lycentia! And it's not that the neophyte intentionally omitted that information. It just never entered his mind to pass this detail onto the innkeeper: the prophecies contained within those parchments may have been written by an ancient enemy of Lycentia!

====================

Deciding that it was too dark to safely maintain their current speed, Patrik encouraged the horses to proceed at a slower pace. "That hostel can't be much farther," he mumbled. "And I do wish that I could determine how much farther." He then let loose of the reins with his right hand to rub his eyes. "I hate getting old … cannot see as well as I used to … especially in the dark! Bah! I cannot make out a blasted thing!" Patrik blurted out. "Galena! I need you! Galena! Wake up and come up here!"

"Now what is the problem?" she said as she slowly sat up and stretched.

"Could you come up here? I should be able to notice at least a few familiar landmarks … but I cannot. I would like to know how close we are to that hostel we stayed at the last time we traveled to Lycentia."

"Since my eyes are much younger – and therefore stronger – than yours, I will use them to decipher where we are," she responded with a hint of superiority in her voice. Since the horses were proceeding at a walk and not a gait, it was not unsafe for her to climb over their belongings and to plop down on the bench-seat to the right of her father. She then squinted and looked first down the road and then to the right and to the left. The forest was not that thick on either side of the highway, but the lack of daylight made it appear to be an impenetrable wall.

"I … I do not recognize anything. Are you sure we are even on the correct road?"

"Don't be absurd, young lady! There is no other road that we could even be on," he responded. But had he been day-dreaming that much that somehow the horses had veered off the highway and onto an obscure side road?

"I suppose we will then keep heading east on this road," Patrik decided with some uncertainty in his voice. "We are bound to soon come upon some place where we may find food to eat and a bed for the night." Galena expelled a long and boisterous yawn.

"Or we could simply turn around and head back to the inn and – " was all she could say before the wagon suddenly lurched forward and then leaned violently to the right. Galena had started to stand up and return to her napping spot in the rear of the wagon when she was thrown violently over its right side and directly into the ditch. The horses, sensing that something was wrong, stopped their forward motion and waited for further orders.

"Galena! Where are you? Say something! Are you alright?" Patrik yelled. He was still in the wagon but barely. "It was good that we were not going too fast," he whispered. "Galena! Can you hear me?" He let go of the reins and climbed down from the wagon. What had been a mostly-sunny day had turned into a murky, cloudy evening, so there was no light from the sky to illuminate the scene of the mishap.

"Galena! Answer me! Please answer me!" He thought he heard moaning and moved towards it, attempting to be careful so as not to stumble and fall on the person he was looking for. "Galena! Can you tell me where you are!" He again heard a soft moan that was a bit louder than before.

"Father…"

"Galena! Oh, thank you, Othleis! I found her!" Patrik knelt down in the water-laden ditch. "Can you hear me, Galena?

"You … you can stop yelling now … and please get off my leg … you are standing on my leg."

"You are alive … good … this is so very good! Thank you, Othleis!"

"Ouch! And it is not … not so good! My head…" she said as she expelled another painful moan.

"Where does it hurt?"

"My head … I think I landed … on something hard … too hard. Father, it really hurts," she mumbled as she began to cry.

"Your head? Maybe you should just lay there ... don't get up too quickly. Are you dizzy? Wait here! And don't move."

"Father, this ditch is full of ... of cold water ... I have to move! Come back and help me to get up!"

"Yes, that would be best," he replied and ran back to help her to her feet. But just as she stood up, she abruptly collapsed into his arms. The innkeeper staggered backwards a few steps to regain his balance then negotiated a stronger grip on her before attempting to climb out of the ditch. He then headed toward the wagon. Once there, he laid her down on the much-drier roadbed behind it and then sat next to her.

"Now what are we going to do?" he asked. For a few moments he stayed by her side and even softy rubbed her head in an attempt to alleviate the pain. "The wagon? What caused it to lurch like it did?" he whispered to himself and then stood up to investigate. It only took a second to discover that the right front wheel had completely come off.

"This is not good ... how ... how are we going to repair this?" Instead of pondering the ramifications of their current plight, he began to rummage through the wagon's contents. He soon located a small oil lamp and, once it was lit, set it on the ground close to Galena. He gasped as the what lamplight revealed: a fair amount of blood had oozed out of a cut on the back of her head onto the roadbed. Thankfully, though. it had already begun to coagulate. Patrik then stood back up, grabbed a rag from out of one of the baskets and started to wrap it around her head.

"Ouch! What are you doing?" Galena suddenly spouted.

"Your head ... there's a cut on the back of your head. I ... I need to keep it clean," he replied.

"But why so tightly? You ... you don't have to make it so tight."

As the two adventurers sat in the middle of the highway, the wind abruptly changed direction from out of the southeast to the northwest. This volume of air was colder, and the light from the lamp flickered with each northerly gust. Galena managed to finally stand up on her own, and she watched her father make a closer inspection of the wagon.

"So what should we do, Father?" she asked as he examined the hub where the right front wheel should have been.

"I suppose I could continue down the road on one of the horses until I run into someone – "

"We have two horses,.. we both could go..."

"No, that would not work. One of us should stay with the wagon ... someone is bound to come along soon."

"I don't like that idea! You surely cannot be serious about leaving me here in the middle of road ... in the middle of the night ... to fend for myself if and when *someone* does come along!" Galena crossed her arms across her chest which told Patrik that she was not going to be persuaded otherwise.

"Then we both sit here ... and we wait," was the only thing the innkeeper could think to say even as the north wind began to blow even harder and colder.

Barely an hour had passed when something coming from the west could be heard. The noise was made by a caravan consisting of a few wagons along with a handful of riders. The travelers stopped just shy of the light cast by the oil lamp that Patrik had set on the back of his wagon.

"Hello and good evening!" Patrik called out.

"And a good evening to you, sir," was the response that came from the first wagon. The greeting was from a short and stocky individual who adroitly hopped down from the wagon and then walked up to the innkeeper. As the man moved into the light that was cast by the oil lamp, his loose-fitting but ornate and multi-colored tunic, dark leathery pants and long hair that was pulled and tied back behind his head revealed that the stranger was surely a Rigarian. Patrik swallowed hard but determined to not reveal any fear.

"What seems to have occurred here?" the man asked.

"A wheel broke away from our wagon," Patrik answered as he pointed towards the damaged area. The Rigarian looked at the bare hub and shook his head.

"And where might you be bound?" he then asked.

"Lycentia," Galena responded. "But it was not my idea." Patrik scowled at her, but the man's expression stated that he didn't see it.

"I am called Khel Tain," the Rigarian said, "And we as well are destined for the capital city. Three days previous we vacated the Plains with our wagons full of wool. Might you be needing any assistance?" he asked.

"That would be wonderful – especially if you could convince my father to turn around and go back home!" Galena quickly answered, and Patrik's face again revealed his displeasure with her for taking the initiative to converse with the stranger.

"Yes, any help you can provide would be greatly appreciated," the innkeeper said. "That is, if you think you have the time."

"Ha! Your wagon sits midst the road, and I think not that my carts might negotiate around it. Assisting you appears to be our only solution." And with that, the Rigarian and who then introduced themselves as his two sons helped Patrik to temporarily reattach the wagon wheel. And while the men labored in the increasingly-blustery conditions, Galena sat in the second wagon with the wool-trader's wife who helped clean the dried blood from Galena's reddish-blond hair,

"Who is in the other cart? The one behind this one?" Galena asked as the Rigarian woman worked on the blondish mat encrusted with blood and mud.

"The wounded," the lady replied.

"Wounded? Where they in an accident like I was?"

"No," was the response. "Robbers … they attacked us … not far from the Plains," she said.

"That's horrible!" Galena said. "Who were the robbers? Did you kill all of them? And those who are hurt? Are they going to recuperate?"

"It depends," the woman said as she continued to work with Galena's hair. "The girl … her left leg … was cut badly. There is hope that there will be no infection. If so, she should recover soon. But the boy…."

"A girl and a boy? Are the wounded ones … all children?" The woman stopped and began to cry softly.

"Our men … they drove off the Haarigoians – "

"The robbers were Haarigoian? But I thought that Haarigoians were at peace with Rigarians?" The woman wiped her eyes and looked away.

"Some Haarigoians ... those evil, dark-hearted Harrigoians ... are animals ... they do not deserve to be at peace with anyone," she offered amidst her sobs.

"But the boy? You were going to say something about the boy?"

"The boy ... his wound is much-more serious," she replied, and began again to cry harder. "Those monsters ... they almost took him! They almost took our little Oriek! They almost took him away from us! But Khel ... he is such a brave and mighty warrior ... Khel rode after the brute that grabbed Oriek! Khel killed him and rescued our boy!"

"Your husband?" Galena asked with a definite amount of disbelief in her voice. "That short man helping Father with the wagon wheel? He rescued the boy? All by himself?"

"My husband is a great Rigarian warrior!" the woman exclaimed. "He not only killed that dark-hearted Haarigoian but also removed *this* from his person!" Khel Tain's devoted wife then reached behind Galena and latched onto a burlap bag. "Here! This is proof of the mighty warrior that is Khel Tain of Rigar!" she announced as she pulled out of the bag a black-haired, black-bearded head complete with golden nose-ring attached.

Once the repairs were completed, Patrik coaxed the horses to move closer to the ditch on the right side of the highway to allow for the wool caravan to pass by. As they barely squeezed to the left of his wagon, Patrik shouted out another word of thanks. Galena then blew a kiss towards the caravan-master's wife. As they watched their rescuers move eastward on the highway, the wind commenced to blow even harder than before. Patrik then grimaced at the few large snowflakes that accompanied it. Galena mumbled incoherently and then reached back into the wagon to grab another blanket to bundle up against the cold.

Neither father nor daughter uttered another word as Patrik signaled to the horses to once again make their way towards the capital city. But Patrik, concerned that the wheel may come off again if they trotted too rapidly, determined to proceed at a slightly-slower pace than before. Before he had a chance to complain again about not noticing anything familiar landmarks, Galena shouted and pointed at a small structure nestled within a stand of cedars on the left side of the road. Although it was not the hostel Patrik had anticipated patronizing, the innkeeper decided to stop and investigate it.

CHAPTER FOUR

"The Creator, Othleis Himself, desires to give the woman victory over the Dark Ones.
Mother, do not despair when the Dark Ones steal your loved ones;
do not lose hope as you mourn your dead.
Your victory comes when you give Him the glory in the midst of your mourning.
For He alone will have the complete victory."

Deep from within a mine almost forty miles north of Noran, a young man clad in thick, protective leather and sporting a crude but rudimentary iron-headed pickax released a loud and long yawn. He then removed one of the leather gloves that kept his hands from being cut as he gathered up the jagged bits of iron ore his pick knocked out of the dark wall. With this bare hand, he attempted to wipe away the gray dust that had collected on his face. To his left were three other young men, all about the same age and all similarly-attired. To his right was an older gentleman who, even though he wore the same uniform as the young man and his companions, closely examined the wall to determine where those who were using pickaxes should next demonstrate their pick-wielding skills.

At the end of yet another long and arduous day, as the young miner was leaving the mine, he failed to duck down right before exiting the dark tunnel and consequently banged his head on the rock above the mine door. A wound like that to the forehead can produce a copious amount of blood, and this wound just so happened to be one of those. The gash was deep enough to keep the flow of blood going at a precarious pace. Even though he thought he had stemmed the flow as he prepared for bed that night, it commenced once again.

As he lay there staring up at the dirt and timber ceiling of his crudely-constructed mountain hut – pressing down on the wound to hopefully stop the bleeding – in that dark ceiling above him he suddenly pictured a strange but vaguely-familiar white creature. Was it a raccoon? A rabbit? The creature stared back at him as he stared up at it.

Then, before he could think anything more about it, the creature began to speak to him. Was he actually using words that could have been heard by anyone? Or were its thoughts being sent directly into the young man's mind? It told him to not be afraid but to pay close attention to what he was about to say. It then began to tell him about the Creator's plans for the people of Betrovia. It told him that Othleis was going to send The Advocate who – through the performing of amazing deeds and powerful preaching – would remind the people of the soon return of Latreies, the Lord of the Great Forest. The creature then declared that The Creator had appointed the young miner to be a messenger of this good news and to deliver it to all who reside in the Great Forest. He also said that if the miner responded positively with all of his heart to this command, he would be rewarded dearly for his obedience.

The young miner continued to listen, enthralled not only by the powerful words but also by the calm, loving and peaceful way in which the creature delivered them. But before he could voice any of the questions that were racing though his mind, the serene, white face quickly vanished.

Because the miner chose to immediately took the vision of the white forest creature to heart, he also chose to put down his pick ax – the tool willed to him by his miner father – and moved away from his mountain abode and the region of many generations of humble and hard-working miners before him. Because he had grown up in and around this particular mine, he could not see himself living in a cabin made of mountain dust and wood. So he left the Rigar Mountains and took up residence in a cave in a remote valley on the northern edge of the Great Forest. While living in that cave, he began to write down all that he could remember the creature telling him. And not long after he had recorded what he had remembered, the creature visited him many times more. After each vision, he would record as much as he could remember of what the creature had shared with him.

Suddenly, this pointy-snouted messenger of the Creator visits stopped. For nearly a month, the creature failed to appear and speak to him. He took this sudden and unannounced conclusion to the visitations as the signal that it was time to move out of the cave and begin to share what he had written on those parchments. Therefore, he headed out of the valley, towards the only logical place to begin sharing with the people of the Great Forest what he had been commanded to share. The former miner headed for Sheu Leun, the only town in the Great Forest that he knew anything about.

When he finally arrived in Sheu Leun, the town that one day would become the great city of Lycentia, he was soon recruited by the Netherenes who had recently begun to seek disciples there. However, at that time in the early history of Sheu Leun, shamans who hailed from the Knaesin Mountains were the strongest source of any spiritual enlightenment for the open-minded residents of Sheu Leun in particular and the Great Forest as a whole. Even though his teachings differed very little from the Netherenes' edicts and precepts, they were accepted by only a few of the townspeople. His followers, however, soon began to outnumber those who took to heart the Netherenes' teachings.

Those who listened to Harrak, the former miner from the Rigar Mountains, those who were excited about the soon advent of The Advocate, chose to emulate Harrak's lifestyle. They chose, like he had, to focus on living a life of purity and love for both the Creator and their fellow man. Not many of his fellow Netherenes believed that Harrak had been appointed by the Creator to be the messenger of this amazing prophesy. Those he considered his friends told him that if was to remain much longer in Sheu Leun, he would have to cease teaching about the coming of The Advocate. They feared that the rank and file Netherene priests as well as the Knaesin shamans envied the former Rigarian mine-worker and that they might soon be driven to act upon this jealousy. Harrak shook off these testimonies of negativity and continued to preach, teach and amass a loyal group of followers.

This Rigarian miner transformed-into-missionary sent to the people of the Great Forest of Betrovia died before he turned thirty. His followers attributed his death to overwork, but there were rumors that his passing was due to something a bit more insidious. Before giving up residence in this world and moving onto the next, he exhorted the members of his inner circle – those who were at his bedside to witness his passing – to take all of the parchments – the compilations of the visions – and to keep them safe.

That small group of followers did more than protect the scrolls: they began to make copies and distribute them in and around Sheu Leun. Not long after Harrak's death, the Netherene leadership – because of their jealousy of the power of the scrolls – summarily outlawed the Rigarian miner's writings. Consequently, the propagation of Harrak's parchments was forced underground. Since the information contained in those pages communicated that a life committed to loving and serving not only Othleis but one's fellow man was such a contrast to the legalistic dogma that for some time had been disseminated from the pulpit of the Sheu Leun temple, Harrak's followers began to refer to themselves as Lyce-Tuereons: the "light-bringers."

======================

After the innkeeper and his youngest daughter had fallen asleep, the gusty, strong northerly winds died down to barely a wispy breeze. But what came once the wind had calmed was snow – much more than the few unorganized flakes that had fallen the previous evening. By the first light of dawn, over four inches of the season's first snowfall was on the ground. And in less than a day, the temperature had fallen over thirty degrees. Summer had officially given way to autumn a few weeks previous, and autumn snows like this were not that unusual for the Central Forest of Betrovia. That morning, Galena awoke before Patrik, and she let out a gasp of excitement after throwing open the curtains.

"Father! Look! You will not believe it!" she gasped.

"Galena? Must you be so loud? Is something the matter? Please! Why can't you allow me to sleep a bit more?" Patrik complained from underneath a patchwork quilt that Galena had crafted the previous winter.

"Sleeping time is over, lazy bones! You must now wake up and come look! You're not going to be pleased with what you see." The innkeeper grunted but slowly complied. Wrapping the quilt around his shoulders like a shawl, he shuffled to the window.

"Snow ... that is most-definitely not what I wanted to see," was all he said before climbing back into the tiny room's only bed.

"Oh, Father! But it's the first snow of the season! And isn't it just so beautiful as it positively shimmers where the scintillating morning rays hit it!"

"It is frozen precipitation ... that is all ... cold, heavy precipitation. And because of it, our mission to the capital city is going to – "

"Our mission? Father, can't you refer to this trip as something other than a *mission*? That word makes it sound ... makes it appear that we are in the militia ... or something like that," she quipped, continuing to gawk through the window's leaded glass at the cold white blanket.

"Bah! I do not want to begin this day arguing with you ... particularly about our *excursion* to Lycentia," Patrik said, again from underneath the warm covers.

"Fine. No argument then," Galena said. "I will get dressed and go check on the horses." And with that, she quickly rifled through the bags that contained her clothes, tossing the ones that she had worn the day before directly onto the bed where her father was attempting to fall back to sleep. Once completely attired, she left the room. And the slamming of the door produced yet another grunt from the groggy and uncooperative innkeeper.

As he lay in bed, Patrik – greatly desiring to fall back into blessed unconsciousness – pondered instead the morning's weather report. "Too much like last winter … it comes early and will probably stay late. Cold … I so detest the cold … and the confounded snow!" He shuddered then wondered if it would be worth it to hitch the horses up to the wagon and force them back onto the highway. "Why did it have to snow?!" he yelled just as Galena came back into the room.

"It is just so beautiful outside! No, it's resplendent! That's what it is! Resplendent! And, most-wonderful Father, it is most-assuredly going to be a gorgeous, sunny day!"

"Yes," he responded, as recalcitrant as any old man should be on the morning of the season's first heavy snow. "And I am up … you don't have to say anything else…"

"I didn't intend to say … oh, never mind!" she blurted out. "And just to let you know, the horses have been fed and watered. The owner of this establishment already ordered his stable hand to take care of them! He really is quite efficient," she then added.

"I refuse to comment," Patrik replied.

Galena continued to reveal her impatience with Patrik as she left and re-entered again as he grudgingly prepared himself to take on the day. She even sang another song, one that she and Tamara had sung when they were younger, hoping that, by doing so, he would speed things up. She exited and entered one more time and was carrying a few slices of bread along with a teapot. As she poured a cup for herself, she asked if he wanted one. Patrik merely shook his head, and then she poured one for him.

"How does your head feel this morning?" he asked her, breaking the silence as they sipped hot tea and nibbled on their breakfast.

"Oh, it still hurts ... but not as bad as last night. I suppose getting some sleep did the trick," she answered, still with optimism in her voice. "I need to do something with my hair, though," she laughed. "Orrin, that nice stable boy, told me that he thinks the cut on the back of my head probably looks horrendous." Bringing up the topic of the accident and her resulting head injury enticed Patrik to quickly button up his coat and walk over to her.

"Let me see that cut," he said, gently pulling the hair on the back of her head away from the wound. "Good ... it appears to be closing quite nicely."

"Of course it's healing! Aren't you forgetting that whenever I have suffered cuts or bruises, I heal fast ... it is what you have always said, Father," she said. She then reached into a small bag, pulled out a barrette and then proceeded to use the barrette to arrange her hair to hide the gash.

"That thing you're using there ... that clip. It looks rather elaborate ... expensive," Patrik said as a matter-of-fact. "Where did it come from?"

"This old thing? Ha! It was one of those trinkets that Edelin bought in Noran to give to Tamara. And she, of course, refused it. So I asked him if I could have it. So he gave it to me – with no questions asked!"

Edelin Bock was another former employee of The Lonely Fox Inn. But the circumstances behind his becoming part of the Vellein enterprise were much different than Kristof's. Edelin was the eldest son of a third-generation thief and con man who successfully eluded prosecution while at the same time attempting to raise a family. The Bocks lived in a village not many miles east of Lycentia. Edelin, unfortunately, did not have many positive role models while growing up, so he soon followed in his father's footsteps. One day, while running from the law, he sought refuge in Patrik's establishment. Since Kristof's tenure there had ended a few weeks prior to Edelin's arrival, Galena – completely oblivious to Edelin's seedy past – begged him to become their new stable hand. They desperately needed someone to help Patrik with the daily chores, she pleaded as she begged him to accept the position. Grudgingly, at first, the young thief decided to accept the offer. But since working at the inn meant being close to not only Galena, but also her very attractive and – at that time – unattached older sister, Tamara, he wondered if his luck was about to change. But, as unsavory circumstances often metastasize for scalawags like Edelin, things didn't pan out as well as he had hoped. And so, just like Kristof before him, he fled The Lonely Fox Inn.

He first ended up in Noran where his carousing with a few other young men in a tavern was interrupted by that rebellious band of Haarigoians and Rigarians who attacked Noran. Barely sober enough to evade the battle, he ran into the livery stable and hid behind some bales of hay. Once the battle was over and it was sufficiently dark, he emerged and headed back to the hostel where he had taken up residence.

That next morning, he volunteered to help with the clean-up and so impressed the owner of the hostel that he was hired by him. Only a week after accepting the position, he thought it would be a good idea to investigate what that hostler might have hidden in his room. He hadn't rummaged in through the man's things for long before he found a small bag of gold coins. Thinking that his luck had indeed changed for the better, he quickly gathered up his belongings, and made a beeline for that livery stable from which he stole a horse. The young thief was headed out of Noran almost as quickly as he had entered. Uncertain about how safe it would be to travel on the Plains highway, he chose to venture west instead via a nearly-abandoned forester's trail. Within a two days, he was riding into a small village on the north-eastern edge of the Plains of Dreut.

The unanticipated late-autumn storm that dropped but a few inches of snow in central Betrovia – the four inches that caused Patrik to become so sanguine about continuing their trip to Lycentia – was the Plains of Dreut's first blizzard of the season. Two feet of the white stuff blanketed the Plains' rocky pastures from the coast of the Great Sea all the way to where it met the Central Forest of Betrovia. Edelin, born and raised in the foothills of the Knaesin Mountains, was accustomed to heavy snow; he laughed at the powdery drifts as he pulled open the door of the abandoned cabin where he had sought refuge from the storm the night before.

"Well, well, well, it seems that winter has come early this year. And what might this forebode? Let's see … at least a foot of snow this early in autumn. How would Grandfather Bock put it? 'A little snow leaves but few tracks, but much leaves many.' Uhm … interesting … I best be very careful today!" Edelin then closed the door, quickly stuffed everything into the bag, then re-opened the door and stepped into the frigid whiteness. "Yes, much snow leaves too many tracks," he said again as he forged a way through the snow towards what he believed was the center of the this hamlet.

The warm rays of the morning sun were beginning to peer through the snowy tree branches as Edelin noticed smoke rising from the rock chimney of one of the pine-wood log cabins. As he stepped into the smoky and dark confines, it appeared that he had stumbled upon a tavern. He took in a deep breath and was about to sit down at a table just inside the hut when a raspy shout abruptly came from the other side of the hovel.

"You! By the door! Whattya think you are doin'?!" The young thief squinted to make out the source of the unfriendly words. "Don't curl up your face at me like that! Speak quick or I be tossin' ya back out into a snowbank!" Before he could respond, a diminutive but stocky man with curly and thick reddish-brown hair grabbed the front of his coat and pulled him further into the building. "Ah, just another traveler. My, and a young one, too. No worries, no worries," the purveyor said as he released his grip and stepped back. Edelin forced a polite smile and bowed awkwardly.

"Sir, please pardon me. It was not my intention to startle you," he said softly, not wanting to further agitate the assumed proprietor of the establishment. He then set down his things and said: "Allow me to apologize for my rudeness. I am Edelin … Edelin Bock."

"Oh posh, I care not who ya be," the tavern-keeper interrupted. "Care not in the least … that is, unless … unless you are related in someway to that dastardly Gandek Tranz!" The proprietor forced out a soft chuckle. "Let me take another look at you. Yes, it appears that you could be a Tranz."

"No, sir, I have no relations with that name. I am a Bock, not a Tranz and – "

"Never mind, never mind," the old man interrupted. "If it's food and drink you're needin', then find a seat and I'll bring it … that is, as long as you have the proper coinage!" He then grunted something unintelligible. Edelin smiled at the man's sudden irritation.

"Probably hard of hearing," he said.

"What's that you say?" the tavern-master asked without turning around.

"Hard to believe all the snow that fell last night."

"Snow? What about snow? Ah, it not be much … there's been more than that for a first snow of the season," he said as he returned to Edelin's table with a plate of dried meat and rather dark and wrinkled tubers. "Now don't ya even think about touchin' that food. Coins first! Lemme see what ya got." Edelin reached inside his coat and pulled out a cloth wallet. He then showed the tavern owner two coppers. "Not enough. Five coppers if you want the food."

"How about one silver then?" Edelin offered.

"Is it Lycentian? I have no use for anything but Lycentian."

"Here! You can have my last Lycentian silver," Edelin said, forcing a smile. The wallet contained many more silver coins than the one he gave as payment for breakfast that morning, but he was not about to let the old man know that he had more than the one. With the Lycentian coin in hand, the gray-haired tavern-keeper returned to what he was doing before Edelin entered his domicile. The thief nibbled on the cold food as he watched the peculiar little man with the great amount of thick hair; he noticed that every few seconds the man would stop what he was doing and glance quickly at the tavern door. A few minutes later, the tavern-keeper returned to the table carrying a pewter mug.

"That ale is all I have for drink this morning ... haven't made it out to the well yet."

"Not a problem with me, sir," Edelin replied. "By the way, what's the name of this village, if I can be so rude to inquire?"

"Name? Why, they call me Grundy, but that's not what I like to be called ... don't need to call me anything. And don't you expect more food or drink ... that is, unless you have more silver coin." Edelin shook his head.

"No, I believe you've supplied me with ample sustenance. And I appreciate it very much!" The old man grunted, mumbled incoherently again then resumed his morning routine. Edelin put the last piece of cold salted pork into his mouth and washed it down with a gulp of the ale and then smiled: the ale was unexpectedly sweet. Thinking that he had stayed much-longer than he should have, he stood up as if to leave. But before he could reach down to grab his bag, the tavern was suddenly awash with white light. Silhouetted at the doorway were two figures, one quite tall and the other about the same height as the young vagabond.

"Grundy! Bring me something to eat! And make sure it's hot this time!" Edelin was momentarily paralyzed by both the timber and the volume of the man's words. "You! What are *you* looking at?" The huge man pointed at the thief, but the response did not come fast enough for him. Without saying a word, the shorter of the two men scurried over to Edelin and shoved him back onto the stool, the stench surrounding the man nearly causing him to gag. "Answer me now, worm! What *are* you looking at?" the taller man bellowed.

"Sir," Edelin answer softly. "You … you entered this fine establishment … so suddenly that I … I could do nothing but stare in your direction. I mean no offense." The shorter man stuck a gnarled finger in Edelin's chest and smiled, revealing ash-colored teeth. But Edelin's attention was drawn instead to the man's larger-than-life bushy black eyebrows.

"Move over there!" the brute commanded, pointing to the far wall of the smoky tavern. "And say nothing more. I'm already tired of hearing your effeminate voice." Edelin quickly stood back up, grabbed his bag, and was about to move to another table when the short man with the super-sized eyebrows pointed at Edelin's bag. "Ah yes, Laithe, you think he has something of value in there? How about we take a gander inside of it then?" The thief unwittingly tried to hide the bag behind him and that was when the brute for the first time since entering the tavern moved; and he moved with such adroitness that it startled Edelin. "Trying to hide it from me, eh?" he said as he grabbed the bag out of Edelin's left hand. "I suppose that means there's something in here worth hiding?" Edelin shook his head.

"Kind sir, this bag contains but a few items of old clothing – "

"Silence! Have you forgotten that I told you to say nothing? Laithe, show this young cuss what he will have to deal with if but one thing more comes out of his mouth." Before he could even think about what to say, the brute's sidekick had pulled out a knife and was holding it precariously close to Edelin's jugular. The skin of the man's hand was like petrified tree-bark.

"Now, now, Naterik, there's no need for Laithe to go stickin' his blade into the traveler," the tavern-keeper said as he walked up to the man who was nearly two heads taller than him. "Here ... have some ale." Grundy held the tankard up, the brute grabbed it, took a whiff of it, then drained its contents in one breath! His accomplice, still holding the cold steel to Edelin's throat, chuckled hoarsely as he readjusted his grip on the blade. "Take a seat. I'll be bringin' you some food shortly."

"*Hot* food, Grundy. You surely don't want to also deal with Laithe." The dwarfish hit-man reacted with a guttural utterance that could be categorized as laughter. "Did ya hear that, Grundy? Laithe still has his sense of humor ... even after your miserable excuse for food nearly killed him the last time we blessed you with our presence!" The man the tavern-keeper called Naterik then glanced over at his partner. "Put away your blade now, Laithe ... I think our *traveler* has learned to stay quiet when told." The knife was returned to its home as quickly as it was exposed. The dwarfish sidekick continued to watch Edelin out of the corner of his least-bloodshot eye after putting a half-dozen feet between himself and the young thief. "Now for the bag! Let's see what's in it," Naterik said.

Edelin remained motionless – and silent – as Naterik untied the rope and proceeded to remove a shirt, a pair of pants and few other articles of clothing. Within seconds, the entirety of the bag's contents was on the table.

"Like I was trying to inform you, I own nothing of consequence," Edelin blurted out, wishing that he had remained quiet. Naterik and Laithe neither looked up nor said a word as they continued to inspect Edelin's things. Laithe suddenly grabbed one of the shirts and put it on; Naterik responded with a guttural guffaw.

"Ha! Not bad! Even though it's a tad small for you!" Both men laughed derisively while Edelin glared at them.

"Here! Hot food for the both of ya!" Grundy announced, interrupting the intruders' moment of frivolity. He delivered two plates of the same meat and bread that he had prepared for Edelin, and one of the portions was twice as large as the other.

"Good! Now … go away!" Naterik shouted as he shoved the contents of Edelin's bag off the table and onto the floor as he sat down. Laithe continued to stand until Naterik finally signaled that he too could sit. "Laithe, you go first … take a bite. Then share with me what you think of our meal." The diminutive hit-man picked up a piece of meat and bit off a chunk. Edelin watched, transfixed, as Laithe closed his eyes and chewed methodically; a small dribble of saliva came out the side of the dwarf's mouth, making Edelin's stomach hurt. After a few seconds of mastication, he opened his eyes and offered his boss a grin, revealing once again his blackened teeth. "Ha! Grundy! You get to live yet another day! Now bring us more ale!"

Edelin continued to watch the freak show as the tavern-keeper first brought more ale and then yet another plate of meat. As the two men were about to polish off the final course, the tavern door opened again; this time, three men in uniform entered. All three were attired in dungarees but sported nearly-identical dark-green coats. These were militiamen, and may have been from Noran, Edelin thought, but was not quite sure. But he breathed a huge sigh of relief that they were not members of the Lycentian brigade who customarily sported uniforms that were generally navy-blue. Even though he felt that they were not looking for him. he still moved behind one of the tavern's oak pillars so as not to be noticed.

Grundy set down the pot he was trying to clean and quickly waddled over to them. Naterik, chewing on one more piece of dried pork, paid no attention to the soldiers, but Laithe squinted menacingly at them, his eyebrows hiding his black-pea eyes. He then, with a greasy piece of bread in his hand, grunted something as he pointed at one of the newcomers. Naterik nodded but didn't look in their direction.

Edelin strained to hear what the tavern-keeper and the men were talking about but couldn't make out a word. Meanwhile, Naterik picked up his mug, drained its contents, then motioned toward Edelin's things on the floor. Laithe grabbed the bag and began stuffing everything back into it. He then shuffled over to the thief and handed the bag to him. He smiled, revealing once again the ashen teeth but again thumped Edelin's chest with a gnarled and leathery index finger. The young traveler made quick eye contact with the henchman: the warning was understood.

"Grundy! We ... are leaving," Naterik said as he moved towards the door. "Put the meal on my tab. We'll settle up ... next time." And with that, the brute and his dwarfish companion sauntered out the door, shuffling past the three newcomers as if they were not even there. Edelin let out a sigh of relief, threw his bag over his shoulder and moved towards the door as well. One of the soldiers stepped in front of him just as he reached the doorway.

"Don't I ... know you from somewhere? You look awfully familiar," he said. Edelin began to hope that his current predicament was less precarious than the previous one. He thought of what to say and then realized that even though he had by that point encountered six different people in this village, his identity was known by none of them.

"If it is my name you desire, I gladly give it," Edelin said with a twinkle in his eye. "I am Elrick ... Elrick Blotch. And I do not think we have ever met."

"Blotch ... Blotch ... sounds Rigarian," the soldier said, "Funny, though ... you certainly don't look Rigarian." Edelin took two steps backwards and bumped into another of the militiamen. Edelin looked to his right; the third one continued to chat with Grundy. The tone of the man's voice wasn't as threatening as Naterik's which inspired Edelin to continue creating this new persona.

"My grandfather's given name was also Elrick, but when he left the Rigars to seek out adventure in the Great Forest, he shortened his family name to Blotch It was originally Blotch-traen," Edelin said. "Surely you are familiar with the Blotch-traens of the Lower Rigars? From the Misrikle Valley" The soldier shook his head.

"Never heard of them. But that is not important," he stated plainly. "Why are you here? You must realize that this village borders the Plains of Dreut. The Plains are a very dangerous place for common travelers like yourself." Edelin couldn't help but smile: he liked where this conversation was heading.

"But, kind sir, I am no *common* traveler. I have recently determined to leave the creature comforts of Lycentia to proffer my services here on the front … to whoever would accept them." Edelin continued to smile as he thought of how professional that sounded.

"Services?" the second militiaman asked. "And what might these *services* be?" Before responding, Edelin turned to face the man directly: his eyes lit upon the soldier's full but well-trimmed carrot-red beard; the man didn't appear to be much older than the young thief.

"I am a lawyer from the capital city … a lawyer who specializes in negotiating contracts … as well as finalizing difficult accords." Edelin wasn't being totally untruthful: being a successful confidence man required more than an average ability for "the mastery of give-and-take," as his beloved Grandfather Bock used to say.

"A man of the law, eh? Did you hear that, Drake? This vagabond says he knows about the law!" the bearded militiaman said. "What do you think you can do with this *knowledge* of the law … way out here where very few people care not for what's legal?" The militiamen who had been chatting with Grundy then approached the two who were interrogating Edelin.

"So what did Grundy find out?" the first soldier asked.

"The old man didn't learn a thing … at least that's his story. Naterik and Laithe hassled the stranger here but took nothing from him. That Haarigoian played by the rules today … for the most part."

"They … those men were Haarigoians?" Edelin interrupted.

"One of them is. The short one is … well, he's just a half-wit Rigarian," the first soldier answered. "You need not concern yourself with either one; they gave up the fight years ago. But we still like to keep tabs on them."

"Stranger," the last of the soldiers said, "Did you say you are a lawyer?" Edelin looked at him and couldn't help but notice the fresh scar that ran from just below the man's left ear to directly under his chin. Unlike the other soldiers, this one sported no facial hair but the salt and pepper hair of his head was tied tightly into a ponytail.

"Not a lawyer completely. I have yet to pass the high court's examinations. But I hope you don't mind me saying but – on many occasions – my advice to clients was treated as viable as any of my employers." Edelin surveyed the faces of all three soldiers and concluded that none doubted his story. He then looked at the one with the red beard. "And now to better answer your question, sir. I would like to volunteer my services to those stationed here on the front. Rumor has it that more than a few militiamen have been accused of numerous illegalities, and I am certain that men possessing my experience and knowledge are few and far between in this inhospitable locale."

The militiamen conversed with one another for a few minutes, whispering for the most part, until the third soldier, the one who had been talking with the tavern-keeper, insisted that Edelin accompany him and his companions back to their camp.

"Our captain may want to talk with you," he said. "To talk with you about your proposal … among other things."

CHAPTER FIVE

"Othleis craves humility; His power is released through the submissive humility of those who love Him."

Patrik expelled a tremendous yawn as he coaxed the horses to pull the wagon across the bridge. This ancient but sturdy bridge of massive rectangular stones and thick oak timbers signaled to travelers that they were leaving the Great Forest of Betrovia and entering the more-populated counties that surrounded Lycentia. Galena, laying down in the back of the wagon but wide-awake, reacted to the noisome outburst by quickly sitting up.

"Father! What are you doing? Are you alright?"

"Look, Galena! We are finally close enough to Lycentia to say that we have arrived. And it's not a moment too soon for me, either. I truly hate riding for any length of time in this uncomfortable and disconcerting contraption." Galena climbed over their things and, like she had done a few times during their ride from The Lonely Fox Inn, plopped down next to her father and wrapped her left arm around his neck.

"But how were you going to get us here unless by this *contraption*? Sometimes you make almost no sense," she said, patting the top of his hoary head with her left hand. "No sense at all."

The few inches of snow that had fallen the night before amounted to barely a dusting around Lycentia. And the small amount that had fallen had nearly melted away, leaving a few puddles in the road and in its ditches. If it wasn't for the tall oaks, cedars and elms on both sides of the highway, the innkeeper and his younger daughter would be able to see the three golden Lycentian temple spires. Even though they had made this trip the previous summer to attend the wedding of Tamara and – at the time of the wedding – *Prince* Ilead, Patrik was more exhausted than he had been, more so than even after repairing the roof of the inn earlier in the summer. "The cold … it has to be the cold … I can't take this cold weather anymore," he mumbled.

"The cold? What are you talking about? It's a beautiful afternoon! And the snow that you detest so much is nearly gone!" Galena interrupted. "Why are you in such a bad mood when we are so close to the end of our little adventure?"

"If it wasn't for feeling the need that I must deliver the scrolls personally to the Netherenes as soon as possible, I would be satisfied to lay down and take a long, long nap … and maybe to never wake up." Galena quickly removed her arm from around Patrik's neck.

"No, no, no! You are not to even think about leaving me alone with nearly everything we own stacked up in this nasty wagon!" she said playfully but emphatically. She furrowed her brow and pointed her right index finger at her father's nose. "This whole *excursion* … it was your idea … and you have to finish this! You *are* going to finish this!" Patrik, much too tired to even construct a comeback, simply sighed and signaled the horses to pick up the pace.

When the horses crossed the second, but shorter, bridge that symbolized the entrance to the official outskirts of the capital city, Patrik quickly commanded them to not head directly to the city gates but to take the side road that would lead them to a village just north of the city.

Lycentia, more than a hundred years before the advent of the innkeeper's adventure, was called Sheu Leun. The original name carried with it no important or even symbolic meaning. It was christened with the new moniker once the trio-spired Netherene temple was completed. The goal of Oliver III's grandfather, Oliver I, was that the city in which the Netherene's most-expansive temple was erected would be called Lycentia, "The City of Light." Oliver I dreamed of centralizing the dispensation of Netherene credos in that city, and constructing the triple-spired temple in the center of Sheu Leun was his method for doing it.

For centuries, Sheu Leun functioned merely as a trading outpost for the denizens of the Knaesin Mountains, and for their counterparts who resided in the Great Forest west of the city. But Oliver I – and the wealthy and powerful Netherene priests that followed him – desired to forever change the town, even if the change was to occur at its literal core. Sheu Leun was to become the site of Betrovia's most-important, and most-elaborate, temple. And that massive structure would be erected in the geographical center of the village,

=========================

Like she had done many times before, Galena demonstrated her gymnastic skills by hopping over the side of the wagon; it had not yet come to a full stop as Patrik coaxed the horses to pull the wagon as close to the livery stable as possible.

"Couldn't you wait until the wagon wasn't moving before getting off? Why do you continually behave like you are still a child? And, more importantly, have you forgotten about your injury?" Patrik scolded as he tied the reins to the iron bar in front of him.

"Oh, Father, you mustn't worry about me! Nor about my *injury*. I am utterly starving and have to find something to eat!" And with that, Galena strutted off, leaving her father to negotiate with the stable master by himself.

"Good afternoon, sir! And what might we able to assist you with?" The man was tall, lanky but middle-aged and was clad in a stained leather apron as well as happily sported a peculiarly-shaped stoneware pipe. He smiled at the innkeeper, took another puff on the pipe and waited for the innkeeper's reply.

"Yesterday the right rear wheel of the wagon came off," Patrik said. "We managed to re-attach it, but I'm sure that it is still not properly repaired. Might you have time to look it over?" The man who appeared to be the stablemaster removed the pipe from his mouth, walked over to the wheel in question and then tapped out the smoldering contents of the pipe on the side of the wagon. He then crouched down by the wheel.

"Right! I see the problem. You are most-fortunate that the wheel did not work its way off again. Tis barely on the hub even now," he said as he stood back up, as he inserted the pipe back into his mouth and took a puff. There was a brief pause as he appeared to wonder why the pipe was empty. While Patrik waited for the man to continue, he scratched his head and sighed. "That wheel itself needs to be replaced," he said as he again removed the pipe and inspected its contents. "Better to replace it instead of trying to repair it."

"You don't suppose you could take care of it today, do you?" Patrik asked.

"Today? For Othleis' sake, this day is quite ended! And I've yet to finish re-shoeing the constable's horse. I must take care of Blaed's needs before taking on this little project. Don't you agree?" The innkeeper had no idea who the constable was or how important he was to the stable-master. And he also assumed that this Blaed creature's needs took precedence over his. So, Patrik merely nodded his head in agreement. "Good! I appreciate you not pressing me to configure a new wheel at this moment," he said. "First thing in the morning! I will tackle your problem! It will be my top priority!" He then sauntered back into the stable, taking yet another puff on the quite-extinguished pipe. "I promise!"

As Patrik stood next to the wagon, pondering what to do next, he noticed Galena exiting a two-story structure west of the stable. But she wasn't alone; walking beside her was a girl who could not have been more than six years old. Galena's tag-along wore a bright-yellow dress and sported a bonnet to match. Her hair, in direct contrast to her clothing, was charcoal black. Patrik watched as the two walked slowly towards him, and, due to color of the tyke's hair, caught himself thinking of Tamara.

"So what's the verdict, sir innkeeper? Do we have to buy a new wagon?" Galena teased. The little girl looked up at Patrik and grinned mightily which revealed at least a one-inch gap between her front upper teeth. Her eyes were dark green, and Patrik again was reminded of his older daughter. Without saying a word, the girl then left Galena's side and pranced into the stable.

"I appreciate your sense of humor ... as I always do, Galena," Patrik replied. "But at this time the wagon only requires a new wheel. That is, if that quirky stable master is to be believed. He plans to take care of it first thing in the morning." He then turned around to see that the stable master had picked up the little girl and had placed her on his shoulders. She giggled as he walked around inside the stable with her on his shoulders as he continued to chew on that stoneware pipe. "That girl ... she appears to be the stable-master's daughter?" Patrik asked, pointing at the young man and the girl.

"Your guess is a good as mine," Galena said. "As I walked into the store, she bounced over to me and latched onto my right leg. She took me completely by surprise, she did! I asked her what her name was, but all she did was giggle. Once she let go of my leg, she asked why I was wearing the scarf. I told her that I had fallen out of the wagon and hit my head on a rock. She laughed this curious little laugh, like she had the hiccups. It made me start laughing with her." Patrik shrugged as he noticed the man gently place the girl back on the ground. Nearly as her feet touched the stable's dirt floor, she scurried back to Galena and grabbed onto her right leg.

"Hello again! Now will you tell me your name?" Galena asked. "Someone who latches onto another person's leg really should be known by name!" The pixie peered out from under the yellow-as-sunlight bonnet.

"Sereal! Papa calls me *Sereal!*" she giggled, again revealing the large gap in the center of her teeth.

"Good! Now I can tell you – " was all Galena could say before the girl ran back into the stable. She stopped just inside the doorway, waved vigorously, then disappeared. "That is one strange little girl."

"Not so strange," Patrik responded. "I can remember two little missies who behaved much in the same way."

"But of course you cannot be referring to Tamara and I! We were the most-perfect little girls!"

"Yes, indeed you were … indeed…" Patrik mumbled. "That girl … what did she say her name was? Did she really say *Sereal*?" he then asked.

"Her name? I think she did say it was Sereal … wait … isn't Uncle Franck wife's name Sereal?" Galena asked.

"Yes, Sereal is his wife's name," Patrik answered. "Might it be a good idea right now to find out where those two live and pay them a visit? What do you think?"

"*Right now*? Didn't you say that the wagon needs a new wheel? Shouldn't that be taken care of before we head into Lycentia to look for Uncle Franck? Or to do anything there?"

Patrik's old friend, Franck Horriatt, had made a name for himself as a free-wheeling and very successful traveling merchant. His forebears, however, eked out a meager existence clearing and then farming a few acres in the Great Forest southwest of Lycentia. But when Franck turned fourteen, he was recruited to leave the farm to be mentored by an acquaintance of the family who happened to be a fairly-well-to-do traveling merchant. Franck quickly learned the ins-and-outs of the trade and, before he turned twenty, had completed his tutelage with the merchant and made the decision to venture off on his own. Moving away from the area around Lycentia to invest some time in Noran to nurture relationships with the hunters and trappers there was how he first came in contact with the Vellein family.

Before too long, Patrik – the young hunter/trapper – and Franck – the novice traveling salesman – had become not just business acquaintances but close friends. Franck appreciated Patrik's shrewdness when it came time to negotiate the selling price of his skins and hides. Patrik, on the other hand, liked how Franck would generally agree to his asking price – even if it meant haggling a bit more than he liked. After moving back to Lycentia, Franck's favorite business route took him from Lycentia through Noran, then to the villages bordering the Plains of Dreut and then back through Noran on the way to the larger markets in the capital city. For years, he attempted – in vain – to persuade Patrik into becoming his partner. But even though Patrik enjoyed Franck's company, he detested traveling. So he instead chose to remain in Noran to attempt to make a living for himself as a hunter and trapper.

That next morning, one day after Patrik and Galena had arrived in the village just north of Lycentia, the pipe-sucking stable-master reassured the innkeeper that attaching a new wheel to the wagon was better than trying to repair the old one. Patrik, not wanting to waste anymore of his precious time arguing, consented. As the replacement was made, Galena nonchalantly meandered around the stable looking for the little girl. But she was nowhere to be found. And except for them and the man repairing the wagon wheel, the square was completely deserted. Patrik was not concerned about the girl's whereabouts and reminded Galena that the first thing they would do once entering Lycentia was to find Franck and Sereal.

Once the repairs were made, Patrik gave the stablemaster one silver coin combined with a few coppers and thanked him for his trouble. He and Galena then climbed into the wagon and proceeded to head back down the narrow road for the capital city. As the wagon approached the first curve outside of the tiny village, Galena pointed at something in a clearing just to their left.

"What is going on over there? It looks like a group of people standing in the middle of that field," she said.

"Now why is that so unusual?" Patrik replied, refusing to even look in the direction of the distraction.

"Father! Stop the wagon! I want to find out what they are doing!" She grabbed the reins and pulled back on them,

"Why did you do that, young lady? We need to be on our way to Lycentia!" Patrik yelled as she leaped off the wagon again before it had come to a complete stop.

"Galena! Come back to the wagon this instant!" Patrik yelled. But it was no use. Instead of yelling at her again, he commanded the horses to move as close to the edge of the one-land road and then also exited the wagon. By the time he had gotten off, Galena was already beside them. About fifteen people, mostly adults, stood in a circle around a large pile of wood. On the top of that woodpile appeared to be a small body.

"It's a funeral," she whispered to the innkeeper as he walked up to join her.

"Funeral? For who?" Patrik asked. Galena tapped the shoulder of a man who was close to her and whispered something. The man replied so quietly that Patrik couldn't hear the response. "What did the man say? Who is the funeral for?" Patrik asked Galena again.

"A little girl," Galena replied. "The man said it's a little girl who died last night." A solitary tear made its way down her left cheek. "A girl who was only five years old," she added with a quiet sniffle.

"Might you find out what did she die from?" Patrik then asked. The man who Galena had talked to heard the question, left the circle and walked over to the innkeeper.

"Poison," he whispered. "That is what we were told."

"Poisoned? How could – " Before Galena could finish her question, the man turned around and shuffled back to the group. Galena tried to follow him, but her father latched onto her arm. Not more than a minute later, an elderly, well-dressed man picked up a torch, lit it and slowly walked up to the woodpile. Surrounded by near-silence, except for the metallic chattering of a fox squirrel perched high above the circle in a brownish cedar tree, he thrust the torch into the woodpile. The pyre of dry tinder and straw exploded into orange and yellow flames.

"Why are they burning her?" Galena asked. "Why aren't they burying her like people in Noran bury their dead? Like … like we buried Uncle Pieter?" Patrik shook his head.

"I cannot explain it, Galena," he replied. "There is nothing I can say to attempt to explain such strange customs."

======================

The ride from the disconcerting ceremony to the gates of Betrovia's central city took less than an hour. Patrik was prepared to talk to Galena about what they had just witnessed but she remained silent the entire time. Once inside the city proper, Galena broke her silence, wanting to talk about other things besides finding out the location of Franck's house.

"Where do you think we should find lodging in Lycentia, Father?" she asked. "Wait! Forget I asked that!" she exclaimed as she grabbed his right arm. "I have a wonderful idea! How about we move in with Tamara and Ilead? Surely there's room for the two of us in that huge palace!" Patrik thrust his right hand into the air, dislodging her grip, and waved it like he was shooing away a pesky mud-dauber.

"*Surely* you cannot be that naive, Galena. No! That will not work! Not in the least!" he stated loudly. "Relying on the king and queen of Betrovia for our housing would most-definitely send the wrong message to the Netherenes. It would not be beneficial to complicate my mission further by connecting Ilead to the scrolls … at least not until I have had an opportunity – if the Creator even provides one – to discuss them with the king." Galena reached behind her neck and untied the scarf that she had been using to keep the bandage attached to her head. She then threw both the scarf and the bandage into the back of the wagon.

"There! That smelly thing is gone! My head is all better now!" she announced. "I throw both of them behind me just like I would like you to toss away your fears!" She exclaimed. "Y*ou* are nothing less than a coward, Father! A simple coward! You must make it a priority to convince Ilead about us moving into the palace. We are her only family. So doesn't it make perfect sense that we all live together in the same house?" Galena then gently put her hand on the innkeeper's shoulder. "You are, in fact, the father of the queen!"

In all of the great city of Lycentia, one place Patrik was familiar with was the central market. And that was the first place where he and Galena stopped to inquire the residence of his good friend, Franck. The first person Patrik talked to was a middle-aged, loquacious woman stationed at a cart overflowing with boots, shoes, purses and other leather goods. Once Patrik succeeded in enticing her to listen to his questions, she said that she knew of the portly merchant but could not remember where he lived. Another lady was not as talkative but still wanted to hawk her wares instead of give away any information. Her merchandise consisted of pots and pans that she proclaimed were meticulously crafted by monks of the Knaesin Mountains. She had recently been introduced to a merchant who matched Patrik's description of Franck but confessed that she remembered neither the man's name nor where he might live.

After talking to a few more vendors, even some patrons of the open-air market, Patrik became disillusioned.

"Galena, this was supposed to be an easy thing to do. But it appears that Franck is not as well-known here in Lycentia as he has led us to believe," he muttered with an obvious sadness in his voice.

"Good! Then it is time for us to head for the palace! They will be so excited to see us!" Galena grabbed Patrik's hand, pulling him in the direction of the wagon. In order to not create a scene, he quickly dislodged his hand from Galena's grasp and proceeded to follow her.

"Sir! You there! Sir!" Patrik stopped and turned around to see who was yelling.

"I beg your pardon, but are you speaking to me?" Patrik asked.

"Are you looking for someone named Franck?" the young man asked.

"Yes, we are. Might you know of him? Even better: might you know where he lives?" The youngster smiled.

"If the Franck I know is the man you are looking for, then yes, I know where he lives. I can take you directly to him if you would like!"

"Yes, I would like that very much! Please take us there! And thank you for your help!"

Patrik soon learned that their guide lived in Franck's and even worked for him when the portly gentleman required his assistance. This merchant's apprentice – who looked to be all of fifteen – rode on the bench seat next to Patrik while Galena occupied her favorite position at the rear of the wagon. As the boy gave Patrik directions, Galena sang and cheerfully waved at those who granted her their attention. Before too long, Patrik was encouraging the horses down a narrow alley that opened up into a large but vacant cobblestone square.

"There! The building next to the one that has burnt! That is where your friend lives!" Before the wagon had come to a complete stop, the boy jumped off and ran inside.

"What is it about this generation that they cannot wait for a man to bring his wagon to a complete stop before disembarking?" Patrik complained. It wasn't but a few seconds later – before Patrik had told the horses where to park the wagon – when a rather-large man burst out of the same door.

"Patrik! And even Galena! What a pleasant surprise!"

"Uncle Franck!" Galena shouted as she then hopped off the rear of the wagon and ran up to the portly merchant. Franck stuck out a pair of oak-branch arms to give Galena a hug. "It's been such a long time!" she said as she squeezed him tightly. "I cannot remember when we last saw you!"

"How long has it been? My. My! I really have no idea. I am so sorry, little one, but my memory is not what it used to be. However, as I look at you, I have to say that it has been much too long. My oh my! You are turning into such a beautiful woman!"

"And you continue to be unable to resist the sweet breads and dark ales," Patrik interrupted, walking up to the two who were still in each other's arms and poking the traveling merchant in the side. Franck gently released Galena from the bear hug and then stuck out a ham hock-hand towards the innkeeper. Patrik grabbed it and beamed. "It is so good to see your cherubic face once again, old friend. More than a few times over the last many months I was sure that I might not ever see it again."

"My oh my! Look at how the typically-stoic keeper of The Lonely Fox Inn has become so incredibly sentimental! Let us resist crying here in the middle of the street, shall we? Come inside, you two! We have much to talk about!" Franck then extended that large hand towards Galena, she latched onto it with hers, and together they strode towards the three-story structure. Patrik, like a statue, mutely watched them. "Well, old man," Franck bellowed back as they reached the stoop. "What are you waiting for? A special invitation?"

Once inside, Franck insisted that he give them a tour of his abode. He first led them through the pantry down a narrow staircase to the cellar where he proudly pointed out his collection of aged wines. "Someday I may even open one of those bottles. Then again, I might not," he said to

Galena with a twinkle of the eye. Then it was back to the main floor where he boasted about the prolific collection of trinkets and whatnots he had acquired during his many travels. Many of the curious items had been placed on shelves throughout the house, shelves for the most part that were as crooked and over-filled. He stopped to draw his guests' attention to a small but intricately-carved image of a shark that by itself occupied one small shelf.

"I was told – and I have no reason to doubt the veracity of the man who sold it to me – that it was carved out of a single tooth. Seems only proper that an image of a man-eating beast such as this should be created from a tooth, eh?" He asked if Galena wanted to touch it; she grimaced and without uttering a word backed away from it. Three rooms were on the second floor of the house: one obviously was Franck's bedroom while the other two both contained beds but not much more. Franck's room was the largest of the three rooms, and while the smaller bedrooms only had small portholes for windows, the window in his room was quite large.

The tour ended on the third floor, actually just the attic of the building, where the merchant disclosed that he was storing some Netherene relics. "There is no doubt in my mind that most of these things are forgeries. Worthless junk. I have exercised a great amount of shrewdness in purchasing these … only one or two actually cost more than I was willing to pay." He then added as he comically rubbed his pink and puffy hands together. "Maybe … just maybe … something in this attic could one day be of great value to even old Oliver himself!"

When they returned to the main floor, Patrik remembered the horses and excused himself to go back outside to take care of them. The innkeeper paused as if waiting for Galena to join him, but she had already wrapped her right arm as well as she could around Franck's waist.

"So, where have you hidden Sereal?" She asked. Franck quickly pulled away from her grasp.

"Sereal ... why she's ... she is not here," he quietly replied, turning away from her.

"She's not here? What does that mean? Oh, I know! She must be at the market. Of course!" Franck's silence told her that she had guessed incorrectly.

"No, my sweet, she is not at the market. She is gone. She has been gone longer than I want to think about." He finally made eye contact with one of his greatest fans, took her by the hand and escorted her back outside. There they stood, neither one saying a word, while they watched Patrik lead the horses up to the stoop.

"Where might I safely bed these two down for the night? I am afraid I need to buy some grain for them since the wagon is void of any," Patrik said.

"Behind that shell of a building ... the one that nearly burnt down ... there's a shack. A well is close by, too. There should be some sacks of corn or something like that in there. That is where my horse is kept. Until the fire I was able to use the large structure." Galena left Franck's side and walked up to her father.

"I'm going to help you with the horses," she whispered as she glanced back at the stocky salesman. Even though the twilight didn't offer much light, they located the sacks of grain as well as a oaken bucket for drawing water out of the well.

"Uncle Franck told me that Sereal isn't here," Galena said as she brought the horses much-needed water. "All he said was that she was gone. You don't think she is dead, do you, Father?"

"Sereal? You mean she wasn't there in the pantry cooking dinner? I thought for sure I smelled something cooking," he replied. Assured that the horses were in a safe place for the night, Patrik put his arm around his younger daughter's waist, and together they walked side-by-side back to the house.

Patrik asked about Sereal right as walked in the door.

"She is gone," Franck said. "And that is all I know."

"Gone? You cannot mean that she is dead?" the innkeeper asked.

"Dead? I certainly hope not! I do not think I could live another day knowing that my sweet cucumber was dead. My oh my! Perish the thought!"

"If she is not dead, then just what do you mean by *she is gone*?" Franck answered by telling his two guests of returning to Lycentia from one of his longer trips a few months before and discovering a note on the pantry table. Patrik asked if he still had the note. Franck said that after reading it, he wadded it up and threw it immediately into the pantry hearth.

"The note ... what did the note actually say? Certainly you can remember!" Galena said.

"The note ... it said ... Sereal ... it said she was leaving ... leaving me for ... for another man," Franck whimpered. A small tear unpredictably appeared under his left eye.

"Now I know you are fabricating a monstrous tale! Sereal? The woman who fell in love with you the first time she laid eyes on you? The woman who would cry a river of tears every time you would leave Lycentia on business? And this is all according to you. Those are your own words, Franck," Patrik said.

"Yes, tis the same Sereal of which we speak," Franck sniffled. "That note … it offered nothing … not a thing about why she had lost interest in me … fallen … out of love with me. There was nothing in that note about what attracted her to that other man!" Galena suddenly stood up and pointed a finger at the him.

"I figured this out! Listen to me! Both of you! I know exactly what happened!" Galena commanded as she stood in front of both of them, hands firmly placed on her hips. "She left you because you were unfaithful to her! Of course that is it! It makes perfect sense! There you are, the salesman who is away from home more than he is at home, and you give in to temptation! Tell the truth, Uncle Franck! Sereal found out about one of your little escapades, didn't she?" Patrik stared at his younger daughter as if she had confessed to a murder: how had this girl of barely nineteen come to learn so much about the sordid life of a traveling merchant? he thought.

"Galena, please show Franck a bit more respect," he commanded. "What evidence do we have that she left him because he was unfaithful?" Before anyone could answer, the young man, who Franck at the onset of the tour of the house had introduced as Walthan, entered the room.

"If you think you are ready, I have sufficiently prepared some food for you," he said.

"There! I knew I smelled something cooking!" Patrik said as he quickly stood up and moved towards the pantry.

During the meal, Galena respectfully cajoled Franck to disclose more about the note as well as why he thought Sereal left. But the trader remained recalcitrant and refused to say anything else about the mystery. Instead, he demanded that they allow him to share something totally unrelated to Sereal's leaving. Before he would forget about it, he said that he needed to tell them about the Ulek the Haarigoian.

"Ulek? Wait! Let me remember. Isn't he the Haarigoian giant that Ilead challenged and then killed that day on the Plains? The day when Ilead ceased to be the youngest son of a charcoal merchant and became a hero of the Lycentian militia?" Patrik asked.

"The one and the same," Franck replied as he stuffed another fork-full of roast duck into his mouth. "During my most-recent excursion to the Plains, I happened to bump into an old Haarigoian … one that I had the privilege of trading with more than a few times. He simply would not allow me to continue my journey until he told me these things about that Harrigoian." Franck then informed his captive audience of the short, but sordid, history of a fierce warrior of The Plains of Dreut.

"Ulek Melak-Sodat was born on a hot summer's night to a Haarigoian fisherman's slave-woman. His mother … unfortunately … died bringing him into the world. The old trader didn't offer much information about the fisherman besides that he attempted to raise him the best he knew how. That is, until the boy reached his teens. By that time, the fisherman had grown very ill and then died. Not long after his death, the adults of that seaside village shunned Ulek because of how large and tall he had grown. I suppose they were afraid of him … the trader stressed that at that young age he was already seven feet tall!"

"Seven feet! At thirteen? I wonder how much he ate on a daily basis," Galena pondered.

"By the time he reached adulthood," Franck smiled and then continued, "He joined a band of migrating herdsmen who followed their herds as far south as the plateau of Ahnak to as far north as the western foothills of the Rigarian Mountains. Before long, the other young men of that roving band made him their leader. And for what reason did they desire a leader? It certainly was not for increasing the size of their herd! My oh my! Ulek's band of mighty men soon became one of the fiercest … one of the most-ruthless group of scalawags that have ever called the Plains of Dreut home!" Franck then reached across the table and picked up piece of dark rye-bread. "Ulek had built a reputation for not only being ferocious in battle but being completely merciless as well." He paused again to take another bite of the duck. "And … this is the best part … Ulek was notorious for cutting off the heads of his enemies. What do you suppose he did with these heads? My oh my! This is the most-intriguing! He ordered the heads delivered to the village where he grew up... where they would become part of his macabre collection!"

"Heads? A collection?" Galena asked. "How could anyone make a habit of collecting the heads of their victims? Such a vile person! Such a vile habit!" she proclaimed a bit too loudly.

"Galena, you might want to think about what he gained with such a … hobby. Might he have kept the heads to establish a reputation for abject brutality?" Patrik replied. "If so, the irony of how he died at the hands of our King Ilead is quite appropriate."

"How did the Haarigoian die? How did King Ilead defeat him?" Walthan asked as he entered the dining room. This time he was carrying a freshly-baked pie.

"He decapitated him," Galena offered with a matter-of-fact tone. "Why didn't you already know this about your king? Some things about King Ilead are *supposed* to be common knowledge. Isn't that right, Uncle Franck?" The young man placed the pie on the table directly in front of Franck and then with his left hand pointed eastward.

"I am very sorry. I do not know much of Lycentian culture," he whispered as he looked down at the pie. "I only recently relocated here. I am from a small village in the Knaesins where – "

"That is correct," Franck interrupted. "And there is nothing else you need to say about yourself at this time, Walthan. Now … please return to the pantry and bring me another mug of ale." The young man, with eyes still down-turned, then bowed and walked backwards out of the room.

"Uncle Franck! How awfully rude of you! Why didn't you let the boy finish his thought?" Galena asked, staring at the man with the bulbous cheeks who began to fill those cheeks with a nearly-half of the dark-purple pie.

"Walthan is … now how can I phrase this? He is *different*," he muttered through a mouthful of plums and pie crust. "It would be best that you not discover *how* different at this point in time, young lady."

"Father! Tell Uncle Franck immediately to send for the boy and demand that he tell us more about himself!" Galena said.

"Oh no you don't! I refuse to involve myself in this," Patrik announced as he pushed himself away from the table. "I gave up many years ago trying to tell this old merchant what to do!"

CHAPTER SIX

"The Creator is patient in keeping his
promise of purity to those who seek
Him whole-heartedly."

Without much effort at all, Edelin Bock infiltrated the battalion of Noran regulars that was stationed on the eastern edge of the Plains of Dreut. As he predicted, a few influential officers actually wanted legal counsel. Before long, the young confidence man understood why the militiamen were still needed there. Ahnak was believed by Lycentia's political and religious elite to be the source of all that was evil in Betrovia. Even though the city had been under Lycentian control for nearly a month, relatively small – but nonetheless hostile – bands of Haarigoian and Rigarian malcontents continued to terrorize the Plains. Militiamen from around the region, not just from the capital city, were stationed up and down the rocky plateaus that served as a natural border between the unruly Plains and the Great Forest of Betrovia. His success at impersonating a Lycentian attorney made Edelin wonder if someday he could become a bona-fide practitioner of the law. His confidence grew even more when the militia commander took the con artist under his wing a few days after the two first met.

"Mr. Blotch, a man with legal training like yourself is exactly what is needed here," Leitser, the commander of the

Noran militia told him. "My men are under-paid, under-nourished and lacking in the materials to combat these Plains vagabonds. I charge you to work as our liaison to bring improvement to our conditions here in the wild. The Lycentian troops have always had access to the finest horses, armor and weapons while we of the village militias must rely on whatever we can find or fabricate on our own. This inequality must come to an end!" he exclaimed.

Edelin had never been in such a situation where he could work side-by-side with the partisans of the status quo instead of conniving and plotting against them. Because of this new-found camaraderie with the military elite, he salivated at the opportunity to craft plans that would separate as many valuables as possible from the commander – as well as anyone else he might choose to victimize. Yes, the young Lycentian had quite possibly never felt this good about himself ... this good about being a thief.

In less time than it would take for a ten-pound ham to cure, Edelin had so endeared himself to Commander Leitser, a veteran officer with more than twenty years of service, that the commander insisted he move his belongings into his tent instead of bunking down with the members of the rank-and-file. Edelin saw this invitation as a perfect opportunity to discover just how "well-off" the commander might be. The third night after relocating to Leitser's tent presented a fortuitous opportunity for exploration.

"Elrick, I generally do not join my men as they venture onto the Plains in search of these rebel criminals. However, for the excursion planned for tomorrow, my presence is required," Commander Leitser said. "Our scouts have discovered not more than an hour's ride west of here a pack of these mangy high-plains mongrels. We believe they are cunning, ferocious and quite ruthless. Of course," he added with a stout grin on his face, "It behooves me to lead our attack against them."

"What do the veterans within your ranks think?" Edelin interrupted. "I mean ... are they as cognizant of the dangers as you seem to be?" Right as he formed the words, he felt it odd to question him, particularly since the commander was about to be Edelin's next victim. He hoped that the expression on his face didn't reveal what he was actually thinking.

"Dangers? What might you be implying, counselor? My officers ... everyone of them ... hail from Noran. They have dutifully served under my command since joining the militia. The recruits from other villages ... from within the larger interior ... would surely attest to these veterans' bravery and sense of nobility in battle. Why, even the greenest volunteers have shown that they know how to follow orders. Even to the death!" Edelin watched Leitser walk to his side of the tent where he pulled something out of a bag next to his bedroll. "I hope you might humor me by allowing me to show you something," he said, motioning the young thief to step closer. Edelin's curiosity was definitely piqued.

"*This* was presented to me ... by Oliver III himself," he stated with a twinkle in his eye. Dangling from his hand was a large, silver pendant embossed with what appeared to be the three peaks of the Netherene temple in Lycentia. "This gift symbolizes the high priest's gratitude of how the Noran militia – under my command, of course – have kept Noran safe from the Haarigoians' malevolent advances.

Even when they have been within but a few miles of town … and appeared to be ready to invade … we have kept them at bay." Edelin couldn't resist from saying what was on his mind.

"That is, excluding the the little incident from a few weeks ago?" From the expression on the commander's face, Edelin was sure that Leitser intended to throw the pendant at him.

"What is that you say? Those incompetent, blundering Lycentian scouts who stumbled upon the Harrigoians! They were encamped in the gorge west of Noran! They are to blame for that disaster! That *Captain* Jarad Kethrein and those other haughty, incompetent Lycentians! They were pathetically outnumbered! And they knew it! But they chose to attack the Haarigoians anyway which sent the horde lickety-split into Noran! I knew the mongrels were in the gorge! According to my faultless reconnaissance, they had no plans to head for Noran. As a matter of fact, I was certain that they were mustering instead to venture north into the Rigars." As he drew in a deep breath, Leitser persisted in dangling the shiny medallion in front of the young thief.

"Up to that day, counselor, the town of Noran had never been attacked by Haarigoians. And *this* pendant is proof of my leadership in this matter!" Leitser coughed and then tossed the pendant onto his bedroll. "I … I must apologize … for losing my temper. I thought I had … forgiven … that Lycentian captain. However, it seems that I still harbor some … animosity … towards him." The conversation ended when the commander succinctly informed him that his services were no longer needed that day, and he told Edelin to leave the tent. Before exiting, Edelin took note of the location of the silvery bauble.

That evening, Edelin did not return to Leitser's tent to dine with the commander and the other officers but ended up instead at one of the campfires of the volunteers and recruits. As he sat there and nibbled on what was probably rabbit or even raccoon, he quietly listened to the men discuss the mission Leitser had referred to earlier that day. An older but fairly-muscular gent sporting an equally-angular frame – and a severely-balding scalp as well – led the informal discussion around the fire.

"The group we will pursue tomorrow includes a few of the traitors who caroused with that monster Ulek," the soldier said. "If we are successful in routing them, we will have dealt a severe blow to the rebels' state of mind. Accordingly, our mission on the Plains should then be nearly complete."

"Your logic is faulty," a much-younger recruit chimed in. This militiaman sported a tattered deerskin hat embellished with similarly-worn feathers; he also wore a long deerskin coat that complemented the hat. "Vicious packs of these beasts are moving about not only on the Plains but are venturing even into the interior counties of the forest." The man spoke plainly and without much emotion. "Ulek may have been an important leader for Haarigo, but these brutes ... for Othleis' sake! They have demonstrated no loyalty to any man."

"Indeed, Pike, but eradicating the last of these rebels who swore allegiance to Ulek should send a definitive message to those who remain loyal to Ahnak," the nearly-bald soldier replied.

"What have you been sippin' there, greenhorn?!" another soldier exclaimed. "I care little for what effect slaughterin' those malcontents has on the others!" This stocky militiaman had a tankard in one hand and a black and greasy chunk of roast wild hog in the other."Mullin' around in this dusty camp just waitin' for somethin' to happen is drivin' me plum crazy! And see my sword here? Why, she's gettin' awfully rusty." He paused and looked into the faces of the men seated around the fire. "And we all know what's the best remedy for rust! Ha! Fresh Haarigoian blood, that's what!" The men responded as one with guttural laughter. That is, all laughed except Edelin. Maybe because of his silence, the one called Pike glared at the thief.

"You there! The one who calls himself a lawyer! You've been sitting there … eating our food and taking in our conversation. It's your turn to share a word with us! What think you about all this, counselor?" Edelin nearly choked on the bit of roasted raccoon and promptly thought how to best respond. He coughed again to give himself more time to craft a credible retort.

"You're asking me? You want to know what I think? While I personally have never taken part in an excursion like the one the commander is orchestrating – "

"Wrong answer, Blotch," Pike interrupted. "And that would be a peculiar name … Blotch. You said that you're Rigarian? *Blotch* sounds Muad to me. Stupid name either way! Listen, men! I wager that this wisp of a willow tree has never wielded a sword in anger … or even pulled back on a bowstring in the heat of battle! And here he is," he said, pointing a finger at the young thief. "Yes, and here *you* are … appearing out of nowhere … to become Leitser's personal advisor. Tell us, *Blotch*! What in all of Othleis' majestic creation gives *you* the right to sit by our fire tonight? Oh, pardon me! I may have already figured this out! Maybe the commander himself sent you to … spy on us? On *us* … his lowly recruits?" Pike then began to move slowly towards the source of his irritation.

"Pike! That ale is gettin' the best of you again! Why don't you just set yourself back down? Even if that Lycentian greenhorn doesn't know which end of a sword to latch onto, it can't be worth upsettin' Leitser by inflictin' any damage upon him." Pike stopped walking towards Edelin but continued to stare.

"Bah! I was not going to hurt the frail sapling … it just needs some … pruning … that's all." Suddenly, in his right hand a long knife appeared. The reddish-orange flames of the campfire danced wildly on its steel blade, giving the impression that the blade itself was ablaze. "This knife … it was my dear old Grandpappa's … and do you know what he liked to do with it? Skin wild hog and deer, that's what!" Pike stopped staring but stepped a few feet closer. Edelin responded by standing up and retreating correspondingly. "But do have you any idea what *I* like doing with it, counselor? Now do you?" Edelin grimaced as he designed his response.

"Whatever I say would surely be wrong, kind sir, of that I am certain. But might it have something to do with the killing of Haarigoians?" The militiamen laughed, all, of course, but the inebriated aggressor.

"Wrong answer … *again*, Blotch." He then put the knife back into its sheath. "I wouldn't want to offend the spirit of Grandpappa by desecrating this fine blade with the blood of any putrid Haarigoian."

"Consider yourself summarily blessed by the Creator, young man, that you do not have to experience what Pike generally uses that blade for," the stocky soldier offered. He then displayed a large knife and pretended to shave his crusty beard with it. "Maybe Pike was thinkin' about usin' it to remove that scraggly bit of hair under your chin?"

"You are most correct, my overly-rotund companion. If a man wants to grow a beard, at least it should look like a beard ... and not like a layer of chamber soot!" Laughter again ringed the campsite, and Edelin, finally realizing that he had overstayed his welcome, bowed to his adversary.

"Kind sir, if you permit me, I will be leaving the cozy confines of your wonderful fire. And as I leave, I promise to do what I can to improve ... the quality of my facial hair."

"Ha! Now there's somethin' you just might be qualified for, Blotch!" Pike shouted as Edelin moved away from his antagonizers and into the darkness of the surrounding woods.

Once he was a few yards from the rear of Commander Leitser's tent, Edelin emerged from the emerald darkness as adroitly as he had entered. "Ah yes. It is time to continue with my original plan," he whispered. Using the tent as cover, he peered first to his left and then to his right. He then crawled on his hands and knees around the corner of the tent and pulled the slit of a door open ever so slightly. "Perfect! He's not here." Still on hands and knees, he entered the tent and then closed the slit behind him. Once erect, he moved quickly in the darkness to the side of the tent where his things were stashed and grabbed his knapsack. "Grandfather's old bag has served me well," he whispered. He reached inside the knapsack and – from a hidden pocket in the bottom of the bag – pulled out the gold coins that he had lifted from the hosteler in Noran. "Leitser's pendant may not be made of gold, but in the long run it may be worth more than these coins." He put the coins back into the pocket and then moved to Leitser's side of the tent.

"Aha! Here it is!" he said after rifling through the commander's bags. The moon was nearly full that night, so as he held it aloft for a moment, suspending the silvery object from its chain, he smiled as he appreciated its fine craftsmanship. Edelin then ripped off the chain and tossed it back into the commander's bag. The pendant then joined the coins in the knapsack's secret compartment. "I wonder … might Leitser have something else worth stealing?" But before he could ponder it further, voices approached the tent. Quickly, he crawled into his bedroll and pretended to be asleep.

"I will be right out. There's something I need to collect from in here." It was Leitser. Edelin focused on remaining still and even drew in air to imitate the deep breathing of one seemingly lost in dreamland. "My, my! The Lycentian lawyer! Sacked out and sawing logs!" Edelin trained an ear to what Leitser was doing and knew that he could not be looking in the bag where the pendant had been located. He took another deep breath and this time exhaled with a low-volume wheeze. Leitser chuckled, and then there was silence. Edelin resisted the temptation to sit up, wanting to ensure that if the commander immediately reentered, he would not find him awake. He waited a few more minutes then quickly leaped out of the bedroll, folded it, and tied it to the knapsack. "I hope to never again meet anyone from this camp," he whispered. Then, like he had entered it, he exited the tent and melted once again into the forest.

Under the cover of darkness, he not only made it to the makeshift corral where the militia kept their horses, he successfully enticed one of mares to accompany him without any of the guards noticing. Fearing what he might encounter if he headed west into the Plains, he instead steered his mount directly north in the general direction of the Rigar Mountains.

By morning of the next day, Edelin rode into a hamlet nestled in a narrow valley below the Rigars. It was not totally unfamiliar, but a few years had passed since he had visited it. One place he was familiar with was a small hostel that, if it had not been demolished, should have been on the village's east side. And, like he had done a few weeks before, he ditched the stolen horse, first making sure that no one saw him.

Like he was born to deceive, the young thief soon endeared himself to a few other young residents of that village who were bored and looking for something to do to make some money. Before too long, the four of them – three Rigarian malcontents and one Lycentian impersonating a run-away Noran militiaman – headed further up into the mountains in pursuit of adventure.

CHAPTER SEVEN

"Othleis has ordained all three Ages: Enlightenment, Misanthropy, and Restoration. Those who succeed in pursuit of His purity have already been Enlightened. And they will thrive through the Age of Misanthropy; they alone will enjoy Restoration."

The day after Patrik and Galena arrived in Lycentia, the second snowfall of the season blanketed the city. This time the white stuff amounted to more than a dusting as it flowed down from the heavens like cream over freshly-picked strawberries. Due to but a hint of a breeze, the elegant white icing coated all of the city's flaws and imperfections. As he sipped hot persimmon tea laced with honey, Patrik spent much of that snowy morning watching Galena and Walthan cavort in the vacant cobblestone square just outside Franck's front door. Their winter games began with pummeling each other with snowballs. They then moved on to constructing snow creatures upon which they channeled their aggressions with more snowballs. Galena's structure of snow was taller than her and was about as thin while Walthan created a caricature of a grossly-overweight man. The innkeeper garnered a smile as he watched both young people first destroy Galena's gaunt snow sculpture then reduce Walthan's to a discordant pile. As the young adults continued to fashion weapons made of the white stuff, Patrik thought that the horses would appreciate fresh water and food, so he grabbed his coat and made his way downstairs and out the front door.

"Father! You have finally come outside! I knew you couldn't stay cooped up in the house for very long!" Galena shouted just as the innkeeper closed the door behind him. Then, with a farcical effort, she launched a snowball in her father's direction; he ducked down to dodge it, and it smacked into the house behind him. "If I had wanted to hit you with that, I would have!" she then added. Patrik laughed, bent over and then scooped up a handful of the white stuff. He held the frozen water vapor in his bare hands for a second then, as quickly as he had gathered it, let it fall back to the ground. Galena's arms dropped to her side, and she visibly sighed. "Why can't you even make a simple snowball? You never do anything fun anymore!"

Galena retreated from the battlefield and followed Patrik to the burnt-out shell of the building next door to Franck's. As they walked away, Walthen shouted out something about needing to prepare the noon meal. Galena turned around to wave at her new friend, but before he could see it, he had re-entered the house.

"Father, what did Uncle Franck mean when he said that Walthan is different? I mean, what is so *different* about him?" Galena asked as she lifted water from the well and poured it into the oaken bucket.

"Walthan?" Patrik replied. "What must you know about Franck's understudy?"

"*Understudy*? Is that what Franck has planned for him? To turn him into an itinerant merchant like him?" she asked as she poured the crystal-clear liquid into the trough.

Before the bucket was emptied, the horses were lapping up the fresh water.

"Uncle Franck hasn't disclosed to me why the boy is living here. I just assume that he is preparing him to become a merchant ... even though I have no evidence to support my assumption." Patrik patted one of the horses on its head and then scratched the chin of the other. Neither beast looked up and continued drinking. "What do *you* think is different about him?"

"Oh, I don't know ... he doesn't appear to be crippled. Nor does he seem to lack any mental capacities," Galena replied. "Maybe Franck thinks he is strange because he likes to cook and do other things like that?" Patrik laughed.

"I doubt that his affinity for cooking has anything to do with Franck's opinion of him. Maybe you should just ask the boy?"

"Fine! I will do just that! But if he gets angry, I will say that you told me to ask!"

Not much later, Walthan announced that the midday meal was prepared. For the first time that day, Franck came down from his room and was the first to take his place at the head of the table. Even before Galena could find a seat, he began to help himself to the food.

"Uncle," she said as she sat down across the table from the portly merchant. "How did you and Walthan meet?" Franck paused, closed his eyes, chewed up and swallowed what was in his mouth, then took another bite. "Uncle Franck! I just asked you a question. Could you stop filling your face for a moment and answer me?" Franck slowly put down the knife and fork, picked up a napkin, and wiped the corners of his mouth.

"Walthan!" he yelled. "Come here! Into the dining room!" Franck then laid his arms across his large chest, furrowed his gray and bushy brow, and glared at Galena. The door to the pantry opened and out walked Walthan carrying a pewter mug. "No, I did not ask for any ale, boy! We only need you to explain something." He then glanced up at the young man standing next to him. "Tell Galena how we met. Tell her how you then came to live in my house." The young man's face turned the color of fresh cottage cheese. "Go ahead! Tell her!"

"How we met? I ... well, it really is not that interesting ... it was just ... we ... Mr. Horriatt and I – "

"Spit it out, boy! Just explain to them what happened that night in the inn." Franck stood up and latched onto the ale that Walthen had delivered. He then threw down a huge gulp. "Tell them," he whispered as he walked away from the table with the tankard lodged firmly in his right hand.

The boy swallowed hard and began to relate what happened one night when Franck was visiting Walthan's village in the Knaesin Mountains. The old traveler had just fallen asleep when he was awakened by the sound of something hitting the floor not far from his bed; Walthan inadvertently had knocked over a candlestick. Franck jumped out of bed and tackled the boy as he was about to escape. They wrestled on the floor until Walthan finally assented. After the owner of the inn and his wife came into the room, Walthan confessed that he could not help but notice the trinkets that Franck was selling in the market earlier that day. He thought that getting his hands on even one of those would help him solve his current predicament. He said that his grandfather had died the week before

Franck had arrived in the village, leaving him completely without any family and pitifully penniless as well.

Franck threw down another bit of ale and then interrupted to add that at first he didn't believe him, but as the boy continued to emphatically plead his case, Franck graciously chose to not turn him over to the constable. Instead, he offered him a choice: either agree to work for him, which ultimately meant relocating to Lycentia, or be charged with burglary. Walthan didn't think long before choosing to become the merchant's trainee.

"When did all this happen?" Patrik asked.

"Walthan has been here in Lycentia for nine … maybe ten weeks," Franck replied. "I must include that his presence has made dealing with Sereal's absence much more-bearable." He then sat back down in his chair, picked up a fork and returned to eating."Walthan has also proven to be as talented in the pantry as Sereal … nearly as talented," he added as he speared another chunk of braised turnip. It appeared that the discussion about Walthan had ended – at least for the afternoon – as Franck changed the topic to ask Patrik why he had come to Lycentia.

"Surely you remember those scrolls, Uncle," Galena said before her father could muster a response. Franck first glanced at her, then at Patrik and then closed his eyes and expelled a loud sigh.

"Scrolls … let me think," he said as his fork found yet another steaming tuber. "Ah yes, those parchments you found in that cave … the cave not far north of the inn? The one in which not very long ago animal – and maybe even human – sacrifices were performed? What was it called?"

"Feleg," Patrik said. "And as far as I have determined, only animals were ever sacrificed there … and not inside the cave proper, but on a crude stone altar that's just below the entrance." The innkeeper took a sip from his tankard and continued. "On that particular day last Spring, Othleis allowed my attention to be drawn to a small area of the cave that I for some reason had chosen to ignore. It was in that narrow fissure that I found the urn ... a crude earthenware pot ... that contained those parchments."

"And where are you keeping these seemingly-rare but mysterious writings? For sometime now I have wanted to examine these things that have given you this new zest for life," Franck said as he pushed himself away from the table. "Might you go find them for us?" he then asked. Patrik excused himself and went upstairs to the guest room. Franck belched, apologized for being so rude and then reached across the table to grab the last piece of black-bean bread.

"Here they are!" Patrik announced as he laid the light-brown leather pouch on the table, nearly spilling the contents of Franck's tankard. "Even though the scrolls were in that cave for many years, miraculously, they are in fairly good shape," Patrik said.

"Fascinating," Franck replied. "Might you read something from them, old man?" Franck said. "Take out a sheet and read something that will prove to my agnostic ears what is so amazing about them." Patrik untied the strings that kept the parchments tucked safely inside the pouch then pulled the entire set out as if they were bound as one document. "And start reading soon! I am about to fall asleep!" Franck yawned with a sly smirk on his face.

"Could you allow me a moment?" Patrik asked respectfully. "You asked for something amazing. Please allow me time to find it." The innkeeper slowly leafed through page after page. "Teophelus, one of the neophyte priests who serves at the temple in Noran ... he has helped me to understand quite a bit of what Harrak wrote. But there are still ... many passages that I have yet come to grips with." Franck shrugged his shoulders, put his hands behind his head and leaned back in his chair.

"Take as much time as you need, old friend," he said. "If you are choosing to give up a good life as an innkeeper to instead be a *scroll-keeper*, then it behooves me to be patient," Franck quipped. "That is, if I can just stay awake long enough."

"Teophelus has been more than kind to help Father learn how to interpret the scrolls," Galena offered. "Isn't that right, Father? Hasn't he been the most-helpful person you have ever met?" She slid over to the side of the table where Patrik leafed through the parchments. "What about this one? Can you read from this page?" she asked, placing her right hand on a piece of parchment that Patrik had already passed over.

"No! Please allow me to decide! And as I've told you before: do not touch these pages!" Patrik nearly shouted. The expression on his daughter's face reminded him of another time when he had gotten angry at her for handling the writings. "Galena, I am sorry. Please forgive me for raising my voice."

"I forgive you," she said softly as she then moved away from the table. "Uncle Franck, now you can see what those papers have done to him. Be careful to not get too close to them or he might just rip your head off!" Patrik glared momentarily at Galena but then focused again on finding a thought-provoking passage. A thin line of sweat formed on his forehead as he struggled to find something worth sharing with the old merchant.

"Here!" Patrik finally announced. "This passage! Last month ... the last time he visited the inn ... Teophelus said that this section is very important. Now please bear with me. It is going to be a rough translation since I have only begun to learn how to read this strange script." He took a deep breath and began to read aloud. *'There is a small island in the middle of the mighty Etruscan. On that island Othleis revealed the future to me. It is a future of blackness, evil compounded by a greater evil. But light, pure light that will destroy all evil – all that is darkness – will again rise from the grave.'* There. I think I translated it correctly," Patrik whispered as he set that page on the table and began to search for another passage.

"*A future of blackness ... evil compounded by more evil* ... interesting ... very interesting, And just what might this *blackness* represent? Death? Disease? Famine? Financial disaster? Maybe all of the above?" Franck asked sarcastically as he again pushed his portly frame out of the chair. "Walthan! Come in here! We are finished," he yelled. "Walthan! What are you doing in there?"

"Sir, forgive me! I am here," the young man panted as he came into the room.

"Mealtime is over. Clear off the table and then draw my bath," he said. "Prepare the water hotter than last time. I am fighting another one of those despicably-irritating backaches. My head is pounding as well."

"Yes sir," was Walthan's response as he started to clean off the table.

"Franck, I have found another important part – "

"Tomorrow, my scraggly-bearded friend, tomorrow," Franck grunted. "I do not think that my brain will allow me to grasp anymore fanciful words from your mystical writings today." Walthan had picked up some the plates when Patrik – attempting to return the parchments to the pouch – inadvertently bumped his arm. This sudden movement sent the plates out of the boy's hand and crashing onto the dark, hardwood floor. "Walthan! What are you doing? You nearly ruined the innkeeper's papers!"

"Papers? Oh, they … they are parchments. What is written on them?" Walthan asked as he knelt on the floor to scoop up the disheveled dish ware. "They appear to be quite old," he added as he stood up and looked at the scrolls.

"They are old … and only *old* people care about what is written on them," Galena quipped.

"What do they say? Can you tell me?" the boy asked. "My grandfather … before he died … would read to me from old papers that looked much like these."

"Your grandfather had scrolls, too?" Galena asked. "Father, did you hear that? Your precious parchments are not that unusual after all!"

"Young man, I can read something from these for you … if your *master* would only allow me the pleasure," Patrik said, gently waving one of the pages at him. Franck shook his head as he left the room. "Here. I will read that same passage that I read a moment ago: 'But light, pure light that will destroy all that is evil, will rise from the grave.' Does that make any sense to you?" Patrik asked.

"It … it sounds … interesting … maybe even familiar," Walthen responded softly. "Grandfather often talked about how the evil of the world was growing, how it was becoming more powerful ... about how the coming darkness would soon consume everything and – "

"Walthan!" Franck bellowed from the top of the stairs. "Have you forgotten about my bathwater!" The young man sucked in a deep breath, collected more of the plates from the table, and scurried back into the pantry.

That evening, tired of listening to Franck and her father catalog their numerous aches and pains, Galena released a tremendous yawn, thereby announcing that it was time for bed. Franck wished her a "good night" and, before long, the merchant first and then the innkeeper made their way upstairs.

The snow that had been falling at a steady rate the entire day subsided around dusk. Not much later, the thick, gray clouds that deposited the white stuff gave way to a moon-lit, indigo sky. Galena, from the window of their second-story room, was admiring the twinkling starlight combined with the shimmering snow when her attention was drawn to a shadowy figure in the yard behind the house. "Father," she said quietly, "Someone is out there ... I think ... I think it is Walthan!"

"Outside? At this time of night?" Patrik asked. "What might he be doing out this late?"

"I cannot tell. He is just standing there in the snow ... and he's not even wearing a coat."

"A peculiar lad, to say the least. Best to leave him be," he grunted. "Maybe he finds pleasure in gazing at the moon." He yawned and then stretched, hoping that Galena would get the hint that he was exhausted and wanted to get some sleep.

"Father! Now he's doing something ... not merely looking up into the sky," she said, the volume of her voice a tad louder than before. "Something ... unusual."

"Unusual? How so?"

"His arms ... he is standing in the snow, with his head up, looking at the moon ... and his arms are raised high above his head. And ... he is ... might he be dancing?!"

When he was finally able to turn down the lamp and climb into bed, the innkeeper could only lay there, unable to fall asleep. So he let his mind wander as he stared at the shadows that the dim light from outside the window created on the ceiling above him. He began to think about Dalneia, and for some reason also began to think about Markus, her younger brother.

"Galena," he whispered.

"Yes, Father?" she replied.

"I am thinking about your mother this very moment ... and also about your Uncle Markus," he whispered. "How different those two are ... brother and sister but so very, very different. Your mother would sing, oh, how she loved to sing!"

"I remember, Father," Galena interrupted. "Can I go to sleep now?"

"And her brother?" The innkeeper continued. "Ha! Not a single, solitary musical bone in his body. They looked like twins but Dalneia was so talented musically. And your uncle.... oftentimes when he was depressed and gloomy, she would sing to cheer him up. But did he appreciate it? No, of course not."

"Why are you now thinking about them? I thought you said you were tired and wanted to go to sleep!"

"Right," he replied. "I am tired. Forgive me for keeping you awake. Good night, sweet Galena."

"Good night to you, silly Father."

The next morning, Patrik was awakened by pigeons outside the window scratching and tapping on its cold frame. Even though warm sunlight had been pouring into the room for over an hour, he was able to remain asleep. He rubbed his eyes and looked around the room. "Bah," he complained. "She's already up and gone. I hope she's not bothering Franck." Before falling asleep the night before, he was thinking that it would be prudent to find Franck and talk to him about Walthan before Galena had a chance. "It appears," he muttered, "That is not about to happen."

Before heading downstairs, he looked across the hallway. "Good … his door is closed. Maybe he is still asleep." As he made his way to the first floor, he heard the clanging of pots and pans coming from the pantry. He then headed in that direction and expected to find Walthan preparing breakfast. But, much to his surprise, it was Galena who was making all the noise.

"Galena, remember what we were talking about before going to sleep last night?" Patrik asked.

"And a fine 'Good morning' to you, too!" she replied.

"Oh, I'm sorry. Good morning, dearest daughter!" he said as he reached out and gave her a hug. "But can I tell you what I dreamed about last night? While it is still fresh in my mind?" Galena moved out of her father's arms and put her hands on her hips.

"Most definitely! We simply cannot allow your dreams from last night to just disappear into nothingness, now can we?" she replied.

Patrik then told her that he dreamed about Dalneia and

Markus' father and how he suddenly passed away during one of the worst snowstorms to ever roar into Noran. Their mother took his death so hard that she was not able to care for the children. When Dalneia was only twelve, her mother's conditioned worsened to the point that she took off one night that following spring. It was rumored that she was seen leaving town with a young and handsome traveling merchant.

"So why are you telling me this? It's not like I did not already know of Grandmother's mental condition," Galena said.

"I had to tell you about it because right before I woke up … before the dream about your grandmother's irresponsibility ended … I then started to dream about Franck's wife, Sereal."

"And why do you suppose that is so strange? Did we not discuss Sereal's leaving just last night? Sometimes, Father, the way your brain works makes me wonder about your sanity," she quipped as she displayed a faint smile.

"My brain is perfectly fine, young lady! And don't you ever forget it!" Patrik exclaimed. "By the way, my sweet younger daughter," he continued. "What are you doing here by yourself here in the pantry? Attempting to get Uncle Franck mad at you for making such a ruckus when he's trying to sleep?"

"Surely not! I'm starving and am merely looking for something palatable to eat," she replied.

"But why can't you just be a good house-guest and wait for the host to have breakfast prepared for you?"

"Father, I do not think that will be happening anytime soon. Look at this," she replied and handed him a piece of paper.

"And what do we have here? A note … let me see that," he said and then began to read it silently, his lips moving as he read. "Bah!" he said after a few seconds. "This must be a joke! That man can be such a prankster! How could Franck depart on another one of his excursions without saying a thing to us about it last night?"

"But he *did* leave that note … as rude as it is … to inform of us of his plans," Galena offered. "What do you think about it saying that we can stay here until he returns. That is, if we really – "

"Walthan? What about the young man? Is he still here?" The innkeeper interrupted.

"Father, do you honestly think that I would be in here attempting to prepare something for us to eat if Walthan was still here?"

"Upstairs? Did you think to look for him upstairs? Ah yes, Franck's door … it was closed…. I noticed before I came downstairs," Patrik said.

"I left our room as soon as I awoke … at the break of dawn. That note … it was laying on the little table by the front door at the bottom of the stairs," Galena offered as she fiddled with her hair.

"But how could they have left without us hearing them?"

"Oh, that would not require much!" Galena exclaimed."You hardly wake up during the night like you used to. You have become quite a heavy sleeper … in your old age," Galena said, pursing her lips as she formed her strawberry-blond hair into a bun.

"Watch what you say about my age, young lady," was all he could think to say. "What about Franck's wagon?" he then asked to get the conversation back on topic. "Is it gone?" She nodded. Patrik left of the pantry, walked quickly through the dining room and then opened the front door of the house. There in the snow was one set of wagon tracks coming from the out-building and heading down the street. "But how did they leave without you seeing them? Didn't you say that you were up at dawn?"

"I guess he decided that they would leave very early, much before daylight. Walthan, after cleaning up from dinner last night, must have prepared everything for them to leave first thing."

"Right. So if I am now such a heavy sleeper, why didn't *you* hear them moving around?" the innkeeper asked.

"Father, I have always been a heavy sleeper," was her quick reply. "Tamara has always been the one to not stay asleep at night for more than a couple hours at a time!"

Even though he was still confused about Franck leaving without saying anything about it the night before, Patrik resigned himself to the fact that he and the old merchant just were not the close friends that they once had been. Soon, the two visitors from Noran were enjoying a breakfast of kettle-cakes – prepared a bit differently than the ones Tamara used to make – which satisfied both the cook and the innkeeper. While they ate, they sat quietly, until Galena suddenly broke the silence.

"Since you had to recount *your* silly dreams, you must allow me to tell you what I dreamed about." Patrik smiled and nodded his head, so she continued. "Tamara was the focus of my dreams last night. And there she was, still wearing that amazing wedding gown … and she was all alone there in that huge castle! No servants, no guards, no one! Not even Ilead! It was so sad that it almost made me wake up crying!" She got out of the chair and wrapped her arms around Patrik's shoulders. "Father, we haven't seen her in so long! Isn't it time that we go to the palace to at least let her know that we are in Lycentia? We have been here for almost three whole days already!"

"Now please do not start talking again about us moving into the palace," Patrik scolded. "Our mission to deliver the scrolls to Oliver must not be endangered by allowing Ilead and Tamara to be associated with Harrak's writings – even if the association is indirect."

"Father! Now don't *you* start talking *again* about this being *our* mission," Galena retorted and then suddenly stood up. "Wait … I have it! It is the perfect idea! I know where the castle is! I can go there by myself! Why, I could even move into the palace with my queenly sister while you continue your all-important *mission* from here! You and your precious parchments can just remain right here in your *old friend's* house!"

After allowing her to construct a few more reasons as to why it was necessary for them to see Tamara, Patrik finally assented. He then said that they even would go to the palace later that morning, but only under the stipulation that she would not bring up the topic of them establishing residence in the palace.

As Patrik was about to leave the house to prepare the wagon and tend to the horses so they could make the cross-town trip to the palace, he wondered again about Franck leaving without telling them. Galena wanted to join him, so he asked her to give the horses some fresh grain and, as soon as she closed the front door, he dashed up the stairs. He hesitated just outside the door to Franck's room. He then tested the latch; it was not locked. Quietly and slowly, he opened the door. What he saw made him gasp for air. On the bed was Franck, still dressed in his nightclothes, appearing to be sound asleep. The air in the room was much-colder than the air in the hallway and when Patrik glanced at the window, he learned why: it was open!

"Franck? Franck! Wake up!" Patrik shouted. Then he began to shake his old friend. "Franck! Wake up!" But the merchant would not move. "He ... he does not appear to be breathing," Patrik whispered. "Galena ... I cannot allow Galena see him like this. Later ... I will deal ... with this later," he whispered again.

Suddenly, like her death had happened only the day before, the image of Dalneia lying in bed, her body without breath, without life, came speeding out of his subconscious and slammed full-force into his mind's eye. Unlike Dalneia, though, Franck's eyes were closed. But even though they were closed, the index finger of Patrik's right hand gently touched the man's right eye, and then the left, as if the eyes needed to be closed – as if the body of his wife was in that bed.

"I ... I cannot....I will not ... let Galena ... see this," he muttered as he backed out of the room and pulled the door shut. He quietly and slowly began to walk down the stairs; half-way down, he suddenly picked up speed and ran down the remainder of the steps, hitting the front door at full speed. He kept up that pace until he reached Galena who was waiting for him in the wagon.

"Father! Why are you so out of breath?" she asked as he climbed up and sat down next to her.

"Please move over and give me the reins."

"Why? Why can't I have the reins? The horses – "

"Do not argue with me!" he shouted. Staring at him as if he had just insulted her, Galena quickly handed him the reins. In less time than it takes to muster a hearty sneeze, Patrik commanded the horses to make their way towards the palace, and the four of them were headed out of that part of the city.

CHAPTER EIGHT

"The Creator promises healing and deliverance
for those who faithfully seek His purity;
He alone is Othleis the Healer."

Edelin was grateful that the constant whiteness floating down from the gray clouds covered the stolen horse's tracks as quickly as it created them. Before long, he had made his way down the mountain. After nearly a month of residing in this quaint but nondescript hamlet, the thief had tired of the charade of pretending to be a member of the Noran militia. The villagers who had accepted him for who he said he was offered little in entertainment nor did they seem to possess anything worth stealing. They were, in his mind's eye, the most-pathetic handful of economically, intellectually-challenged men he had ever come in contact with. Was his disgust towards them fueled by his Lycentian upbringing? More than likely, it was fostered by an ego voluminous enough for three men.

Edelin had planned on partnering with these rustic roustabouts longer than he did, but could no longer force himself to listen to their monochromatic drivel for even one more night. So, in tune with his current modus operandi of staying in one place for not more than a month, he slinked off in the dead of night and scurried away, snagging one of their mangy, but sure-footed, mountain ponies in the process.

The snow began to fall about the time he dismissed himself from the others and came down even harder as he mockingly waved "Good-bye!" to the insipid handful of inexperienced miners, hunters and trappers who – without reservation – had taken him into their fold. As he continued down the trail, he thought about one trapper who had shown a considerable amount of intelligence compared to his peers. This somewhat-adventurous soul had recently returned from delivering pelts to a trading post about ten miles northwest of Ahnak. During his brief stint with Commander Leitser and the Noran militia, Edelin had learned that the ancient Muad citadel was finally under Lycentian control. But he had not yet put two-and-two together concerning the fresh possibilities for trade between the previously-opposed cities. It was this realization that inspired him to vacate the Rigarian hamlet.

As the grade of the mountain trail became less-precipitous, the northwest wind then picked up. This gave the impression that the flakes were coming down in greater volume compared to earlier in the day. Edelin wiped wind-blown snow from his face, and from a distance he thought he heard the lonely, but ominous, cry of a wolf. For some reason, that lonely wail reminded him of Patrik. So, his thoughts turned to time spent at The Lonely Fox Inn, to the salt and pepper-bearded innkeeper and to his daughters. The memory of Galena's unsought affection made him chuckle, and he quickly pushed away any sentimentality associated with that relationship. But – and this made his heart skip a beat – he began to dwell on Tamara's uncommon beauty.

He thought of how she walked, the way her espresso-brown hair would flow from side to side like molasses would flow on a cool day. He also tried to categorize the tint of her eyes, "Were they green?" he said softly. "Yes, they had to be green. But what shade, what splendid hue of green? The green of a newly-sprouted maple leaf? No, no. Not dark enough," he pondered. "But," he quickly added. "They were the most-beautiful shade of green. Ah yes, they certainly were."

When the light of the impending dawn revealed the depth of the snow around him, Edelin wished that once he was completely out of the mountains and into the forest the snow would subside. However, the exact opposite occurred. The white stuff came down even harder as he moved further south – even forcing him to look for a place to find cover. He hopped off the pony and led it under a large oak tree that had not completely shed its dead, brown leaves from the previous summer. The leaves – at least momentarily – kept much of the snow on the tree's mighty branches and from accumulating on the forest floor below. While he waited for the wind and snow to recede, he pulled a cracker out of his duffel bag and took a bite. "Argh! Stale and mushy!" he said and, instead of tossing it on the ground, offered it to his companion who bit onto the offering wholeheartedly. So as he waited, he noted how many crackers were pulled out of the bag and used that number to gauge how long they took shelter under the friendly tree.

"Fifteen crackers," he said to his four-legged partner. "We've been standing here too long. Even though the snow hasn't stopped, it's slowed down enough." And with that, he climbed up onto the brown and white-speckled pony and coaxed it back onto the snowy trail.

He again heard a raspy howl, and Edelin felt that whatever made it was closer than before. He looked to the right, and then to the left, shrugged his shoulders, patted the pony on the head, and thought nothing more about it. As he had hoped, the snowfall finally could only be classified as light flurries. This improvement in the weather made him feel like his luck had changed for the better. He also felt that the slope of the mountain trail wasn't as severe; this too convinced him that the hardest part of their journey was over. He squinted to examine the path ahead and noticed that they were approaching a small brook. "I bet you're more than ready for a drink of fresh water," he said as he patted the pony's slush-covered head once again.

Upon reaching the brook, Edelin dismounted and, while the pony helped himself to the transparent mountain water, he looked for a spot where he could relieve himself. The warm stream of his yellowish waste created a fine white mist as it splashed on the snow-covered rocks. After his bladder was sufficiently drained, Edelin stretched and yawned. "I rode the entire night … sure don't want to do that again anytime soon!" Then, as he bent over to work out the kinks in his lower back, he was suddenly knocked, face-first, into the brook. The shock of the icy-cold water in his face made him quickly forget his stiff muscles. Without thinking, he stood up – still in the middle of the shallow brook – and turned around to see what had made him fall.

It was a wolf!

Not more than ten feet away, the grayish, blackish creature was crouching, front legs down and hind end poised for what was for sure to be another lunge. He menacingly peered into the young thief's eyes and bared his yellowish teeth. Edelin quickly scanned the area to see if the wolf was alone; he hoped that none of his pack were in the vicinity. He knew that if he didn't solve this problem soon, other wolves were bound to join. However, for some odd reason, the pony was still lapping water out of the brook, seemingly oblivious to what was transpiring. Edelin took a deep breath of cold air and thought that he had also caught a whiff of sulfur. He then thought of diverting the beast's attention away from him and onto his sure-hoofed companion, but quickly realized that if his mount ended up seriously wounded or worse, his method of effective transportation would, of course, be eliminated.

As he stared back at the crazed creature, he bent down to feel for anything at his feet that could be used as a weapon. "Strange," he whispered as he squinted to examine the wolf more closely. "Quite a bit of the animal's fur is gone." His hand found what might be helpful if the wolf attacked again and subsequently latched onto a palm-sized rock. Edelin then repositioned it appropriately in preparation for a successful launch. But before he could begin to judge how hard he would need to throw the rock, the wolf lunged at him, his fangs nearly grabbing onto his left shoulder very close to his neck but biting into Edelin's left forearm instead. He felt the teeth sink into his woolen coat but hopefully not past his chamois shirt and linen undergarment.

With the wolf's jaws still attached to his arm, he smacked the back of the beast's head with the sharp rock. The wolf didn't let go, and so he hit it again, this time with even more force. Edelin gagged when he again breathed in that sulfuric stench; the wolf replied with a sickening yelp since the rock's jagged edge must have inflicted serious pain. The beast then let go of Edelin's arm and unexpectedly retreated back into the forest. Edelin let out a huge sigh but didn't release the rock. With it still in his right hand, he inspected his arm to see if the wolf's teeth had made contact with his skin. He felt little pain and took that as a good sign. Since he could not safely remove his coat, he could not be sure. The young thief looked back to where the pony had been standing; it was no longer there. "Not good," he said. "But at least the wolf didn't go after him."

When his feet screamed out in pain, Edelin remembered that he was nearly knee-deep in the frigid waters of the mountain brook, so he consequently moved back to the dry bank. But he ended up on the opposite side of the brook, keeping an eye on the spot where the wolf had re-entered the thick undergrowth. Edelin then looked at the jagged edge of the rock; it was stained bright red. With the index finger of his left hand, he wiped off a smidgen of the blood and examined the dark liquid. "The hide-skinning knife that I took out of Patrik's barn is in my duffel bag … which just happens to be on that pony!" he said. "Here's hoping that the wolf doesn't come back. I was very lucky that this sharp rock was just where it needed to be … *right* when I needed it," he added as he tossed the rock back into water. In less than a second, the swift current of the shallow creek cleaned off every speck of wolf's blood from it.

Edelin felt it was safe to now remove his coat, and, sure enough, the beast's teeth had penetrated the coat and shirt as well as the militia-issued undergarment. On his arm were two small red puncture marks that were colored with a small dabble of his own blood. Keeping his eyes on the spot where the wolf took off back into the forest, Edelin scooped up some water from the brook and cleaned the wounds. "Yes," he reaffirmed, shivering from the impact of the ice-cold water on his bare skin. "I am one lucky man."

Because of the thick blanket of wet snow, it didn't take

him long to locate his mount. And once reunited with it, Edelin guided it back to the trail. As he rode, he thought about why the wolf had attacked him in the first place and also wondered if the beast was just hungry. "But what about that awful odor? And what happened to his fur?" he whispered. Then he realized that he was quite hungry. Consequently, he reached into the duffel bag to search for anything besides the stale crackers to satiate his hunger. He pulled out a small hunk of ox jerky and – even though he disliked both the briny taste and grainy texture of it – forced himself to take a bite.

Directly above him, strong sunlight peeked out from behind the thick, white clouds. The resulting sound of snow melting off tree branches and hitting the ground below made Edelin feel like the weather had finally changed for the better. "And if I can keep up this pace, I should be in Ahnak in two days," he announced. He continued to nibble on the jerky and periodically rubbed his left forearm. "Why did that solitary wolf attack me, a grown man, in the first place?" he asked himself again. "Wolves in a pack would not hesitate to attack if hunting but a lone wolf?" he conjectured. "Surely he didn't have the fever. No, I have been too lucky these last few months to be bitten by a feverish wolf." He looked up at the tree branches and shielded his eyes from the lemon-yellow rays filtering through them. "I wonder, though … when might my good luck run out?"

It was close to dusk as the trail became more like a road when Edelin heard what was not the lonely howl of a wolf but what appeared to be human voices not far ahead. He quickly got off the pony and lashed it to the trunk of a small willow tree. He then knelt on one knee and strained his ears; he was positive that it human voices. "Shouting," he whispered. "And they are shouting." He cautiously moved from tree to tree, and once he had reached the origin of the noise, he crouched behind a cluster of rocks and fallen timber.

In the middle of the trail – at this point twice as wide as it was just a few miles north – were two groups of men. One group was clothed in uniforms that Edelin was not happily familiar with while the others were clothed in the dark, thick leathery garb of Haarigoian warriors. Edelin could not help but smile as he noticed that the Lycentians appeared to be slightly outnumbered. He was entranced as he watched a half-dozen Lycentian militiamen equipped with shiny double-edged steel swords defend themselves against Haarigoians armed with cruder but just as lethal weapons: single-edge axes, spiked clubs, and wooden staffs. A solitary Lycentian was on horseback and was barking orders at the others, directing the battle from his vantage point in the middle of the road.

"Here! Scrimpf! Over here! Scrimpf! Now! Lend a hand!" the officer shouted. "See! Just like I told you! These brutes are all bulk and no brain! There! He's finally down! Good job, men!" With a glistening Lycentian-steel scimitar in his right hand and a shorter but thicker broadsword in the other, the officer on horseback orchestrated the battle – first to his left then to his right. One of the Haarigoians pushed aside the foot soldier with whom he was entangled and lunged towards the officer. Without a word or even making eye contact, the officer thrashed down mightily at the attacker with the saber, driving the cold steel into the left side of the Haarigoian interloper. The militiaman who had been in hand-to-hand combat with the Haarigoian then drove his short-bladed sword into the man's midsection.

"Aha! You bastardly son of a Muad prostitute! That should teach you to never attack an officer of Lycentia!" The captain continued to belch commands while no other Haarigoians attempted to attack him. Edelin smiled in unpredicted admiration as he watched and, just when he thought that the attackers had been driven off and the Lycentians had won, the officer suddenly screamed.

"Argh! An arrow! In my side! I have been hit!" When the officer spun his horse around, Edelin saw the feathery end of a solitary shaft in the officer's right side; it bobbed up and down as the captain dismounted, nearly falling out of the saddle.

"Scrimpf! There he is! Behind that tree! Go in there and get him!" he shouted as he collapsed in a brackish puddle in the center of the road.

"Captain Kethrein! Let me help you!" one of the militiamen said as he pulled the officer out of the frigid water and to the side of the road.

"Scrimpf!" the captain continued to yell. "Did you get that blasted archer yet?" The militiaman-medic told the captain to lie down and asked that he be quiet. He then snapped off the shaft as close as possible to where it had entered and tossed the broken piece into the woods. "Scrimpf! I can't hear you! Did you find that archer?!"

"Sir, if you continue to scream like that, you'll only make it bleed more," the man said.

"Who's … screaming? I certainly … am not … screaming! Argh! What in Othleis' name are you doing to me?"

"Captain, I have done nothing but break off the shaft. It is now up to you to remain as still and as calm as possible so we can hopefully slow down the bleeding. It appears that the arrowhead is merely lodged between two of your ribs. I don't think that it hit anything important."

"You ... you are a funny man, Klatch, that you are. Of course the *arrow* didn't hit anything important! If it had, would I be sitting here yelling at you right now?!"

"Sir, you are most-definitely yelling again. The bleeding, sir ... you must be quiet, so I can slow down the bleeding." Edelin nearly laughed out loud as he watched the militiaman push on the captain's chest to make him lie down.

"Captain!" a voice then came out of the forest. "I found him! I have located the archer!" The foot soldier called Scrimpf returned to the road, and he was escorting a short but thin man who sported a long, black ponytail.

"A Rigarian! I should have known!" the captain bellowed as he was being stretched out on the soggy grass on the edge of the road. "Bring...," he then coughed. "Bring the confounded traitor ... to me!" He coughed again and then spat some blood onto the grass.

"There, captain, I told you that you would only complicate your wound even more if you continued to move about," the medic chided. "Now will you believe me and try not to say anything else? At least until we can slow down this bleeding?"

"Right," Captain Kethrein replied. "Scrimpf! We cannot take any prisoners with us. I believe you know what to do." And with that, the one called Scrimpf pulled out his sword and thrust it entirely into the archer's midsection. He then pulled it as the Rigarian collapsed at the captain's feet.

"Now," he commanded, "Tend to the other wounded while I figure out what to do about the remainder of our mission."

Still hiding safely from behind the rocks, Edelin continued to take in all the details while the medic and another militiaman tended to the three other wounded Lycentians. It appeared that the captain was the only one with a somewhat-serious wound.

"Klatch, have you finished with me yet?" the captain asked.

"Jarad … I mean … Captain," the man quickly corrected himself, "The arrowhead remains lodged between two ribs. And unless it is removed as soon as possible, infection is bound to set in. You do remember that the Rigarians love to dip their arrowheads in hog slime?"

"You just had to remind me, didn't you?" Jarad replied.

As dusk turned into night, the Lycentians successfully relocated all but one of their horses. "It appears that our mission to Noran is now awash. Therefore, we must then return to Fort Poulean," the captain said. "Thanks to this ridiculous arrowhead stuck in my side." And with that, the Lycentians mounted their horses – with the captain sharing a mount with the medic – and moved down the road in the same direction that Edelin had been heading.

Edelin was completely aghast that his good luck had not run out. "Actually, it has improved immensely," he said. This battle scene reminded him of the Haarigoian tradition of leaving men wounded in battle to die where they had fallen. As far as he could ascertain from his vantage point, the attackers were already dead, and because of this, he was so happy that he nearly giggled. So the moment when the militiamen were sufficiently out of earshot, he ran out from behind the rocks and began to rifle through the clothing of the dead Haarigoians. The young thief found nothing of interest until he looked in the small pouch that the Rigarian archer carried on his back. Inside that pouch was a dozen or more gold coins – all of Lycentian origin! "This is simply astounding! My good luck continues to flow!" he exclaimed a bit too loudly. "It would be one thing to stumble upon some gold coins, but for all of them to be Lycentian! It was definitely worth waiting for the soldiers to leave!"

He returned to the pony, untied his duffel bag and opened it. He then placed the newly-acquire coins into the secret pocket. But before closing up the bag, his attention was drawn to the purloined pendant, the silver medallion embossed with the three steeples of the Lycentian temple. Edelin looked up and noticed that the moon was directly above him. And in that orb's cold but bright light, he was once again entranced by the silvery medallion.

"Leitser's pendant … presented to him *personally* by Oliver III. Yes, this is the reason for my outlandish good luck. Yes, this is my lucky trinket. No doubt about that," he whispered as he placed the pendant back into the duffel bag, closed it up and put it back on the pony. For the rest of that night, the moon's ethereal light illuminated the path as he continued to make his way towards Ahnak.

CHAPTER NINE

"Celebrate when those who rejected the pursuit of His purity have humbly returned; the Creator passionately desires to reconcile them to Himself."

Anyone looking out of the twelve-foot high wall of windows of the palace's master bedroom would be reminded of why the windows were installed there in the first place. The top floor of the palace, the second-tallest structure in Lycentia, was illuminated by the natural light filtering through those windows. And that top floor consisted of only room: the master bedroom. Anyone peering out that glass wall would have no choice but to notice the tallest structure in Lycentia: the temple of the Netherenes. When the sky was free of clouds, the reflection of sunlight off the temple's three golden steeples would deliver as much light into that bedroom that anyone could ever want. And the morning that Patrik and Galena pulled away from Franck's house heading for the temple was such a morning.

Tamara, the queen of Betrovia, was never one to indulge in the juvenile narcissism of sleeping much past sunrise. And this was a good thing since the architects of the palace insured that its occupants would have to install very heavy curtains over the windows – or just board them up entirely – to indulge in such frivolity.

On the day when Patrik and Galena left for the palace, Tamara was out of bed and downstairs an hour before any steeple-reflective sunlight had an opportunity to awaken her. Tamara enjoyed scavenging the palace pantry for something to eat without any of the palace servants there to pester her. Kept warm by a thick, burgundy virgin wool and satin robe, she prepared a modest breakfast of fried eggs and potatoes, quietly humming one of her mother's favorite songs in the process. Her husband of only a few months, King Ilead Tetrokeu, was off on another adventure with the Lycentian militia, so she felt no guilt in cooking just enough food for one person. The palace pantry was so spacious that the entire first floor of The Lonely Fox Inn – pantry and dining area combined – would fit easily into it with many square feet to spare. And this was another thing that she missed about the inn: its cozy but friendly ambiance.

"Madam Tamara!" a voice unexpectedly rang out in the dark but airy pantry. "What are you doing?" The raspy voice belonged to Voldina, the palace head cook. Tamara grimaced as she quickly put another bite of potatoes into her mouth.

"I ... I woke up over an hour ago ... and discovered that I was quite famished. So I came down and prepared some eggs and potatoes. That is all ... really," she said as she stood up from the table.

"But Madam," the cook replied, "Palace protocol demands that the food prepared in the palace must be prepared under direction of the palace cooks. It is the rule, Madam, a very old rule. Madam surely does not want to disobey a very old rule." She was a middle-aged, short but thin, strawberry-blond woman with a splotchy-freckly facial complexion to match. Voldina was promoted to the head cook position a few months before King Justen – Ilead's predecessor – was assassinated. Maybe it was because she was still fairly new in her position that she was such a stickler for enforcing the rules. Tamara may have been miffed that morning with the cook's attention to "protocol," but she appeared to be fighting the temptation to show it.

"I apologize, Voldina … would you please forgive me?" she nearly whispered. "I promise that I will never do it again." Without saying another word nor making eye contact with her queen, Voldina removed Tamara's breakfast dish from the table and placed it in a wooden barrel by the door.

"The queen of Betrovia must show proper respect for Lycentian protocol," she offered as she began her morning routine. "What might the servants begin to say – and do – if the Queen herself cannot … how to say it? Abide by the rules?"

"I said that I was sorry," Tamara said with a hint of irritation. "It … it was just a few eggs and a small potato. No rules were broken and – "

"Madam, you must excuse me now. I have to be about my duties," the head cook said as she latched onto Tamara's left arm and began to lead her to the pantry door. "Breakfast will be served within the hour, Madam."

"Breakfast? Why … I just had my breakfast."

"Protocol, Madam, protocol," was the cook's response, and she abruptly closed the door. Tamara sighed deeply, shrugged her shoulders, and walked slowly across the massive dining hall.

"Protocol ... rules ... etiquette," she complained. "Is this what a queen is forced to reckon with?"

When Voldina's breakfast had been prepared and served, Tamara forced herself to eat at least some of the food. She then went back upstairs to the master bedroom to get dressed for the day. Even though she was fully-clothed when she left the bedroom before fixing that little before-breakfast snack, she still wore the burgundy robe when she came back downstairs. Every room on the first floor of the palace contained a large fireplace, and by the time Tamara had come back downstairs, the damp and cold air of each room was being warmed by a roaring fire. She first entered the stateroom where the king was supposed to greet and entertain important visitors. She sat down in one of the half-dozen or so heavy, overstuffed chairs and looked around the room. The wall opposite the door was decorated with shields of various sizes and shapes. One particularly caught her eye: a large oval seemingly solid gold shield. In the center of the shield was the image of warrior and a large bear in combat. She stared at it for a few minutes and then shook her head. "I can't remember the last time I saw a bear ... or even heard someone say that they had," she whispered.

She then went across the large central hall and entered what had been King Justen's private office. Even though she and Ilead had lived in the palace for nearly three months, that room was in the same condition as it was the day Justen was killed. The books were in the exact spots on the dark walnut desk where he had placed them. Even a pewter tankard, half-full, resided still on that desk. She walked over to the desk, picked up the tankard, and gagged from the odor emitted by the stagnant ale. "Horrible stuff," she announced. "An ungodly liquid even when it is fresh out of the barrel … completely horrendous." Instead of returning the tankard to its place on the table, she carried it out of the room and delivered it directly to the pantry.

"Hello, Madam," a short, dark-complected, gray-haired woman clothed in a floor-length, off-white smock said as Tamara re-entered.

"Hello..?"

"It's Natiasha, Madam," the woman said with a polite grin.

"Hello, Nat … Nati…"

"Natiasha," she repeated. "But you shouldn't worry about my name, Your Highness. It is not that important."

"Natiasha," Tamara finally said, "This was in the king's office." She then held up the tankard. "It contains the foulest-smelling liquid and I – "

"Give it to me, Madam," a voice from behind Tamara commanded. Once again it was Voldina. "The queen of Betrovia should not concern herself with such domestic issues." And before she could say another word, the tankard was removed from her hand and summarily deposited in the same barrel as the dish from earlier that morning. "Where did Madam find the mug?" Voldina inquired.

"Where? Oh, it … it was in the king's office – "

"King Justen!" Natiasha interrupted. Voldina scowled at the older woman.

"Does it matter where the mug came from?" Voldina asked. "Now, does it?"

"No, ma'am. it does not," Natiasha replied, her eyes glued to the floor. Voldina then explained to Tamara that the older servants, the ones who had worked in the palace since Justen achieved the throne, were superstitious about touching anything that belonged to him. She was the only member of the palace staff who would even go into the king's private rooms. She concluded by adding that their fear was rather illogical. She deemed it unnecessary to press the issue about removing Justen's things from the chambers until the current king desired to utilize it.

"Now that you, your Highness, have removed that odoriferous item from the room, do you feel that the king will want us to prepare the chambers for his use?" Voldina asked.

"The king? Ilead? I … I don't know," Tamara stammered. "There's so much – "

"Madam! Madam!" a gaunt, long-haired old man wearing a dingy overcoat and a floppy brown hat exclaimed as he burst into the pantry. "There's someone at the front gate, and he says … he says that he … is your father?"

"Father? Now why would – "

"Brock!" Voldina yelled. "What are you doing inside the palace ? Don't you see that you have – " The head cook, looking quickly over at Tamara, lowered her head and continued. "I am sorry, Madam. I interrupted you." Tamara reached over and touched Voldina's left arm.

"Oh, it is fine," she said. "Brock, would you go back out and escort the man … I mean … my father … into the palace?"

"But Your Highness," the old man complained. "It is above my station to usher guests into Your Highness' presence. I am merely your humble gardener," he said as he backed out of the room, bowing in the process. Tamara crossed her arms and sighed.

Not much later, after Voldina had escorted Patrik and Galena to the reception area and made sure that they were comfortably seated, Tamara came into the room and stood directly across from them.

"Father, you and Galena have to move into the palace," she commanded. "Immediately. Since Ilead is gone so much … fighting the Haarigoians or whoever General Demirain says he needs to fight … I am all alone in this monstrously huge and impersonally cold mausoleum!" Galena laughed.

"Alone? We have seen nearly a dozen people in and around the palace since we arrived," she said. "How in the world can you say that you are alone?" Tamara sternly pointed a finger at her younger sister.

"You have no idea what I am forced to endure here on a daily basis!" she complained. "From sun up to sun down … and even later … until I have finally closed my bedroom door at night … I am hounded by this servant and that servant, and then I – "

"Tamara, sweet, overly-sensitive Tamara," Patrik consoled. "I never would have guessed that this would be your reaction to living in a palace … to living the life of a queen." The queen then pointed her finger at the innkeeper.

"I certainly do not appreciate your sarcasm," she replied. "Answer me now … before you say another disrespecting word! Are you going to come live with me in the palace or not?" Patrik chuckled and stood up from the dark-leather chair.

"Dearest elder daughter," he replied. "We cannot move into the palace while we are attempting to convince the Netherenes ... Oliver, I mean ... of the importance of Harrak's scrolls." He scratched his head and began to pace back and forth across the overly-polished white oak floor.

"The scrolls? They ... they cannot be that important to you anymore, can they? Why Ilead is already a very spiritual man ... and I can't say that I've met anyone as spiritual ... even compared to that young priest from Noran. What's his name? The one who displayed an interest in my little sister here?" Tamara asked, glancing quickly at Galena.

"Teophelus," Galena chimed in. "And he's been helping Father learn all about the truths ... the important things that are going to happen in the future ... that are hidden within those scrolls." She grinned from ear-to-ear as she said it. Tamara shook her head, looked at her father and then continued.

"Ilead desires to be the king that Justen never was ... the king who will work diligently to make Betrovia a better place for all who live within her borders. He wants to be a much-better king than Justen ... the king who was more concerned with stuffing the coffers of select Lycentian merchants than improving the lives of all Betrovians. Just about all one could say that he accomplished was filling his gardens with the most-elaborate, but inedible, flowers and plants." Patrik stopped pacing and nodded his head.

"I agree that Ilead has proven, in a very short while, that he has in mind what is best for Betrovia. And it is not my place to criticize anything that King Justen did or did not accomplish." He cleared his throat before continuing. "But it would be simpler ... and easier ... for all of us if Ilead would agree to the validity of the scrolls. If he would do that, Oliver and the rest of the Lycentian Netherenes would have to proclaim their efficacy since they would not want to be accused of disagreeing with the king. Yes indeed, agreeing with the king would strongly imply that they agree with Harrak's prophecies." Tamara moved towards one of the windows and began to look outside of it.

"The high priest ... Oliver," she said, quickly turning around and looking back at Patrik, "And even Viktor, the one they call *the Prophet*, have come here too many times to talk with Ilead ... to promote their views of some obscure and ancient doctrines. And Ilead himself told me that he has never heard of those strange teachings! Both Oliver and Viktor have demanded that he stay away from anyone who detracts ... who contradicts ... from the things they want him to learn." She paused to look out the window again.

"And that Viktor ... he is one cold-hearted old man!" she continued. "With that long, white beard ... and that thick and overly-depressing gray robe. I simply detest how he glares at Ilead when he talks to him ... with such an irritatingly condescending attitude! Oh, and his eyes ... they are black ... black and dead ... cold, dark and dead! And whenever he is here, he refuses to even acknowledge my presence!" she exclaimed. "He ignores me entirely! It is ... it is like I am not even in the room with them!"

"Harrak's scrolls," Patrik said, smiling as he interrupted her, "As I am beginning to understand them ... with Teophelus' help, of course ... conflict in many ways with what I have learned about the *doctrines* taught by these Netherenes." He stood up and walked over to Tamara who was still looking out the window and gently placed his right hand on her shoulder. "But one thing Teophelus told me about Viktor is that both his teachings and Harrak's scrolls refer to the advent of a 'commoner king.' He said that the Netherenes teach of a king who will conquer Betrovia's enemies with a demonstration of brute force that has never been seen before and then rule the entire region with an iron fist." Tamara turned to face her father, but before she could say a word, he quickly continued. "However, this future king described by Harrak is one who will be an advocate of the people of Betrovia … one who through effective diplomacy … not through brutish might and bloody war … will finally unite all the peoples in the land."

"And that is the kind of king Ilead will be, Father! The kind he desires to be! I just know it!" Tamara finally blurted out. She then she grabbed his right arm and squeezed it so hard that the innkeeper grimaced. "But … but all the General wants him to do now is head out to the front and hunt down and kill Harrigoians!"

"Hopefully, General Demirain will soon understand that because Ahnak is under Lycentian control, any power the Harrigoians had in the Plains has been reduced significantly." Patrik stepped back from Tamara who took the hint to let go of his arm. "I am no expert in these matters, Tamara, and I feel that Ilead is a fine warrior as well as a just king. But he also must be a spiritual one. Once the general recognizes this spiritual side of him, he must encourage Ilead to take on the more essential role of uniter of the kingdom." He walked back to the maroon chair and sat down. "And talking about this reminds me of something. According to Teophelus, no king of Betrovia … not even Ilead … can fulfill this role of 'purifier,' as specified in the scrolls," he added with a more serious tone.

"According to Harrak's scrolls, The Purifier has already come."

"Then!" Galena chimed in, "Then Teophelus must have been referring to Justen! Now I am beginning to understand this whole mess! King Justen could have been the one to fulfill the Netherene's prophecy!" she exclaimed. "He could have been the one to work for a diplomatic solution to the conflict with Harrigo. Didn't he have the power? Didn't he have the talents to work for a peaceful, more diplomatic, solution to the problem?"

"No," Patrik responded. "The prophecies do not point to King Justen. The fact that he was assassinated proves, according to Teophelus, that he wasn't the purifier Harrak wrote about. Even though he worked hard to strengthen the Lycentian economy – "

"But how can Ilead become the spiritual leader of Betrovia?" Tamara interrupted. "How can he be seen as more important than Oliver? Or even Viktor? He is a good man ... an honest man ... but he is far from perfect." She appeared to be almost in tears.

"Teophelus has said that 'the commoner king' would first undergo a 'rebirth' which would make him a more-effective leader. But that *rebirth* would not qualify him as The Purifier."

"*Rebirth*?" Galena asked. "Now what does that mean? How can anyone be born ... again?"

"Father, the more that you read from those scrolls, the more ludicrous you sound." Tamara said, looking then at Galena. "And the same goes for whatever that neophyte priest says." Galena then interrupted to continue with her line of questions.

"If Ilead would be *re-born*, how would he then be changed? What kind of a man ... what kind of a king would he then be?" she asked with impunity while Tamara glared menacingly at her.

"I am still quite puzzled about this 'rebirth' thing that Harrak wrote about," Patrik added. "And it is therefore one thing I need to ask Teophelus about when I see him again. Hopefully he should be arriving in Lycentia any day now. And once he is here ... and he has helped me to understand a few more sections of the scrolls ... then I should be prepared to go to the temple and deliver them to Oliver." Tamara suddenly glared at her father and again shook a slender finger at him.

"Mother would not appreciate what you have become," she blurted out. "Here you are, talking about all this scroll nonsense like it was everyday news, and what do you have to show for it? All she ever wanted you to do was to become a good artist ... to draw and to paint and ... and what have you become? It's ... it's like..." she drew in a deep breath. "It is like you have become just the opposite! You've turned your back on art ... on putting onto paper the things that are beautiful in this world. All for what? The writings of a crazed hermit ... a heretic that no one cares about!" Patrik ran his right hand through his thick white hair as he crafted his words carefully.

"You ... you don't understand," he said, looking at the floor instead of garnering for eye contact with either young lady. "Dalneia ... your mother ... she knew why I sketched ... why I painted. And it was not to please her ... it was not to in some way relieve her of any pain." Then he raised his head and looked straight into Tamara's dark green eyes.

"If she were here, she ... she would be supporting me whole-heartedly. I just know it." As the innkeeper continued to defend his decision in becoming the conveyor of Harrak's scrolls, Voldina came into the room.

"Madam, the mid-day meal has been prepared," she said. "And in honor of your father and sister blessing us with their presence today, I made it a point to order a very special treat." Tamara smiled as Voldina left the room.

"See, Father? What did I tell you? They never leave me alone!"

The special treat that Voldina mentioned were succulent fruits and berries that Patrik could not ever remember seeing before. Even though the fall harvest in general throughout Betrovia was sparse, the innkeeper was surprised by the quality and variety of the things set before them. And as he began to take a bite out of a perfectly-formed nectarine, he suddenly remembered that a dead body still lay in a house not far from the palace.

"Father!" Galena said. "What is the matter? Why are you coughing?"

"I ... I was thinking ... just thought about...," he stammered.

"What?" Tamara asked as she reached for another warm piece of dark rye bread. "What could you be thinking about that would cause you to spit out your food?"

"Franck," he said. "I was thinking about Franck." His face turned red, and he coughed a few more times.

"What about Uncle Franck?" Galena asked. The innkeeper struggled with what to say. It was not his intention to wait this long to report on what he had discovered in Franck's bedroom earlier that day. And the image of Dalneia's frail and lifeless body lying in bed in the attic of the inn would not surrender to the image he at that moment grappled with. Patrik picked up a crystal goblet, took a long drink, and then looked at Galena.

"This morning … when you were in the wagon waiting for me … I … I went back into the house … and into Franck's room. And there … there he was."

"There he was *what*, Father?" Galena asked as she picked up a dark-purple plum.

"Dead," he said softly, his eyes glazed. "She was there in bed … and she was dead." The memory was too potent: Dalneia's eyes were wide open and as bright and inviting as the day he proposed to her.

"*She*?" Tamara asked. "Now who are you talking about?"

"Franck!" He nearly shouted. "It was Franck … not Dalneia. She is gone … long gone. It was Franck! And … and he is dead."

That night, Patrik tossed and turned as he lay in bed. The images of the bodies of his wife and his best friend lying intermittently on the same bed, both bodies lying face up, one with eyes closed tight, the other with eyes starkly but peacefully open; these images were what kept him from falling asleep. But he was determined to fight it out, to force himself to gain unconsciousness somehow even though the effort appeared to be fruitless.

An hour before dawn, the innkeeper finally was able to fall asleep. The images of the bodies then disappeared and were rudely replaced by the white, pointy-snouted visage of an albino fox. The innkeeper himself was in this dream, this nightmare, and he lay in the bottom of a ravine, like he had done not many months before, staring up, immobile – as if chained to the ancient rocks that were the floor of that ravine – forced to listen to whatever the ghostly creature had to say.

"*The pure life only comes after death*," the ethereal creature said in a voice too similar to that of his dear, departed wife. "*There is no eternal purity ... no life that will last for an eternity ... without first experiencing death.*"

CHAPTER TEN

"Othleis will ordain His Advocate, and the Advocate will be the channel with the Creator as the Source. And who is this Advocate? He is the Pure One, the One to usher the faithful into the Creator's perfect will."

The three constables who arrived that evening to investigate Franck's death concluded in less time than it takes to griddle a batch of kettle-cakes that the traveling merchant had died of natural causes or, as the veteran investigator of the trio said, "Too much rich, sweet and fatty food ingested by one person in too short of a time."

Two days later, when less than a dozen people showed up for his old friend's funeral, Patrik was more than surprised. But the more he thought about it, it all made sense. Because Franck had seemingly spent the majority of his time on the road, he had not invested in building relationships with the residents of Lycentia. Only one of the mourners introduced himself – one of the vendors from the Lycentian market – and he even apologized for not knowing much about Franck. The Netherene priest who performed the service was the only one Tamara could find at the last minute, and he only agreed to meet them at the cemetery when Tamara promised in return a sizable donation to the temple.

But what made the early afternoon ceremony even worse was a another misty shrouding of the wintry white stuff. The first day of winter was more than a week away, but, up to that day, the capital city had been blessed in total with nearly a foot of snow. Once the short ceremony was over, Patrik was the last of the attendees to leave the gravesite; he, however, remained with the cemetery workers to assist filling in the grave with the moist, black topsoil that had been christened with the newly-fallen snow.

That night, after refreshing the horses stock of corn, oats and well-water, Patrik trudged back through the four inches of new snow. He tried not to think much about the events of the day. Once inside the house, he removed his overcoat, slipped off his boots, and nonchalantly plopped them just inside the front door.

"Galena! Would you like to share a pot of tea with me?" he hollered up the stairs. There was no response. "Galena! Can you hear me? Galena! Where are you?" Silence. He walked up the stairs, mumbled about now being too exhausted to prepare tea, and opened the door to their bedroom. And there she was, in a fetal position, lying on the hardwood floor! "Galena! What happened? Wake up! Can you hear me? Please say something!" He knelt down, put his ear to her mouth and released a sigh of relief when he was certain that he could hear breathing.

"Galena," he then whispered into her ear, "Wake up. You must wake up." A few seconds later, her eyes fluttered.

"My … my head," she muttered softly, turning her head towards him. Her chocolate-brown eyes then slowly opened, "What … what happened? My … my head hurts … why does it hurt so much?" Patrik slipped one arm under her neck and the other under her waist and attempted to pick her up; he growled because his socks were wet, and therefore gained no traction on the wood floor. He repositioned his right foot and tried again to lift her onto the bed. With a grunt and a heave, he succeeded but nearly fell on top of her in the process.

"How ... how long," she started to gasp for air, "How long was I on ... on the floor?"

"How would I know?" Patrik replied. "I went out to the barn to tend to the horses. Maybe I was there half an hour, maybe less." He wanted to rub the part of her head that hurt but didn't want to touch it and then make the pain worse. "What were you doing before you fainted?"

"I ... I...," she stuttered. "I don't remember. Was I getting ready for bed? I..." she grasped at every breath. "And why can't ... why can't I breathe?"

A few minutes later, she was fast asleep but still clothed in the outfit she had worn to the funeral. Because her breathing had returned to normal, Patrik ceased to worry about leaving her alone. So he quietly closed the door and thought about making the trip back down the stairs. "No," he said softly. "I am much too tired to go down and then travel back up. If I go down, I will sleep there ... somewhere." He then looked across the hallway. "Franck's room?" He sighed loudly, shook his head and then grumbled as he walked back down to the first floor of the house. The only place suitable for any kind of sleeping was the tiny room, basically a closet, where Walthan had stayed. Patrik crawled onto the narrow straw-mattress bed and attempted to get some shut-eye.

That night, the caustic north wind whistled and howled which drove the white-stuff across the vacant street and up against the house. Patrik slept but only fitfully because of the noise. More than once, when he was finally asleep, he was revisited by the white fox. During each visitation, the creature would speak with Dalneia's voice and repeat the message from its previous visit. By morning, the wintry winds had created a three-foot drift up against the front door of the traveling merchant's house.

And like that morning a few days before, the snow had ceased, the wind had died down to barely a whisper and the clouds misted away. The sun, egg-yolk yellow set within a turquoise sky, sent warm rays into the house. But before that light could fully awaken Patrik, Galena bounded down the stairs and into the pantry. The noise of pots and pans banging and clanging was the impetus for Patrik to lumber out of Walthan's closet.

"How do you feel?" he muttered as he rubbed his eyes and shuffled into the pantry.

"What? Me? Oh, I cannot say that I've ever felt better!" she replied as she ran to him and hugged him tightly. "And thank you so much for asking!"

"But ... but last night ... your head ... you complained of pain ... and you had fainted again."

"Fainted? Did I? Why, I don't even remember! Where was I when I fainted?" The innkeeper nervously scratched his hoary-white cheek.

"You ... don't remember?" he replied. "I found you sprawled out on the bedroom floor. I picked you up, nearly throwing out my back in the process, and set you in bed. And ... you say you do not remember?" She smiled as she threw open the window drapes, inviting even more of the sun's rays to warm up the pantry.

"Now don't you get angry," she scolded. "I was only teasing. Of course I remember you helping me into bed." She hugged him again and this time also pecked his cheek. "You really should work on that sense of humor of yours, Father. I'm sure it would in the long run be nourishing to your spirit."

"You were passed out, completely unconscious, and even complained about having a hard time breathing. How can you – "

"Father!" Galena interrupted. "What would you like me to cook for breakfast? How about some kettle-cakes? We haven't had them in such a long time! I promise I will try not to burn any of them!"

"I am not that hungry … maybe later…" He sighed loudly and sat down on a rickety hickory-wood stool. "Maybe I should find a physician to take a look – "

"Do you know what was on my mind as I woke up this morning?" she asked. Patrik could only shake his head. "I was thinking about Teophelus … about him arriving soon to help you again with those parchments. He should be here any day, right?" She began to quickly open and then close cabinet doors. "When do you – My word! In the name of Othleis himself!" she exclaimed, slamming shut one of the doors. "Where did Uncle Franck keep the wheat flour? How can anyone possibly make kettle-cakes without flour?" Patrik shielded his eyes from the blaze of light coming through the pantry window then scooted the stool a few feet to his right to move completely out of the rays' path.

"Might you care to learn what I dreamed about?" he suddenly blurted. He then grimaced, wishing that he had thought about how to phrase it better instead of just letting it saunter out.

"Tamara was incorrect, Father," Galena continued as if she hadn't heard his question. Patrik sighed and smiled.

"About what?" he then swiftly asked, thankful that she seemingly had not heard his question.

"The more I think about it ... those parchments may be as important as you make them out to be. So if Ilead ... the king of all Betrovia ... would someday agree to help you promote them to the Netherenes," she said, her voice tapering off as she pulled out a large earthenware container from one of the lower cabinets and set it on the table. "Here! Wheat flour at last! It is kettle-cake time after all!"

"Yes," the innkeeper agreed. "It would be best for all concerned if the king became as adamant as we are about the scrolls and – "

"There you go again, Father!" Galena interrupted.

"What did I say now?" he asked.

"*We* are not adamant about the scrolls," Galena said as she began to mix up the batter. "*You* are infatuated with those moldy things ... not *we*."

So, as Galena prepared kettle-cakes, at least for herself, Patrik tried to come up with something to talk about to distract her from asking about his dream.

"When your mother and I," he started to say but paused to wait for her reaction. "When we began to talk seriously about our relationship ...." Galena appeared disinterested, humming one of her melodious childhood tunes as she stirred the batter, "Please feel free to stop me if you have heard this. And for the life of me, I cannot remember if I have ever told you about it," he added.

"Your relationship? Between you and mother?" she asked. She appeared to be listening after all.

"Yes, your mother and I … well … for the most part … even though she was just about the prettiest girl in Noran at the time … I can not say that I had much interest in her. That is," he paused again, anticipating that she would interrupt. "Until that day she came to our house delivering that crock of soup and loaf of black-bean bread. It was then that I realized I had some … feelings … for her. But I wasn't … I did not know how … how to tell her of those feelings." He stopped to watch as she tested the thickness of the batter and then sprinkled in a bit more flour. "A few days after my health improved, I thought to ask Pieter how I might tell her."

"Uncle Pieter? What about Uncle Pieter?" she asked. It appeared that she was barely paying attention, so he determined to make the story more interesting.

"Yes, your Uncle Pieter," he said. "He suggested … and you will laugh when I tell you … that I sketch a portrait of her and then give it to her … give her a portrait that would serve as a symbol of my affection towards her." Galena didn't laugh; she didn't even smile. But she did glance in his direction. The only sound in the pantry at that moment was the scraping of the wooden spoon on the side of the stoneware mixing bowl.

"So did you?" she asked softly.

"Did I what?"

"Father!" she exclaimed as she shook the batter-covered spoon at him. "Did you give her the sketch?"

"No, I did not. There was no sketch to give. At the time, I was very…" he struggled for the right words, "I was quite shy about my artwork and would not show it to anyone except Mother. And whenever he pestered me about it … to Pieter." Patrik then paused as he watched the kettle-cake batter being poured into the hot black kettle. "A few days after sharing his idea with me, he challenged me again to follow through with it. He was certain that once she saw the evidence of my talent, she would fall in love with me." He then scowled but only to emphasize the point of the story. "But I did not follow through with it."

"Uncle Pieter wasn't serious," Galena said with a smile. "He didn't expect you to give her the portrait. He always was such a kidder, don't you know?"

"Yes, he surely was." Patrik agreed. "And then one day … not too long after that … the two of us … Pieter and I … we went hunting." The innkeeper didn't realize that this new topic was hardly related to the first, but that didn't hinder him from digressing. "We grabbed our bows and arrows and headed into the bean field east of town. And we did not have to wait long before a huge buck came within range. Oh, and he was a massive buck, I tell you! At least a 10-pointer, he was! I remember Pieter saying that this was the beast that we had been scouting for a few years. And much to our amazement, he stopped not more than twenty yards from us. Oh yes, this was the day! So, as the beast nibbled on some clover, I quietly placed a shaft into the bow and began to quietly pull back on the string when – "

"When you shot him dead! And there he died! With a muzzle full of clover stuck in his craw! The arrow went right into the heart!" she exclaimed. He was so startled by her sudden excitement that he was forced to pause to reconstruct his thoughts.

"No, not even close," he mumbled. "Just as I was about to release, Pieter let loose with a scream that would rival the war-cry of any crazed Haarigoian axeman. And I never saw that buck again!"

========================

Around the middle of that same day, there was a knock on the door. It was one of the constables who investigated Franck's death. He apologized for the unannounced visit and then explained that he had returned to ask a few more questions. He also said that he needed to ask Patrik and Galena about why they had come to Lycentia. Patrik explained to him, with as few details as possible, that he had come to Lycentia to talk with Oliver III, the Netherene high priest. The officer chucked and replied that it was common knowledge that no one sought a meeting with the high priest; if the high priest wanted to talk to someone, then he would have them summoned.

"You did say you are from Noran?" the officer asked.

"Yes, primarily from Noran, but more recently we had been running an inn on the Plains highway south of the village."

"And might I ask who besides your daughter here assisted you in that endeavor?"

"Besides Galena? There was … no one, no one else … actually." He caught himself right before saying Tamara's name. He wasn't certain that the constable knew that his elder daughter was queen of Betrovia and if he didn't know, he didn't want him at that moment to find out. Why he intended to be so secretive about their relationship wasn't apparent at the time, and he hoped that the man would not question him further about it.

"Let me see … you and your daughter were the only two people running the inn? Am I understanding this correctly?" Patrik cringed as he noticed a thin bead of perspiration on the man's forehead.

"Oh, do you mean who else *besides* Galena and I? Besides the two of us," he mumbled, "There was Edelin." As soon as he said the name, the officer's expression morphed from casual disinterest to sincere fascination.

"Edelin? Interesting … I have recently met with someone who mentioned that name," the constable replied. The investigator then told Patrik about a man who had been arrested for multiple burglary and larceny offenses and was due to come before the judge to receive sentencing for his crimes. The criminal's name was Dedialas and, up until his apprehension the previous summer, had been one of Lycentia's most-wanted second-story men. According to the constable, the man had become a part of recent Lycentian folklore due to his ability to sneak into a house – no matter how well-guarded it was – and remove as many valuables as he desired, and then exit without anyone even knowing he had been there. It wasn't until the victims would look for their prized belongings that they discovered what had been stolen.

While he tried to listen to the officer, Patrik pondered why the man was telling him so much about this Dedialas person. All he had done to initiate this train of thought was mention the name "Edelin." But since the officer chose to talk about this criminal, it meant that he wasn't choosing to ask more questions about him or Galena. And this was just fine for the innkeeper.

But, the constable added, the thief made the mistake of finding his way into the mansion of Luis, the city administrator. While he was in Luis' bedroom – with Luis in bed at the time – the administrator suddenly awoke. He saw the man and then called for his servants who then captured him even before he made it out of the bedroom.

"That's right ... the malcontent chose to burglarize the administrator's house that night ... but it was at the wrong time," he concluded. "According to the servants, the whole time they held onto him – right up until we arrived to cart him off – he bragged about his exploits, even boasting that if Luis had not discovered him, he would have taken every bit of the man's collection of rare amulets. And what an expensive collection the administrator has, I can tell you!" The investigator then smiled. "But once we put him safely away in the prison, he became very quiet. Even when we threatened to make him talk, he wouldn't volunteer a single word."

That was, the man said, until he was thrown into the catacombs under the prison. And in those dark, cold and moldy confines – where only the deadliest and the most-hated criminals were deposited – Dedialas experienced a change of heart. The weeks locked up there were excruciatingly long. But he was not alone. In the cell with him – and this is where the constable shook his head – was a man who had been deposited into the catacombs by Viktor the Prophet himself. Because Dedialas would not talk about his crimes nor share any information about other Lycentian thieves, he was locked up in the special section of the catacombs where Viktor would leave his enemies to rot. The man chained to the wall in that cell was no thief, nor extortionist, rapist or even murderer. So just what was his crime?

"He was a Lyce-Tuereon."

"A what?" Patrik asked.

"Lyce-Tuereon," the officer repeated. "The prisoner was a member of a sect that Viktor has been trying for decades to eradicate. I cannot say that I know much about their beliefs, but if the Prophet is so adamantly opposed to their doctrines, than these people must be as evil as they come." He added that even though Dedialas' cell-mate was threatened with hideous torture and even death, he refused to either name other members of the sect or to renounce his belief in its teachings. The night before Viktor finally ordered the recalcitrant prisoner's execution, Dedialas demanded to speak to the Prophet himself to beg for the man's life.

"Viktor, of course, wanted nothing to do with paying a visit to the prison, so he suggested that Luis, our glorious administrator, speak with him instead." The constable then stood up and appeared to be ready to leave the house. Patrik stood up as well.

"So, what happened?" Patrik asked. "What did they do with the two men?" By this time, he was more than a little curious about the fate of both the Lyce-Tuereon and the one called Dedialas. Before the constable would leave the house, Patrik especially wanted to find out the connection between this Dedialas character and Edelin.

"I have told you more than I should have, sir," the constable confessed.

"Please! There is one thing I must know. If you do not feel at liberty to tell me more about the fate of this Lyce-Tuereon, could you at least tell me about the thief?" As the request left his lips, Galena came down the stairs.

"Hello," she said softly and politely. "I'm Galena. And what is your name?" was the next thing out of her mouth followed by a long yawn.

"My name is not important," the constable said. "But for the record, you can refer to me as a Constable of Lycentia." Galena smiled but yawned again.

"It's a pleasure to meet you, Constable," she said. Patrik was both pleased and surprised that she chose to inquire nothing else about the man's identity.

"Galena," Patrik said as he wrapped his right arm around her waist. "The constable was about to tell me something about a man who claims to know Edelin." Galena's mouth dropped when he said the young thief's name.

"Edelin!" she cried out. "What do you know about Edelin, kind sir? Please tell me what you know about him!" The officer smiled and looked down at the floor.

"Young lady, I do not know a thing about this Edelin person," he replied. "Your father mentioned the name when I asked about your experiences at the inn south of Noran. When I heard the name, I was reminded of a man ... a prisoner ... who was in one of the cells of Lycentia's dungeon."

"*Was* a prisoner?" Patrik asked. "The one called Dedialas was released?" The constable again would not look at either Patrik or his younger daughter.

"No, sir, he was not released. When Luis arrived to meet with Viktor's prisoner, he discovered that not only had the thief confessed to being a lifelong, habitual criminal, but that he had also confessed to becoming a Lyce-Tuereon. And because his confession, Viktor signed the order that both men residing in that cell be executed the same day."

"I don't understand ... the man was sentenced to death because he decided to become part of a religious order ... a sect, as you called it?" Patrik asked.

"Yes, that is what occurred," the man shared. Then he finally looked up and found Patrik's pale, blue eyes. "And before he died, he asked that we would tell the last-surviving member of his family what he had done."

"That he had confessed to being a hardened criminal?" Galena asked.

"No," the officer replied. "He requested that if we could ever find this Edelin person to tell him that he became a member of the Lyce-Tuereons … and that he should do the same."

"Edelin!" Galena again said loudly. "How are … I mean … what else did the man say? Did he say how he and Edelin were related?" she then asked.

"Dedialas, the newly-confessed member of the Lyce-Tuereons, said as he was about to die … that this Edelin person … was his son."

====================

That night, after Galena had already gone upstairs to bed, Patrik ventured into the pantry to find something to eat before going to bed himself. As he rummaged through the cabinets, he couldn't help but think about Edelin. Where was he? What was he doing? Was he even still alive? "Of course he is still alive," he muttered. "The young man is very intelligent … has a good head on his shoulders." The only choices for the late-night snack was a slice of apricot pie or a cold, under-cooked turnip. He savored the last bite of the pie as he continued to think about Edelin. "What if," he whispered. "What if Edelin was in Lycentia at this very moment? But if not, where might he be?"

For the second night in a week, the innkeeper chose to sleep in Walthan's dark but cozy closet-of-a-room. The lack of any windows in the room had made him wonder why he had never thought before about how convenient it was to sleep in a room without windows. A few hours before it would be time to get up, Patrik tossed and turned. His sleep was interrupted this time not by another visit from the white fox but by memories of Pieter, his younger brother – his only brother – who died while joining in the defense of Noran the past summer. But the image of burying his brother in the Noran cemetery was not the only one that kept him from getting a good night's sleep: he was completely awake as he then began to think about Dalneia.

It was not going to be worth fighting the temptation, so he sat up in bed. The images took the innkeeper back to a time before they were married, back to a time before they were even close friends. Dalneia, like the innkeeper, also had a younger brother, Markus. When Dalneia was twelve years old, she saved Markus, her only brother, from drowning. The rescue occurred one muggy summer day when the four of them – Patrik, Pieter, Dalneia and Markus – ran off to the spring-fed pond only a few Norans knew about. The pond's spring-fed water was too cold, no matter the season, for fish to thrive in it, and this was why the few who knew of it cared little about it.

But on that particular summer day, it was the perfect place to escape from the mundane routines of the little mining town. The water was so cold that none of the youngsters were able to remain in it for more than a few minutes. But the fact that it was both inviting – because of the heat – and formidable made for an interesting challenge.

Patrik smiled as he thought about how good a swimmer Dalneia was and how both she and Pieter, a "fish out of water" himself, made a contest out of daring Patrik and Markus – the youngest of the foursome – to dive down to the bottom of the pond. The evidence of success would be whatever rock or smattering of sediment could be brought back up to the surface. Patrik didn't enjoy putting his head under water, so he was never tempted to take the dare. But Markus boldly declared that he was not afraid of going underwater. And that day he finally took the dare.

The three of them watched from the bank as he quickly swam to the fore-selected "staging area." From that point, the "contestant" was instructed to await the signal. Since Dalneia had designed the game herself, she had to be the one to give the go-ahead. So, on that hot summer afternoon, she raised her hand high over her head and then let it drop to her side, the metaphoric message to dive to the bottom. But after what was possibly only five seconds, Patrik remembered that he began to panic. Before he could say a thing, Dalneia had reentered the frigid water, piercing its silvery surface.

The pond's water was crystal clear, but it was more than ten feet deep at its center. In what had seemed to Patrik like minutes but had only been a few seconds, both Dalneia and Markus reappeared, Markus, shirtless and coughing spasmodically, and Dalneia gasping for breath as well. Once back on shore, Dalneia explained that his shirt had gotten snagged by a submerged tree branch, and he could not pull himself free. Upon finding him, she merely pulled the shirt off, thereby releasing him from what could have become what Pieter later teasingly called "Markus' watery grave."

"Watery grave ... Ha!" Patrik chuckled as he laid back down on the straw-mattress. "All Markus had to do to save himself ... to get back to the surface ... was to merely take his shirt off," he muttered as he fell back to sleep.

Once he had gotten out of bed that morning, Patrik announced that he was going for a walk and that he would be back shortly.

"A walk? Since when do you take walks? And where might you be headed on this walk?" she asked.

"Nowhere in particular ... just going for a walk," he replied. "I need some fresh air." And with that he exited the house but then quickly came back in.

"Your overcoat?" she chided. "Sometimes, Father, your lack of concern for your personal health and safety concerns me."

Now that he was sufficiently bundled up against the brisk, wintry morning air, he went back outside again. "Yes, this good, quite good. I must force myself to do this more often," he said, allowing a slight grin to possess his face. "Taking a walk is an excellent way to begin a new day."

Before long, as he headed west of Franck's house, the innkeeper found himself in the open-air market just east of the Lycentian temple gate. A few vendors were already setting out freshly-baked rolls, pies and breads, while others were bringing out of their shops sundry meats and even some late-season fruits and vegetables. Patrik waved and smiled politely at the strangers but walked past the food; his goal was to merely walk and not to talk to anyone about their wares. As he had told Galena, he wanted to take a walk for the benefit of getting fresh air. And that was exactly what he was going to do.

"Sir! Sir Patrik! Here, sir! I am over here!" The innkeeper was suddenly brought out of his "going for some fresh air" stupor by a high-pitched and panicked voice. Patrik stopped and squinted to see who might be calling out his name; the voice appeared to be coming out of a shadow-filled alley to his right.

"No! Not there! I'm here!" the voice repeated. He turned around and then saw the source of the interruption. It was Walthan, Franck's assistant! And he was quite disheveled, a crass contrast to the polished young man who greeted him as he had arrived at Franck's house a few weeks before.

"Kind Sir Patrik, please ... please do not call for a constable," the boy pleaded. "I am only asking for something to eat ... I am so incredibly starving."

"Walthan! Is it really you? Where in the name of Othleis have you been? And where did you go that night?" Patrik inquired as he reached out and gently tried to grab the boy's forearm.

"Please, Sir, please do not turn me over to the authorities," he cried. "Can you buy me something to eat?" Before Walthan could say another word, Patrik succeeded in grabbing his arm and leading him to the closest baked-goods vendor. He then told the boy to pick out whatever he wanted. Both the white-bearded innkeeper and Franck's former assistant were soon nibbling on steaming-hot butter buns.

"Now that you have something to relieve the hunger pangs, would you kindly explain to me what happened the night Franck died?" Patrik asked.

"That night," Walthan said softly, "The night before we were to leave for the Plains, I found Sir Franck…" The boy's voice trailed off.

"Yes, yes, go on!" Patrik urged. "You found Franck, yes, I am listening! Now please continue!" Patrik demanded as he took another bite of the roll.

"That morning … before daybreak … I hitched up the horses to the wagon. The night before Master Franck said that we were to leave when it was still dark. So I got out of bed much earlier than normal and merely waited in the wagon for him." He paused to stuff the remainder of a roll into his mouth. "I waited and I waited. The darkness was about to be chased away by the oncoming day as I still waited." He paused again but would not look at the innkeeper. "This was so not like Master Franck."

"What did you do?" Patrik asked.

"What else could I do? I got off the wagon and went into the house. I thought that he might be in the pantry. But he wasn't there. Maybe he was in the attic? Or in the cellar storeroom looking for one more thing to take to the Plains? But he was not in any of those places."

"Then you went to his room?" Patrik prompted.

"Yes! I went up to his room!" the youth exclaimed. "But I knocked first! I truly did! Even though the night before he warned me to make no noise so as not to awaken you and Mistress Galena. I knocked and knocked … so very very quietly I knocked … but there was no response. I … I did not want to open the door but – "

"But you did," Patrik whispered. "You did open the door."

"Yes! I did open the door and ... Master Patrik, I was so afraid of what I saw that I can barely remember what I did afterwards," Walthan confessed.

"Afterwards?" Patrik asked. "After what?"

"After I saw him lying there in bed," he said with a hint of irritation in his voice. "After I saw him, I suppose I did something ... something irrational like – "

"Like opening the window and sliding down the roof outside it?" Patrik guessed.

"Yes! That is exactly what I did!" Patrik nodded his head: that explained why the window was open when he went into his old friend's room.

"Sir Patrik! I was so afraid, so frightened, that I could not comprehend. I have never seen ... a ... a dead body. Honestly I have not, sir! Sincerely, sir, I was not thinking very clearly, and so I vacated the room through the window. I am so thankful that there was an ample pile of snow below the window or I might have been seriously injured."

"Indeed you would have, young man!" Patrik had to add.

"Oh yes, Sir Patrik, it was quite fortuitous for the snow to be that deep under his window. After I climbed out of the drift, I ran directly back to the wagon. I do not know why, but I made the horses pull the wagon so dangerously fast, sir! They really did pull the wagon much too quickly for these snowy streets! And before the sun had come up over the mountains, I was out of the city!"

Patrik listened patiently as Walthan then told him of the greater part of his adventure. He said that when he was a few miles east out of Lycentia, he was accosted by bandits who commandeered the wagon, beating him in the process, and then leaving him for dead on the side of the road. The boy was nearly in tears as he explained that he managed to stagger back into the city and had been hiding in and around the shadowy alleys of the east-side market ever since. "Sir Patrik, it was the purest favor of the Ancient Ones that allowed me to recognize you this wonderful morning!" At that moment, Patrik knew exactly what Walthan needed to hear.

"The constables," he said with confidence, "The Lycentian authorities ... they determined that Franck died of natural causes. Therefore you have nothing to fear, young man! Nothing at all to fear! You are not being hunted! You are not a suspect in Franck's death!" Patrik exclaimed as he put his arm around the boy's shoulders. "And no one but you and I will know what has happened to Franck's horses, wagon and the things on it."

"No, kind Sir Patrik, that is not completely true," Walthan said as he stepped away from the innkeeper. "I appreciate you buying me these extravagant butter rolls ... they were so good ... but no, Patrik sir, no. I cannot agree with you."

"What? You cannot agree with me? What do you mean?" Patrik was flabbergasted. "And who are these Ancient Ones?" Before he could think of anything else to say, the boy ran down the shadow-filled alley and was gone, leaving the innkeeper to once again ponder the strange behaviors that epitomized the young man.

CHAPTER ELEVEN

"Give no credence to the ways of the Shadow
Lords by relishing their deeds; instead, give
the Creator glory by seeking His purity. Do
not listen to the Dark Ones' teachings nor learn
of their customs; by doing so,
you will thereby receive
their reward of Utter Destruction."

What drives a man to become what he never imagined? Is it greed – the desire for unfettered wealth? Or might it be the lust for power? Or maybe even the pursuit of the perfection of beauty personified within a certain woman? What could be this impetus for driving a young man away from heeding the call of his ancestral mores and instead drawing him towards a monstrously dark and gaping precipice from which he may not be able to return?

Around the same time that Patrik and Galena moved into Franck's house, Kristof and Dalten were only a few miles from Lycentia. While the innkeeper's purpose in being in the capital city was entirely altruistic, the motivation behind these two former members of the Noran militia for traveling there was much more devious than selflessness. Yes, they were no longer militiamen, having not been formally released from their duties and so should have been considered deserters – absent without leave – which was most-assuredly a traitorous offense in light of the state of military jurisprudence in Betrovia. In light of the effect of their choices upon their consciences, Dalten made it a point to remind his recalcitrant partner-in-crime that they would soon be rewarded for their efforts with fame and fortune, something nearly impossible for them to achieve if they had dallied even one more day in Noran. However, Kristof's heart desire was to discuss, to debate, to deliver a dissertation that would somehow convince Dalten that he wanted nothing to do with being complicit with murder. But the desire for the remainder of the promised gold coinage prevented him from uttering a single word.

As they approached the capital city, close enough to make out all three golden spires of the Lycentian temple, Kristof asked if they were going to visit the same hamlet where, coincidentally, Patrik and Galena had spent the night before venturing into the city.

"No," Dalten said. "We cannot. Lycentian militiamen often stop there. It's too risky. The chance of us being discovered if we showed ourselves there is too great. Remember!" he then commanded. "We are fugitives from justice ... at least until we have successfully completed the mission assigned to us by that old man. And then, my friend, once that is done, not only will we be exonerated of all guilt, we will be considered heroes! Heroes of Betrovia!"

"Then where?" Kristof asked. "Where can we go to get a decent night's sleep? I am so tired of bunking down in the forest!"

"Would you cease with this incessant complaining!" Dalten bellowed. "Trust me, Kristof," he then said in a calmer tone as he sought eye contact with the former stable-hand. "I not only know my way around Lycentia, but … and this is even better … there is another village … one that is very secluded … one that no member of the militia would ever want to patronize. It is to the east of the city, nestled ever so secretly in the foothills of the Knaesins." He then laughed. "Ha! Take solace in knowing that I will garner a safe place for you to rest your weary bones before we go to Lycentia to find that man Helt to learn of the rest of our little … adventure."

So, instead of entering the city through the western gates, they took a narrow path through the forest around its northern walls. Soon they came upon a village consisting of a half-dozen or so ram-shackled shanties, one much-smaller than the hamlet in which Galena encountered the wonderfully-loquacious little girl. Intent on drawing no attention to themselves, Dalten convinced Kristof that it would be best to not seek out a room but to bed down in the stable with the horses. Kristof, too tired to argue, was glad that he would at least have straw for a bed instead of the forest's cold, hard ground.

The next morning, while it was still dark and the snowfall had tapered off to sporadic flurries, they left the village to head for Lycentia. The previous evening, Dalten determined that it would be better to sell the horses and then complete their journey on foot. The stable master – coincidentally down to his last mare – was happy to pay what Dalten believed was a fair price for their mounts. Kristof grumbled when he remembered that frosty morning that he was going to be forced to walk through the white stuff instead of riding comfortably over it.

"Once inside the city, might we ask someone to help us find this Helt character?" Kristof asked as he pointed towards Lycentia's massive eastern gates. Dalten latched onto his companion's arm and glared.

"No! We cannot merely strut into Lycentia and start asking questions! Haven't you figured this out yet? We are deserters! Do you want to go to prison? Let me decide who we talk to and when we talk to them. I know a few people here. Hopefully, at least one of them can give us directions to Helt's place of business." He let go of Kristof's arm, dusted off the few flakes that had accumulated on his hat and then sat down on a nearby stump.

"But we first must gauge our situation. Leitser certainly has alerted the Lycentian authorities that two deserters may be headed here." Dalten then laughed. "Also, besides being acquainted with a few important people here, over the years I am sure that I have also made a few enemies." Kristof attempted a consoling smile but could only manage a polite grin.

Because the former stable-hand had no one to rely on but Dalten for finding their way around the city, he reluctantly determined to stay quiet and as nondescript as possible. So they made their way through the city, keeping to the dark and narrow alleys and side streets. More than a few times, they were forced to quickly duck into shop doorways and even under carts and wagons in order to stay out of sight of the militiamen and even the city constables. Fortuitously, by the end of their first day inside the city's walls, the sole heir of the Molic family fortune had learned the whereabouts of the man who would inform them of the rest of their mission.

In a small but relatively new red brick-and-mortar building that housed on its first floor both a law office and a seamstress shop was the proprietorship of a well-dressed, soft-spoken, dark-complected man of medium height and build. He appeared to be using the top floor of the three-story building as both domicile and a place of business. This Lycentian businessman who introduced himself as Helt at first stared at the two young men, then scowled at them. But when they finally sat down opposite him in thin but identical cherry-wood chairs that squeaked in protest, his countenance sweetened.

On the rustic and dark oak table in front of him was a large platter of roast duck, potatoes and candied pears; Kristof could not keep himself from staring at the food. Before this host said a another word, he slowly cut off a piece of the delectable fowl, took his eyes momentarily off the young adventurers and peered – as if transfixed – at the meat before nibbling on it.

"I don't expect either of you to know this but Nestric, that rapscallion ... the man who blessed you with this assignment ... is a dear old friend of mine," he said as he chewed up one slice of the duck. He then stood up, walked over to a chest in the far corner of the well-lit room, pulled out a large black leather satchel and set it on the floor in front of Kristof. "To be completely truthful, I consider him more than a friend. Oh yes, he and I have much more in common than friendship," he continued as he then reached into the bag and pulled out a short, double-edged sword that sported a golden hilt and guard. With that sword, he stabbed one of the potatoes and then pointed the tuber-adorned sword at Kristof.

"This fine blade here ... one of the finest swords in all of Lycentia ... once belonged to that scoundrel Nestric Pustcheon." He then brought the tip of the sword to his mouth, inserted the tuber, chewed it for a few seconds, swallowed, and ended the demonstration by cleaning the sword's Lycentian-steel tip on his black silk trousers. "It *used* to belong to him ... that is, before he determined to stake a claim to the iron mine in Noran. And if it hadn't been for that irritatingly-inquisitive Commander Leitser...." He then glared again at Kristof as he put the short sword back into the black bag and returned to his dinner. "But that is not something you are concerned with now, is it?"

"Master Molic," he then said, looking at the slightly-shorter but more rotund of the two young men. "If that even is your real name. And while I'm thinking about it ... if you could excuse my little digression ... why *are* you here? Might you be able to explain why a member of the prestigious Molic clan, a family that has made a fortune out of excavating that Noran mine, would want to be involved in an escapade of this nature?" He paused to partake in another tender bit of the roast duck. "Surely you two cannot be the ones my dear friend Nestric has recruited. The task before you is much too weighty," he added while chewing, "Much too important to be completed by young men like you ... the spoiled children of rich parents." He popped another piece of meat into his mouth and then licked his fingertips.

"Do we need to show you the gold coins?" Dalten angrily and suddenly blurted out. "We have them! The Lycentian coins that ... that foul-smelling man gave us!"

"Interesting ... it seems that the young traveler possesses a temper," he replied as he leaned back in his chair. "Now what would showing me a smattering of gold coins prove?" Helt answered, pointing a candied pear-ladened fork at him. "Unless those coins were minted by Nestric himself! Ha! Now that is something I don't think the old codger has ever attempted ... not that he might not attempt it someday. Ha!" Helt returned the cutlery to the desk, looked up at the ceiling, closed his eyes and sighed. "Very well then. Let us suppose the only reason you have come to our wonderful city is to seek an audience with me. I have never set eyes on either of you before nor will I hope to see you – "

"But you will see us again!" Kristof interrupted. "After we have finished this –" The entrepreneur stood up, turned his back on the obstreperous waif and cleared his throat.

"Fine, fine," he countered. "Since you are so certain of yourselves ... certain of your abilities ... certain of your chances to complete your assignment, I will now tell you who you are to eliminate." Helt turned back around and faced them; his large, dark-green eyes became mere slits. "Before the month is over ... if you sincerely want the balance of the payment ... the man who requires your attention is a young priest who recently has been studying here in Lycentia. And the priest is coincidentally from Noran, if my memory serves me correctly."

"A priest? What priest? Are you expecting that we just guess who you are referring to?" Dalten inquired.

"The priest's name is Teophelus," Helt quickly announced. As if he was spring-loaded, Kristof shot to his feet.

"What?!" he shouted. "How could a neophyte ... an understudy of a priest ... barely an acolyte ... be considered a threat to Lycentia?" he asked. Helt then crossed his arms and closed his eyes.

"Over the last few months, this certain priest has demonstrated an unhealthy interest in something." He paused, re-opened his eyes, and looked directly at Kristof. "He has revealed a hazardous affinity for some documents that have been deemed incendiary. And, consequently, possession of these documents has been outlawed."

"What documents?" Dalten asked. Helt responded without looking at the young man.

"Suffice to say that the information the neophyte has taken an interest in has been judged by the Netherenes to be heretical."

"But it's just the writings of some crazy – " Dalten quickly clamped his left hand over Kristof's mouth. Dalten and Kristof were both well-aware of what Teophelus had been helping Patrik with. While he was in Noran working at his family's haberdashery, Kristof had learned of the innkeeper, his former employer, discovering some ancient writings, and he shared this information with Dalten.

"If Helt says that the writings are banned, then they are banned," Dalten said. Kristof pushed Dalten's hand away but remained silent long enough for his partner to continue. "If the Netherenes pronounce that anyone promoting those writings is an outlaw, then that person needs to be dealt with."

"But killed?" Kristof asked. "Why would talking about some old writings necessitate a death sentence? If he really is so dangerous to the Netherenes, why don't they just arrest him? Take him to court? Lycentia does have a trustworthy court system, doesn't it?"

"The Netherenes cannot involve the Lycentian courts in this matter," Helt replied softly but sternly. Picking up a silver goblet from the table, he peered into it, inhaled deeply, then took a long drink. Holding onto the silver vessel, he explained. "There is nothing within the laws of

Lycentia prohibiting people from talking about things that others may disagree with."

"Indeed," Dalten said. "I have to agree that the courts would want nothing to do with this. It is completely in the hands of the Netherenes. It's a religious thing, Kristof, don't you see? It's about preserving the efficacy of their belief system. And if there's a heretic running around spouting things against the Netherenes and what they believe, then it's up to the Netherenes themselves to take care of the problem."

"Why, Dalten?" Kristof stammered, "Why … why are you suddenly so concerned about what the Netherenes teach? Or what someone is talking about that is deemed contrary to their teachings?" Kristof was nearly dumbfounded by the topic of this conversation. "I do not understand why you are agreeing to this!"

"Before I joined the militia … actually, it was before we ever met … I myself was preparing to become a Netherene priest," Dalten calmly shared.

"No! Preposterous! I cannot believe it! You? A Netherene? I cannot … I will not believe it!" Kristof shook his head then sat back down. "How long have I known you? Three years? Maybe four? And how could I not know that you had … sometime in your short life … been preparing to become a priest?"

"You should believe it, Kristof … because it is true," Dalten said as he remained standing. He glanced at Helt who had returned to his chair behind the desk where he took another bite of the candied pears. "I can remember … when I was inside the Noran temple … a discussion between some of the older priests. They were talking about this Harrak, the heretic Netherene priest who supposedly created those scrolls. I distinctly remember them saying that Harrak's teachings are diametrically opposed to the core beliefs of the Lycentian Netherenes."

"Master Molic is correct," Helt added. "Other priests ... other malcontents ... others like this Teophelus ... who have expressed interest in the meanderings of that heretic have been ... how to say it? Taken care of?" Enjoying another bit of the tasty fruit, he got out of the chair, walked over to Kristof and stood behind him. "And this is how some things are done here in Lycentia," he whispered. He then remained behind the former Noran militiaman as if waiting for a response. Dalten said nothing but continued to stare at the entrepreneur clad in black silk.

"If," Kristof muttered as he stared at the floor. "If I agree to go along with this ... mission ... and we succeed ... won't the constables come looking for whoever murdered the priest?"

"Kristof! Teophelus must be dealt with in order for the memory of the heretic Harrak and his scrolls to be destroyed! Once and for all!" Dalten interrupted. Helt looked up at the ceiling again, then took another sip from the goblet.

"Unless we put a stop to him immediately," he said, "the neophyte will continue to malign the tenuous balance between what Oliver III preaches and what Viktor the Prophet promotes. For decades, all of Betrovia has benefited from this peculiar but necessary juxtaposition. If the populace, especially those here in Lycentia, begins to feed on the heresies laid out within those scrolls, our beloved but quite precarious Netherene system just may collapse," Helt added. "And the dissolution of the

Netherene system would be disastrous for Lycentia … for all of Betrovia."

"But how can the teachings of one sect … even one man … possess such power?" Kristof asked even softer than before.

"But they do have power, Kristof," Helt said with a fatherly, but condescending, tone. "I, too, am a student of the Netherene system, and I believe it is the glue to our unified Betrovia. Certainly, without it … without that power structure … there would be no Betrovia … there would only be the dark chaos that held the region in its steely grip merely a hundred years ago." Kristof put his hands on his head and leaned forward; he felt that his stomach was about to erupt.

"If Teophelus is such a threat to the peace of Betrovia, then I … I suppose he must be stopped," he said with his head still in his hands. "But why … why does he have to die? The scrolls are the problem, are they not? We … we could just steal the scrolls from him, couldn't we?"

"Even if we believed … which we don't … that he possessed the parchments, merely taking them from him would not solve the problem," Helt replied. "We are certain who now possesses them, and are just as certain that he presents no serious threat. However, the young priest has determined to press the issue … he knows too much about Harrak's heresies. What you have been given to accomplish is the only way to silence him … for good." Dalten glanced at Helt, cleared his throat and then looked at his fellow deserter.

"Kristof, think about it. We have twenty gold coins … not low-quality coins minted in Noran but Lycentian gold coins! And have been given the opportunity to earn twenty more! Do you realize what this means? Our yearly wages with the Noran militia would barely equal that! All we have to do is take care of Teophelus for the Netherenes, and we will get that other twenty!" Dalten reached over and grabbed Kristof's shoulder. "We will be rich!"

"Alright then," he conceded. "I agree … I agree to go through with this." The possibility of gaining a total of forty coins finally persuaded him that assassination – for the sake of maintaining the peace of Betrovia – was the only solution. "But other people are … involved," he added.

"Other people?" Dalten asked with irritation in his voice. "Who are these *other people*? Who are you talking about?"

"Galena," he whispered and then cleared his throat again. "And her father, Patrik. Teophelus is a close friend of the Vellein family."

"But they are in Noran!" Dalten responded irritatingly. "So how could they hinder us – "

"Bah, I am tired of these petty excuses," Helt interrupted. "Allow me to remind you that the only way you will ever see the remainder of that gold is by ensuring that the priest's death appears to be accidental." Kristof let out a loud sigh while Dalten scratched his forehead. "If anyone else is injured or even suspects that the priest's death was anything but a random act of nature, then you will have earned nothing more." Helt took one more bite of a pear, pushed the nearly-empty plate away from him, then stood up and walked towards the apartment door. "This meeting has ended. There is nothing else to say besides 'Othleis be with you.' I do not expect to see either of you ever again – even if the mission is a success."

"What?" Dalten asked. "Then how … how will we be paid?" The entrepreneur smiled as he opened the door.

"When the mission is complete, you will be recompensed. You have my word," he said softly as the two adventurers exited the room. "And under no circumstances do you come back here … ever," he said as the door closed behind them.

Once they were outside, where the sun was about to come out from behind the thick clouds of another cold, early-winter afternoon, Dalten put his arm around Kristof's shoulder.

"Don't worry about this," he whispered in Kristof's right ear. "I have a few ideas to help ensure that our mission is successful."

"But … but how are we going to make killing him look like it was just an accident?" Kristof said as he pushed Dalten's left arm off his shoulder.

"Like I said, I have some ideas. Let's not worry about the details now," Dalten responded. "After watching Helt eat his dinner, I have developed quite an appetite. Think we can find some roast duck for ourselves?" Dalten asked. He then started to walk briskly down the cobblestone street. Kristof sighed, shook his head and followed after him.

"Wait, wait for a moment," Kristof said. "Since my brain is completely void of any ideas, I guess I must trust your insight in these matters." Dalten stopped and turned around. "Please allow me to again stress my concern for Galena. You know that I used to work at The Lonely Fox Inn. Patrik and his daughters were … were like family to me." He paused to craft his next words carefully. "Galena helped me to learn the value of a hard day's work. She also helped me, though it was all for naught, to get her sister

Tamara to like me – or at least to admit that I even exist!" Dalten laughed.

"Now don't you start babbling about Tamara again!" he said. "You told me more than a few times about your passion for that girl! It was humiliating to listen to you go on and on about her. Yes, it certainly was," Dalten cajoled as he started to walk away again.

"But I'm not finished with what I intended to tell you!" Kristof blurted out.

"Let's find something to eat first, you sap! I promise that I will try to pay closer attention after I take care of these hunger pangs!"

Kristof followed Dalten into the closest pub. No roast duck was to be had there, so they settled for ox-meat stew instead. So while they ate, Dalten fulfilled his promise to listen to Kristof account for this relationship with Galena. After giving the former stable-hand a few minutes, he then interrupted to point out that once Teophelus was dead, Galena would need someone to comfort and console her. This made Kristof being to think about his feelings for Tamara and then realized that as he pictured Galena, he experienced many of the those same feelings! Dalten then pointed out that Kristof could console the younger of the innkeeper's daughters just when she would need consoling.

"This is becoming quite interesting," Kristof said. " Talking with you about this is making me feel much better, Dalten. We may have stumbled upon a way to help me finally let go of my feelings for Tamara."

"Do you think it is even possible?" Dalten quipped. "I mean, she is only *married* to the king of Betrovia!" Kristof's face turned beet-red.

"Don't deprecate me," he whispered. "Of course I know she is the queen of Betrovia. But … but since the first day I saw her." Dalten slowly tapped his right temple with his right index finger, the same finger that sported that large, gold ring willed to him by his miner grandfather.

"Think, Kristof, think!" he adjured. "You can finally forget about Tamara and realize that Galena is no homely handmaiden! Don't you see that she will need someone to take the priest's place in her heart once he is gone? You already have a relationship with her!"

"There was one … until I ran away from the inn," Kristof mumbled.

"Forget that you ran away! She will have forgotten about it as well when she sees you once the priest is out of the picture! And when we have attained all forty gold coins, not only will you be there for emotional support, you will have the money to solidify your commitment to her!" Kristof looked at Dalten and smiled. The idea of transferring his affection from Tamara to Galena seemed possible. No, it seemed more than possible: it was perfect! Why had he not released his feelings for Tamara up to that point? He had learned about her courtship with Ilead while the forester turned war-hero was just a captain in the Lycentian brigade. But Kristof had not resigned himself to the fact that attaining Tamara's affection was completely out of reach. And then, even after the two were married, he continued to harbor – even if it was unintentional – this fantasy that someday she still would be his. Yes, he could give up having Tamara as his own, and his heart would not be broken in two. He at last could actually believe that someone other than Tamara could make him happy.

As he finished his dinner of lukewarm stew and stale rye bread, Kristof remembered the songs Galena would sing, songs that would bring pleasure and solace to his heart when he needed it most.

> *"Keep your eye on the sky, my friend,*
> *Keep your heart on the stars.*
> *Fill your soul with your dreams…"*

"What? You are singing?" Dalten interrupted.

"Yes, I am singing. What about it? It is one of the songs that Galena would sing when I … when I needed relief from my sorrows."

"So, then. Sing, you sap!" Dalten announced. "As long as it makes you happy! Who am I to keep you from singing? To keep you from pacifying your lost dreams?"

The plan seemed almost divine: Galena would become his heart-song, his melody, the love of his life, and ultimately his wife. And the irony of it all was he had no one to thank for this stupendous revelation than the portly young man sitting across from him – the man who had convinced him to become an assassin.

CHAPTER TWELVE

"Othleis searches in the mountains, on the
plains and throughout the valleys;
He pursues those who with pure hearts and
motives yearn for Him."

Three drifters first knocked on and then demolished the flimsy door. They then proceeded to ransack the cottage it was hinged to, killing all but one of its inhabitants in the process. The sole survivor, a youngster not yet the tender age of two, was paradoxically was left alone, unharmed, as some kind of taunting symbol to the remaining residents of the hamlet. His father's mangled body lay to his left while his mother's was to his right. Without tears, without any outward show of emotion, his eyes were glued to the renegades as they crammed gunny sacks with what little booty they could find and then crushed the remains of the cottage door as they exited as quickly as they had entered. Silence then filled the cottage as the boy sat, immobilized, in the center of the room juxtaposed between the bodies of the only members of his family. He sat there until neighbors – once they were confident that the bandits would not return that horrific night – ran to the cottage to determine what remained of it. All they found that was worth saving was the barefoot toddler who still displayed no emotion, clad only in a tattered, woolen tunic. But from his neck hung a small pendant, a circular medallion that was identical to one that was wound too tightly around the neck of his father's bruised and bloodied corpse.

The village elders agreed that the boy should be given to his mother's older sister who had remained childless up to that point. His aunt lived in an isolated cottage a handful of miles west of the village, but not far from the scene of the heinous crime that took place that smoke-laden, hot summer's night. The aunt's cottage was much like his parents': a single room with only two holes cut into the walls that could count as windows. The hut faced a dusty high-plains pathway that was a rarely-used branch of the road that connected the rocky seacoast with Ahnak. Much to the disbelief of his village's elders, the toddler flourished in that crude abode where the skilled spinster taught him how to hunt, to fish and even how to coax a small garden planted into the plateau's yellow clay into producing a surprising number of melons, gourds and vegetables.

This path on which the cottage was located meandered lazily through the rolling hills and high plains of the western half of the Plains of Dreut. But it was merely a tangent from the commercial thoroughfare that ran directly from Ahnak to the Great Sea: those who traversed it were few and far between. This meant that traders did not often venture down the spinster's narrow path, and so the things the boy and his aunt needed but could not find or grow on their own had to be procured via other means. The woman owned neither horse, mule nor ox, so she had no way to effectively transport both herself and the boy to the nearest village. However, and only when necessary, they would walk to the few cottages of their closest neighbors since the village was too far to walk to except in the most-dire situations. But, when adventurous travelers did choose to traverse the spinster's side-road, she would display a gift for discerning which travelers to negotiate a trade and from which to remain safely secluded. When she deemed it prudent to hide from the visitors, they would seek refuge in a small cave nestled in a rocky outcropping a hundred yards or so south of their hut.

The majority of those who came down her road were pleasure-seekers exploring the hills and plateaus of the high plains that lay west of Ahnak. But now and then, Muad shepherds following their herds would stumble upon the cottage. Overall, for the ten years in which they entertained very few visitors, the two of them survived, some years by the skin of their teeth, while others with more than enough food and other goods to spare.

By the time the boy was twelve, thanks to the tutelage of this multi-talented female naturalist, he had developed into a competent hunter, a crafty fisherman and an accomplished gardener. But his favorite activity had to be fishing. He whittled his own hooks out of thin but sturdy shards of animal bones and spun fishing line using plant fibers harvested from their garden. Even though the fruits of his fishing labors were not as bountiful as the other vocations, fishing allowed him the time to sprawl out by the edge of the cool waters of the spring-fed stream that flowed north to south behind their cottage. From that bucolic location he would ponder his future.

When the memories of his violent past crept into his thought-life, he determined to force them deeper and deeper into his subconscious. As he cast his line into the resplendent waters of that isolated stream, it was as if he was launching those images into deep water. When he was rescued from the scene of his parents' death, he possessed but two physical reminders of his life with them. The tunic he wore that fateful night had long been burned up with the garden waste. But his aunt insisted that they retain the pendant, the small, circular bronze medallion embellished with the faint image of a wolf. She wanted him to keep it as a way to remember his parents. At least once a year, usually around the anniversary of the attack, she would tell him that the medallion could symbolize for him the life he might have had with them. When she did this, the boy would merely stare at the round piece of metal, saying nothing.

One gray winter day, the boy and his spinster aunt were returning from a rare but necessary re-stocking trip to the hamlet that was located on the thoroughfare to the Great Sea northeast of their cottage. When they finally left the village, with their bags full of the items they would need for the upcoming winter months, the weather was pleasantly warm for that time of the year, and the wind was nearly nonexistent. But as they turned off the main road and onto the cottage's narrow side-path, the wind – as if to somehow push them back in the direction from which they came – roared viciously over the high ridge that separated their shallow valley from the Great Sea many miles to the west. To make matters worse, as they came in sight of the cottage, a pack of mangy plateau hounds came howling and growling over the hill behind them.

Before she could make it to their garden that was planted in front of the hut, the mongrels tackled the old woman, driving her tired body mercilessly to the ground. Right before they pounced on her, she commanded the boy to run for the cave. To keep them from grabbing onto him, the woman lay where they had forced her to the ground, where she then remained passive, allowing herself to be bitten, clawed and ultimately ripped to shreds. Before her life-breath reached its end, she yelled to the boy that she loved him.

Obediently, he ran like he had never run before to the only place where he knew he could be safe: the cave just up the small ridge not too far behind the cottage. Not even once did he venture to look back; he knew that if he chanced it, he would suffer the same fate. As he scurried up the ridge to the mouth of the cave, one of the hounds latched onto his left ankle, nearly pulling him down from the rocky outcropping. Instinctively, the boy reacted and pulled a skinning knife out of its sheath that hung from his waist and subsequently buried it to the hilt into the cur's bristling neck. The hound released a blood-curdling shriek but thankfully relinquished his grip which allowed the boy to enter the cave basically unscathed.

From inside the sanctuary of the cave, the barking, snarling and growling of the remaining hounds continued to leap up to him. He resisted the urge to peer over the ledge to look out at them, knowing what he would see if he did: gangrene-ladened maws dripping with the blood of his mangled caretaker. Once again, he was alone; once again, he sat motionless; once again, he could do nothing but wait. As he waited, his attention was drawn to that medallion that hung from his neck, that round piece of metal imprinted with the crude image of a wolf.

The following morning when the boy awoke, the only noise that invaded his sanctuary was the encouraging cacophony of the field birds as they whistled and chirped. Before going back to the cabin, he forced himself to examine what was left of his dead aunt. All that remained was a blood-stained woolen cloak and one leather sandal. Even the smattering of provisions that they had traded for in the hamlet were gone. He picked up the cloak, stared at it for a few seconds, then nonchalantly tossed it into the underbrush. It hit a scrawny and gnarled cedar where it attached itself to the dusty conifer as if the nearly-dead tree was a hallway coat-rack.

For more than five years after his aunt's demise, the boy lived alone in her cottage which must be categorized as a hermit's life of his own choosing. When it behooved him to trade the spoils of his fishing, hunting and gardening exploits, his neighbors would ask about the old woman. He told them that she was too old to do much any more but was in otherwise good health. In the span of five years, he grew from boyhood into young adulthood by honing those skills as well as from perpetuating the charade that he did not reside alone in that hut. Most nights, he would climb up into that cave of refuge above the cottage and look out over the hills and valleys of the dry and dusty Plains of Dreut. From that vantage point, he would ponder his future.

One hot and humid afternoon, as he occupied his favorite fishing spot on the edge of the crystal spring-fed stream, the sky suddenly grew dark, and the wind began to blow fiercely. It was that ferocious wind that reminded him of a terrifying night not many years before. He made a dash for the cottage, and as he was about to reach its door, a diamond-white shaft of blazing-hot electricity slammed into its roof's dry thatch. The heavenly spark immediately set it ablaze, and consequently knocked the young man to the ground. The sudden storm's fierce wind mercilessly whipped the lightning's energy into a vortex of orange and yellow, and all the young man could do was lay there and stare at his home while it was consumed by the tongues of flame. Even before the fire was extinguished by the cool rainwater that soon followed, he had resolved that the door to him continuing to reside there on the high plains had effectively been shut. As the much-needed rain of that late afternoon dissipated, he started walking eastward, marking the beginning his passage to the great city of Ahnak.

The young man had listened to his aunt talk about this place, a city full of people and things that seemed impossible to even imagine. He desired to learn for himself if such a place could even exist. So he walked eastward, following the path that he had come to know quite well. He then turned onto the not-so-familiar highway that – on which if he would have turned northwest – would have delivered him instead to the frothy shores of the Great Sea.

Because he showed little interest in the village he and his aunt had visited only a handful of times – as well as not wanting to be recognized by anyone from there – he chose to veer south of it. A few days later, he reached the eastern edge of the Plains of Dreut which also served as the southwestern edge of the Great Forest of Betrovia. The idea that so many massive trees could be crammed into one place had never entered his mind. But he resolved to resist this fear of the unknown and therefore moved further into its towering emerald shadows.

At the end of his first day inside the Great Forest, he came upon a village. Having not eaten much at all in nearly three days, he decided to stop there to seek out food. But that night, he was nearly killed by villagers who accused him of stealing a chicken. Beaten nearly unconscious by that handful of angry men and subsequently left for dead, he managed to crawl into the nearest hovel. This place of refuge just happened to be the home of the village's only priest. The priest, a young Netherene, was also a fairly-new member of the village. Up to that point he had converted none of its residents to the faith, so he deemed it advantageous to take pity on the boy, believing as well that it his duty to nurse the young chicken-thief back to health. Consequently, the priest also indoctrinated him with the essentials of the Netherene faith – even though it was against the rules of the Lycentian Netherenes to proselytize someone who the villagers believed to be a Haarigoian.

Within a few weeks, the priest was not only amazed by the youngster's fast rate of recovery but also by his ability to retain the Netherene precepts fed to him. Before long, it became obvious to the priest that the young Haarigoian hungered for more than just spiritual enlightenment. The villagers were similarly flabbergasted by his quickly-expanding knowledge of the faith.

Mostly out of fear of the young upstart than respect for his unusual skills, they were soon encouraging him that this obscure clearing in the forest was not the best place for such a young man with talents like his. Lycentia, they emphasized, was where he needed to go. Surprisingly enough, the young high-plains neophyte Netherene instead expressed interest in visiting Ahnak. The village priest emphatically reminded him that Lycentia was the hub of the Netherene faith. So, if he desired to learn more of what it meant to be a Netherene, Lycentia was the place to which he must go.

As this orphan of the Plains of Dreut ingested more and more of the Netherene faith, and as he internalized more and more of its edicts and precepts, the depth and width of his anger grew stronger and stronger. This passion also grew darker. His animosity towards everything that had happened to him on the Plains became a power that frightened the villagers, and it especially was disconcerting to his tutor and his only friend. When he ventured to ask about the boy's past, even daring to learn the history of the medallion and what it could reveal about the newcomer's past, that dark ferocity would erupt and the boy would then offer no information at all.

The priest learned very little of the boy's past the first few months of his residing in that forest village. But one thing he had learned early was the Haarigoian's strong resentment towards the Creator. It was paradoxical that even though the boy hungered for more and more of the Netherene faith, the boy never attempted to stifle his bitterness. The boy fiercely resented losing his parents and then his aunt. This twice-orphaned boy from the Plains of Dreut – who much-later in this curious servitude to the Creator would become Viktor the Prophet, Oliver III's chief spokesman – exhibited no compunctions about espousing this rage towards his past.

So, when Viktor the Harrigoian finally left that nondescript woodcutters' hamlet to venture not to Ahnak, the city of his dreams, but to make a pilgrimage instead to Lycentia, the young priest was relieved. The day he left the woodcutters' village that was securely nestled on the southwestern edge of the Great Forest, everyone was overjoyed.

In a valley of gray dust and equally-gray cliffs and rifts – many miles west of the cool shadows of Betrovia's Great Forest – lay Ahnak, the ancient city of the Muads, the lords of the Southern Deserts. This dark and foreboding amalgam of dusty shops, raucous pubs, and seedy hostels was built by the Muads to provide for themselves a waypoint between their homelands farther south and the Plains of Dreut that were populated primarily by sheep-herding Haarigoians. In the center of the city was what had originally been the northern palace of their mustaf. After the Muads abandoned the northern palace, this monstrosity of gray stone became the home of the Shadow Lords, the leaders of the Shadow Hordes. On one cold but sunny early winter's morning, in the center room of that ancient stone bastion, Ilead, the king of Betrovia, and General Demirain, the chief officer of the Lycentian militia, discussed the fate of those Shadow Lords who at the time of the fall of Ahnak were the sole-proprietors of this former Muad trading post.

A little over three months had passed since Ilead and the General commanded a unified Betrovian force to breech the walls of Ahnak in order to defeat the Haarigoians and Rigarian rebels who had taken refuge there. Since the day of that miraculous and historic victory, two of Betrovia's leaders had returned to Ahnak one more time. The General's purpose in returning was to convince Ilead of the most-politically preferable treatment of Ahnak's leaders. The day after the Shadow Lords relinquished their control of the city, General Demirain ordered their immediate execution. But, much to the general's chagrin, the King of Betrovia countered that order, stating that they instead would be incarcerated until further notice. Not only was this the first time King Ilead had over-ruled a direct order given by the

General, it was the first time anyone had ever over-ruled the General. Not even King Justen, Ilead's predecessor – even at the height of his power and popularity – had dared to overturn any Demirain directive.

Illuminated by the first light of day on a early-winter morning, the two men stood facing one another in the largest room of the Shadow Lords' former temple.

"Does the king desire more tea?" General Demirain asked as one of his officers entered the room carrying a freshly-brewed pot. Ilead looked down at the curiously-colorful mosaic stone floor and shook his head.

"Tea? No, thank you. This one cup is plenty," he responded. The large room was void of any furnishings except a massive mahogany hexagonal table in its center. On that table were now two identical ivory porcelain decanters. "I have not acquired a taste for tea," he added. "Growing up, tea was such a luxury in our house. But broth," he said smiling, "The essence of meat broth, actually, was the only choice of a warm beverage on a cold morning. Besides water, of course," Demirain sighed.

"Yes, yes, but we must to get right to the point, your Highness," he interrupted. "And might I remind you that you are the king of Betrovia because of both political and military necessities? You were crowned our new king only because I, the leader of the most-powerful army in the region, single-handedly persuaded Oliver, Viktor and Luis that the crown be presented to you." Demirain exhaled again, crossed his arms over his barrel of a chest and waited for the king's reply. For a moment, the only sound in the room being the General's melodious wheezing, Ilead stared motionless at his counterpart. He then stepped over to the table and gently placed on it the ceramic cup that was much too small for his large, muscular hands.

"Yes, you overstate the obvious, General. It was because of your wonderful powers of persuasion that the men you mentioned agreed to my nomination. On the other hand, as I considered your offer of the kingship, I prayerfully sought the will of Othleis in this matter. Therefore, I believe it was due to His plans ... more so than your persuasiveness ... that I accepted the crown." Demirain put both of his hands into the air and waved them as if shooing a petulant insect.

"Of course, of course!" he exclaimed, continuing that peculiar gesturing. "I am not about to debate you concerning the Creator's will in this matter. But I also must remind you of the political ramifications that would be the result of any discord discovered between the head of the Betrovian military and the crown!" He then picked up the teacup that Ilead had placed on the table and held it to the light that was beginning to pass through the room's east window. He gazed at the delicate, lily-white vessel as if it was a precious jewel.

"Justen, your predecessor, struggled with this exact same problem," he nearly whispered as he slowly turned the cup back and forth. "But he was perturbingly hard-headed, rashly stubborn, and basically a fool for caring so little about strengthening ... or at least maintaining ... the tenuous union between the crown and the Lycentian militia!" Demirain proclaimed. Ilead again looked down at the floor and then moved toward the daylight that was now pouring into the huge room.

"I must confess, General, that I have learned very little of Justen ... or of his motives. But overall, I respect the man for what he accomplished during his time as king. It is because of his efforts that my family, the Tetrokeu family, has fared as well as it has." He looked up and faced the general. "And it is my duty ... my royal duty ... to demonstrate a very similar attitude." Demirain smiled, set the cup back onto the table, and then wiped his forehead with a cloth that was also on the table.

"Your Highness," he whispered, "This impetuousness is as I predicted. The king possesses not only a voluminous heart but a disenchantingly loyal one at that. If Justen were here with me in this room right now ... instead of you ... his words would certainly echo those you have just spoken. Even though this attitude is quite disillusioning, I must admit it is justifiable ... even reasonable. So, if it is your desire that the Shadow Lords be allowed to remain alive ... at least for the time being ... then so be it!" Demirain exclaimed. The expression on Ilead's face revealed surprise as well as relief.

"However," the General continued before the king could say anything. "Those black-hearted shamans must be removed from Ahnak and immediately transported to Lycentia for ... how should I put it ... re-education? And I recommend," he said, pointing at the king with the handkerchief still in his hand, "That *you* be the one in charge of determining the process ... and final outcomes ... of their re-education."

"General, I ... I do not understand what you are intending with this ... *re-education*," Ilead said as he once again stared at the floor. A unsettlingly quiet reigned in that room for more than a few seconds. Then, Ilead looked directly into the eyes of the General and continued. "But if it is your wish ... as my contribution to this compromise ...

I will take these old men back with me to Lycentia. And once they are there, I will do my best to convince them to renounce their evil practices," he said as he again looked at the floor. "As well as to demand that they express loyalty to the holy precepts of the Lycentian Netherenes." Demirain laughed.

"Ha! Now wouldn't that just make Viktor's day?" he chuckled. "Yes, wouldn't he love to see you make converts to the Netherene faith out of those decrepit vestiges of the Shadow Horde?" He picked up one of the teapots and into the same cup that Ilead has used a few minutes previous, poured himself a cup. "Yes, oh yes," he whispered as he sipped the hot beverage. "That would be a quite a sight to see."

The next day, with yet another unwelcome dose of early-winter snow falling from dense, white clouds at a rate of nearly an inch per hour, Ilead and a dozen or so of General Demirain's personal attachment herded their prisoners – ten Ahnak Shadow Lords – onto two covered ox-drawn wagons. The shamans, as the General referred to them, were clothed in satiny, maroon hooded robes that shrouded their faces. Their skin – what could be seen of it because of these large, flowing robes – was whitish, ghostly pale. Similar to their reaction to learning of their earlier fate, they remained mute as they were assisted onto the wagons. By noon, the caravan was headed out of the gates of the Muad's former fortress. Even though the officer in charge of the militiamen argued against it, Ilead rode in front of the prisoners' caravan. But, because of the near-blizzard conditions, the journey from Ahnak to Lycentia was destined to be cold and time-consuming.

CHAPTER THIRTEEN

"Did not the Creator form us as He sees fit? Why then do we complain? How then can we expect to attain purity if we complain about how He made us?"

The morning that King Ilead and his charges left Ahnak for the capital city, Luis – Lycentia's chief administrator – was alone in his bedroom. As he looked out over the plaza from one of the windows on the room's north side, he noticed the snow falling at a rapid pace. "Not again," he grumbled, closing the window and even pulling the curtains over it to return the room to its preternatural state of abject darkness. He sat down at the large desk, much too-large for the modest-sized room, lit a oil lamp, and then pulled something out of the upper desk drawer.

It was a small statuette, one of many that the administrator had collected since young adulthood. Luis went to great measures in keeping his collection secret because he knew that if any of his associates learned of his little collection of religious relics, he would surely be drummed out of office. The icon he chose to fondle that morning – carved out of a thin piece of bone – was in the shape of a fox; it even sported the essence of both a fluffy tail and a pointy snout. He held it close to the oil lamp and allowed his mouth to take on a childish grin as he marveled at the sharp, artistic edges of the finely-carved image. Yes, he knew that the Netherenes especially would be disgusted by his collection: one of their oldest edicts forbid the collecting of any such trinkets associated with the animistic belief systems of the Knaesin Mountains clans.

Luis staunchly believed that every piece of his aggregation was made by the most-talented and dedicated Knaesin shamans and were thereby anointed with possibly even human blood during the creation process. Knaesin mythology dictated that these miniature totems were made as wards against evil. But Luis held to the notion that the icons – imbibed with spiritual powers or not – had been outlawed by the Netherenes simply because of their monetary value and not because of any ethereal connotations. The standard diatribe of the Netherene faith was to be true to their version of belief in and faith towards the power of Othleis, the Creator. Anyone who possessed Knaesin-crafted wards, they would say, definitely could not be considered a dutiful believer of Othleis. Therefore, because of this, Luis knew that he must maintain at least an air of religiosity especially when in the presence of a Netherene priest.

Some of the totems in Luis' cache were crafted from the teeth and bones of ferocious beasts of prey while others were formed out of emeralds, amethysts and even rubies. The most exotic, and therefore most-valuable, were fabled to have been made from the bones of fearsome mountain creatures similar to the seti – the hairy men of Himalayan lore: half-man, half-beast creatures that were the stock of children's nightmares. But by far, Luis' favorite icon was the one he caressed that morning. The mythology of the fox not only intrigued him but had even driven him to borrow a large amount of money to purchase a neck-piece sewn entirely from the fur of a rare white fox. Even though it would be more than acceptable to flaunt such a valuable item due to winter's early onslaught that year, the administrator could not bring himself to don the fox-fur item and then wear it in public out of fear that it may become soiled or something even worse.

As he continued to admire the fanciful trinket, someone knocked on the door. Assured that it was sufficiently secure, he remained quiet to create the appearance that he was still in bed and consequently fast asleep. But the door, as if it was not only unlocked but not even closed, suddenly popped opened. Before he could utter a word of outrage or even consternation, Viktor the Prophet walked into the room.

"Why Viktor! Come in! Please come in! What a surprise!" Luis exclaimed as he quickly stood up, throwing the statuette back into the desk drawer in the process.

"Administrator," Luis' impromptu visitor said softly. "It appears that you have been spending too much time in your chambers as of late." Viktor was clad in his traditional gray robe and carried in his left hand a finely-carved wooden walking stick. As he walked further into the room, the only sound that could be heard was the tapping of that cane as it struck the oakwood floor. "Even your staff has expressed their concerns about this unfortunate sequence of public absence," the Prophet added as he moved closer to Luis.

"My staff? *They* have complained? Now why would they do such a silly thing such as that? What might they have to complain about? I pay them well, provide for their meals, their housing. Why, if it wasn't for me, they would be out in the street and begging for coin!" The tapping ended just as Viktor stopped no less than three feet from where Lycentia's administrator leaned on his desk.

"Luis, your sense of humor never ceases to entertain me," he replied as he looked down at Luis' right hand that was still gripping the brass handle of his desk's top drawer. Luis noticed that Viktor's gaze was fixed on the drawer and he subsequently took a large step away from the desk. "And it is quite interesting that you have brought up this issue of renumeration," Viktor continued. "But delving deeper into that matter at this time is not why I have come, Luis." The administrator cringed; one thing he detested about Oliver's right-hand man was how he overused his name. It was as if Viktor intended to repeat it to somehow remind Luis that he must have forgotten what it was.

"I hope you do not find it rude of me asking, *Viktor*," Luis said with a tinge of sarcasm in his voice, "But just why did you come to talk to me at such an early hour this cold and snowy morning?"

"Good! Very good," the Prophet replied. "It warms my old heart that you desire to get right to the issue at hand." He then let out an sigh of irritation as he plopped down in Luis' desk chair. Luis' lips parted slightly as he watched Viktor's eyes land once again on that top drawer. The parted lips morphed into an impish grin as Viktor's eyes left the drawer and met his. "Luis," Viktor continued, "I have come to your house to illicit your assistance with a problem that has come to my attention."

"Why yes, Viktor! Certainly! As always, you can count on my help with whatever you need!" Luis replied.

"Ah, such encouraging exuberance," Viktor said. "But, as I have already mentioned, I am much too-familiar with your petulance. So, if you wouldn't mind, I would prefer that you immediately shelve this penchant for sarcasm and display a more-somber attitude!" He then stared at Luis as he waited for a response.

"It should be obvious to you that I had just risen out of bed not more than a few minutes before you burst into my room, Viktor!" Luis responded. "So if you desire more civility than I am now exhibiting, please allow me to get dressed and then to eat my breakfast! Not that it matters at all to you, but I battled a bit of a stomach issue last night, so I went to bed without much dinner."

"Very well then … very well," Viktor said as he planted the cane firmly on the floor and leaned on it to stand up. "It is logical that one's appetite may hamper one's ability to effectively partake in a civil discussion. Therefore, I allow you one hour to dress and to fulfill your desire for nutritional sustenance. I will be patiently waiting in your office downstairs."

It was a little more than seventy minutes later when Luis walked into the room where Viktor was seated. The administrator looked at the prophet and pulled the door shut behind him. "I am here, *Viktor*. Now, for what do you require my assistance?"

"As you may well know, I have been dealing with a issue that up until recently has not required much of my time or energy. But for some reason … and it may be due to my age and subsequent health issues … I cannot seem to stay on top of this problem." Luis nodded a silent reply, put his hands behind his back and continued to listen. "So I will get right to the point. The prison population is growing larger, Luis, and dealing with these criminals is beginning to exact its toll on me." Luis smiled.

"The number of pick-pockets, thieves, murders and political dissidents of various types residing in the city's prison has never amounted to more than a few dozen at any given time," he replied. "So, just what *criminals* might you be referring to?" Viktor drew in a deep breath.

"Those impudent dissenters!" the Prophet exclaimed. "As of yesterday, over ten of them were taking up precious space in the dungeon that you have alloted to me! More than ten! Less than a month ago there were only two – maybe three!"

"I see," Luis replied. "And the agreement has always been that any of these *heretics* you want to place in the city's care must be kept apart from the ... common criminals?"

"Indeed they must be kept apart!" Viktor exclaimed. "The false religion that they espouse must be kept away from the flaccid intellects of society's malcontents! And up until this week, successfully keeping them apart has not been an issue."

"But the more dissidents your men drag into the prison, the less room we have for all of the prisoners. As I see it, Viktor, you need to stop arresting so many of them," Luis said with a wry smile.

"That is easy for you to say, administrator!" Viktor replied. "The charges levied against those your officers have detained are obvious ... and can easily be supported in court. What these heretics are being charged with is not so easily-justified. The leaders of Lycentia have made it clear that they want the thieves and murders kept locked away. But these men who continue to propagate heresy against the temple? The issue is not as black-and-white."

"Then tell me, kind sir, what do you want me to do? If the prison lacks the necessary space for incarcerating all of Lycentia's criminals, how do you propose we solve this problem?" Luis asked as he sat down and put his hands behind his head.

"I have been mulling this over for quite some time, Luis, and here is what I have determined," Viktor replied. "Someone closely related to the king possesses something that should require him to join the other dissenters in the prison. But because of his relationship to the king, it would cause harm to the already-tenuous relationship between the temple and the crown if he were arrested."

"What does this person have that is so controversial?" Luis asked.

"There is nothing *controversial* about those parchments!" Viktor immediately shouted. "It has always been my policy that anyone found with those pages of heretical lunacy would be immediately executed!" Luis smiled again.

"Might you be referring to the writings of that Harrak character?" Luis asked.

"That is exactly what I am referring to!" Viktor said.

"But I thought that was taken care of years ago," Luis added.

"Up until this year, it had not been a problem," Viktor replied. "And I am not exactly certain as to why there seems to be more of these heretics now than before. But how many there are is not the issue, Luis. The problem is the number of these enemies of the temple who are so determined in making copies of and distributing those writings! This is what has to stop!" Luis leaned over.

"Again I ask, Viktor, what is it that you want me to do? Besides adding another wing on to the prison?" Luis asked.

"Please refrain from the sarcasm, administrator," Viktor replied with irritation in his voice. "I feel the solution to this problem is very simple. I want you to make the necessary arrangements for King Ilead to procure a copy of those documents."

"The king? You want me to find a copy of Harrak's writings and deliver it to the king? Now how would doing that take care of the over-crowded prison?"

"Luis, you have already said that you would do anything necessary to help me take care of this problem. Will you or won't you do this?"

"Let me see," Luis replied. "If I said 'yes,' just where might I be able to find a set of these *controversial* papers?"

"The king's father-in-law," Viktor replied. "He is the relative of the king that I alluded to before. I believe he has recently arrived here in Lycentia and should be easy to locate."

"King Ilead's father-in-law … I see," Luis said. "So I should send my men to find and then arrest him … since he currently possesses those outlawed documents?"

"No!" Viktor shouted. "I already said that arresting him would most-certainly upset the king. The man cannot be arrested nor can he even be detained. And it is vital that he not be allowed to do what he has intended to do with those parchments."

"And just what might that be?" Luis asked as he leaned back again in the chair.

"He intends to deliver them to Oliver," Viktor whispered. "That most-certainly must not be allowed to happen."

"Speaking of our faithful father," Luis interrupted. "How is his health? Is he still bed-ridden for much of the day?"

"Oliver's health is about the same as it has been," Viktor said. "And that is why we need to ensure that it not be allowed to regress. Therefore, keeping those incendiary writings away from him is mandatory."

"But why? Doesn't he already know about the increasing popularity of these heretics?" Luis asked.

"Yes, he is aware of them," Viktor replied. "But we have been successful in keeping him in the dark about the ridiculous resurgence in the distribution of those writings. Both his father and grandfather fought diligently against Harrak's prophecies, and as long as I am alive and able, I have vowed to keep Oliver III from having to concern himself with them!"

====================

After Teophelus had completed the list of duties given to him by the head of the Noran temple, he consequently thought he was at liberty to return to Lycentia where he could then rejoin Patrik and Galena. But the morning before leaving the village, his plans to travel directly to Lycentia were again put on hold as the priests ordered him to do yet one more thing.

He was told to ascertain who had recently taking up residence in an old forester's cabin ten or so miles east of Noran. Even though he thought the task was a bit unusual for a priest-in-training, he chose to not argue about it with his superiors. He wanted to continue assisting the innkeeper to better understand Harrak's writings, and he wanted to do this before the innkeeper attempted to deliver them to Oliver III. But he also believed that time was not on his side. So to speed things up, even though it was rumored that Rigarian rebels might be in the area, he chose to take the foresters' path that ran directly east of the village into the forest. But in reality, this trail was both rarely used and fairly unknown to anyone but Noran hunters and woodcutters. To add to the difficulty of the task, another late-autumn snow added a few more inches to what had already been deposited there previously. Once he realized that his decision to take the foresters' path instead of the main thoroughfare had become quite problematic, he had already traveled on it too far east to reverse directions and return to Noran.

After trekking through the white stuff barely five miles, with the sun setting behind him and dark clouds moving in menacingly from the north, the young priest whispered a prayer of thanks as he noticed a dim light emanating from the windows of a cabin just ahead of him and a little off the path. He breathed another prayer that this was the cabin he had been assigned to investigate. He didn't give it a second thought as he wrapped his horse's reins to a nearby tree and walked up to the door. Simultaneously, he stomped the snow off his boots and knocked. But there was no response. "Please open the door," he said. "Someone must be in there because light is coming through the window!" He then pushed on the door; it appeared to be bolted from the inside. So he knocked again, this time with a bit more force and much more irritation. He stopped once he heard movement from inside.

"Go away!" a raspy but angry voice shouted from behind the pine-wood barrier.

"Please! Might you open this door? It is very cold out here!" Teophelus pleaded. "And it's starting to snow again."

"More snow?" the voice responded. "Exactly what we do not need ... more snow." And then the door opened but only partially. "What do you want?" Light came out of the opening, but the source of the voice still could not be determined. "Now no trying to force yourself in here! We are heavily-armed and know how to defend ourselves!"

"There's no reason to be fearful," Teophelus said as he creaked his neck around the edge of the door, trying to determine with whom he was chatting. But before he could move out of the way, the cabin door suddenly swung open almost all of the way – and it would have opened completely if it had not come in contact with Teophelus first!

"Be careful back there!" he shouted. "That was my head you just hit!" He moved back from the now-opened doorway and rubbed what would soon be a sizable knot on the right side of his head.

"Who ... who is this? Why ... why is it Teophelus? Is it really you? Yes, yes! It is you! Othleis be praised! Now what in all of creation are you doing way out here?" the voice from behind the opened door asked. The neophyte squinted through watery eyes to see who he had been arguing with.

"Dridel? Dridel Nurflett? It is you! And we all thought ... I ... you're supposed to be dead!" he stuttered, continuing to rub his scalp as he was finally allowed to step inside. Standing in front of him was a thin man of average height with scraggly white hair and an equally-scraggly unkempt but short, white beard. He was attired in a floor-length, but heavy multi-colored patchwork robe and held a short double-edge sword in his right hand. The old man, upon realizing that the visitor was certainly friend and not foe, quickly set the sword down on a crudely-crafted table and stuck out the now-empty hand.

"Dead? Now why would you think that?" The old man asked. "Who was it that said I was dead?" he asked as the two priests shook hands.

"Everyone in Noran! Everyone believes you are dead … especially all of the priests. Last summer you left for … or at least said … that you were leaving Noran to move into the Rigars. And that was the last time we saw or heard from you." Teophelus took a deep breath and glanced around the cabin. Except for the table where the sword now resided, a similarly-crafted chair and a tiny cot, the cabin contained little else.

"Did anyone find a body? Did anyone from the Rigars come into Noran claiming that I was no longer alive? What evidence was there that I had died?" The questions were presented vigorously and with frustration. "Just because no one in Noran has seen me since I left does not mean that I am dead!" Teophelus laughed.

"Of course not," he said. "But it was just assumed – "

"Too many assumptions in this world, that's what. Too many miscalculations and mis…misconstruments. And to alleviate any doubts about my traveling skills, I actually did make it to my intended destination high up in the Rigars."

"But … but why didn't you ever come back to the temple in Noran?" Teophelus asked as he moved closer to the small fire that was burning in the equally-demure fireplace.

"What purpose would it serve to head back there … when my life's mission is finally complete!"

Far into the late-night hours, the old priest explained to Teophelus what had transpired there in one of the villages in the Rigar Mountains.

"Latreies? That is a familiar name. The last time I was looking over Harrak's scrolls with Patrik that name appeared. So tell me … what is the significance of this Latreies?" Teophelus asked.

"Oh, he is very important," Dridel continued. "And it would not take a genius to ascertain why our fellow Netherenes are opposed to anything said about him. It is because of Latreies that Harrak spent those many months writing everything down that he had learned." The white-bearded priest took a deep breath and continued. "Latreies was Othleis' chosen one, the son of the Creator himself. Hundreds of years ago, he was born in a remote village in the Rigars but as a young man relocated to the Great Forest … many years before it was ever called *Betrovia*. It was there – in the Great Forest – where he ministered … where he healed sick people and performed many other wonderful miracles as he taught about the love of the Creator. And he eventually died there. He humbly and selflessly served the people of the Great Forest, demonstrating not only a powerful love for Othleis but also a sacrificial love for his fellow man. And before his death, he completed the mission assigned to him by Othleis."

"Mission? He had a mission? Something besides being a great example of what it means to be a true Netherene?" The old priest laughed.

"Latreies lived many years before anyone was ever called a *Netherene*. At that time, the only spiritually-minded people living in the Great Forest were the Knaesin animists ... along with a smattering of the pathetically-fatalistic Rigarian monks! Since the monks had always been monotheists, it has been taught that Latreies would be born to a Rigarian woman." Dridel then furrowed his shaggy brow and smiled. "The term *Netherene* came about not many years after Latreies' death ... when people living in the Nether Valley east of the Rigars learned of his miraculous life and began to propagate his teachings and even emulate him."

"I ... I simply do not understand. You are wanting me to believe that the uneducated peasants of the Nether Valley were the first Betrovians who believed in him?" Teophelus asked.

"Yes," the old priest answered. "As preposterous as it sounds, they were the first serious followers of Latreies. And anyone who believed the same way as the believers from the Nether Valley region were then also called *Netherenes*."

"This ... this is just too amazing," Teophelus declared. "Only a few weeks ago Patrik and I were looking over Harrak's scrolls and ... and my heart began to beat faster as I started to understand what it could mean to be a true Netherene. So much of what Harrak wrote is contrary to what I have been indoctrinated in. Harrak's teachings are pure ... maybe a bit simplistic ... but are much easier to understand than the dogma taught by the Netherenes.

Because of his writings, I … I was soon losing interest in applying for membership to the Lycentian temple!"

As the north wind blew and the snow completely covered Teophelus' horse's tracks, Dridel also amazed Teophelus with the news that the scrolls Patrik found in the cave were merely copies. As far as he knew, he continued, the original set that Harrak penned was hidden somewhere in Lycentia – quite possibly even in the temple itself! Teophelus was flabbergasted as he continued listening to Dridel tell how Lyce-Tuereons – followers of Harrak – had made it their mission to copy the beloved parchments – before the originals were violently confiscated by the Lycentian Netherenes.

Harrak's followers then traveled throughout the Great Forest – and even into the Rigar Mountains – as they made more copies from the ones they were able to hide from the Netherenes. They even hid those copies wherever it was deemed appropriate. Dridel added that he came upon one such copy the previous summer during his trip into the Rigars. He too believed that he had come upon the original parchments until – while still in the mountains – word of Patrik's discovery came to him. Before the summer was over, not one but two different Rigarian Lyce-Tuereons – at two different times – revealed to Dridel their secret association. Because of their understanding of the powerful truths contained in Harrak's writings, they soon convinced him to become what they were: Lyce-Tuereons. The parchments that Patrik discovered probably had been placed in Feleg only a few years before Patrik began to seek solace there.

"But why Feleg? What is so unique about that cave that would make someone want to stash copies of the scrolls there?" Teophelus asked.

"I have heard rumors ... rumors of terrible things ... horrible things that happened there ... but I never allowed myself to believe them. Now I am certain these rumors are true. Feleg – along with other caves throughout the Great Forest – have been used for human sacrifice! Yes, it is to be believed! Such a horrendous activity! Sacrifices performed by none other than disciples of the Shadow Lords!"

"The Horde? The Shadow Horde was active that far north of the Plains?" Teophelus asked.

"Indeed they were! Even before the Netherenes became the only valid source of information about the Creator, not only denizens of the Horde but even those despicable Knaesin animists roamed the forest. Yes, yes, living in the Great Forest has been quite a dangerous vocation!"

"But, I still do not understand," the neophyte murmured. "What would be the purpose of hiding copies of the scrolls in a cave where human sacrifices had been performed?" the acolyte asked.

"A desperate act of purification ... to somehow nullify the black acts of the Shadow Hordes that were performed there," the old priest softly responded. "Even though there is nothing in Harrak's writings to support this, the earliest Lyce-Tuereons believed that placing the copies in those caves ... or wherever ... would purify those sites. But this practice, of course, has since been abandoned."

"Abandoned? But why?"

"My son, it is because true purity can only come when a man's life has been changed from the inside out ... made pure through faith in Othleis ... faith in what Latreies accomplished in his obedience to the Creator's directives. It makes no difference what transpired in a dismal cave yesterday or even a hundred years ago!" Dridel said. "What matters is what is in the heart of a man ... and what Othleis wants to do for that heart ... and the eternal soul ... of a true believer!" Dridel then walked over to a corner of the cabin and picked up a small satchel. "In here is the copy that I came upon while in the mountains." Teophelus forced himself to remain attentive as the old man pulled out one of the dry pages and read from it; he wanted to ask more questions but also wanted to listen to the old priest translate Harrak's writings.

"'*Purity comes only from passionate, consistent aggression towards evil. Utilize the light that has been given you. Utilize it against all forms of darkness'.*" The young priest smiled in admiration of how fluently the older priest translated the text; the voice coming out of the spindly old man could not have been the same voice that he had been listening to the entire night. "'*Manipulate the light to eradicate the evil. Courage and boldness is required'.*" Dridel then placed the parchment back into the satchel and sat down on the cabin's only chair. "I believe it was that passage in particular that inspired the early Lyce-Tuereons to assign spiritual powers to the scrolls themselves." Teophelus scratched his head but then softly whimpered as he inadvertently scraped the tender lump.

"Explain this to me, Dridel ... and I confess that I still am struggling to understand. Why *did* you become a Lyce-Tuereon?" The old priest's expression brightened, and he then stood back up.

"When I was a young man, even a bit younger than you are now, Teophelus, I was so excited about becoming a

Netherene priest! I wanted to learn all that I could about the priesthood and thereby become the best Netherene priest that anyone could ever be. Before long, however, I realized that all my studying and memorizing was only gaining me knowledge about Othleis. And I know so very much about the Creator, oh indeed I do! But I wanted more than that knowledge! There just had to be something more than just *knowing* about him!"

"That ... that is exactly what I have been thinking about ... exactly how I have been feeling!" Teophelus interrupted. "And this feeling has to be connected to my helping Patrik to decipher the scrolls!" Dridel walked over to Teophelus and put a hand on the young man's shoulder.

"Before we go on, I must tell you that the Lyce-Tuereons are a secretive and protective group ... and this is all for a very essential reason." He then let out a huge sigh as he returned to the chair. "Lyce-Tuereons ... *light-bringers* being the crudest but most-accurate translation ... are being persecuted by Viktor and the rest of the old-guard Lycentian Netherenes."

"But why? This ... this makes no sense," Teophelus complained. "Why would some powerful – but altogether few – Netherenes want to punish other Betrovians for what they have chosen to believe about the Creator?"

"It is a sad state of affairs ... indeed it is," Dridel replied softly. "Those who have placed their faith in Latreies ... those who have taken what Harrak wrote as the only way to follow Othleis ... they desire their worship of and service to him to be pure and sincere ... not just the keeping of a voluminous compilation of rules ... not a conglomeration of ritualistic habits and traditions!" Dridel's voice grew louder as he continued. "We ... I mean *Lyce-*

Tuereons ... especially do not appreciate how the temples are currently being operated! It has become all about the money! Acquiring great quantities of silver and gold ... and the political power that ultimately comes with it!"

"I think ... I am beginning to understand," Teophelus reverently whispered. "Through his writings Harrak emphasized that the first Netherenes had followed the path of purity as it was taught and demonstrated by Latreies – "

"But because of the temptation of acquiring gold and the power that can come from hoarding it, too many of the Netherene leaders have deterred from that path," Dridel interrupted to conclude. He then added that the "light-bringers" have resided in secret throughout the Great Forest but their exact numbers could not be determined due to the sinister vindictiveness of Viktor and his henchmen. Once Viktor found out that a priest – or anyone for that matter – had aligned themselves with the Lyce-Tuereons, and if they were captured, they were secretively disposed of. Dridel then added that many "light-bringers" have been of Rigarian descent and the majority during Harrak's lifetime were as well. Even a few followers of Latreies were converts who were born elsewhere and then migrated to the Great Forest.

"What about the Knaesins? Have any of their clans found the way of the light?" Teophelus interrupted to ask.

"The way of the light? Now that is an interesting way to put it! No, not many Knaesins have become Lyce-Tuerons," Dridel replied. "Because of Harrak's strong condemnation of animism, the Knaesin clans' irascible attachment to their animistic beliefs has hindered too many of them from trusting in his writings." Daylight leaking into the hut announced that morning was approaching. As the

snow tapered off to a mere dusting, the two Noran priests continued their discussion over a hot pot of Rigarian herbal tea.

As sunlight began to finds its way into the tiny cabin, signaling that the night full of amazing revelations was about to reach its end, Dridel walked over to Teophelus who by that time had sat down in the cabin's solitary chair. The old priest then bent down on one knee and put his right hand on the younger priest's shoulder.

"My good friend," he began. "And might I even be so bold to call you *brother*?" Teophelus smiled but continued looking at the floor. "Brother, we have spent the entire night talking about some very important and – of course – very dangerous things. And I do not think you will be surprised by what I am about to ask of you."

At this, the neophyte looked into the old man's pale-green but vibrant eyes. "That day … in the Rigars … the day that I finally understood what it means to be a true Netherene … a complete Netherene … what it means to be a true believer in Othleis … I finally became alive! Yes, it is true! I now know why I was born and have discovered my purpose for living!"

Dridel then stood up and put both hands on the young man's shoulders to coax him out of the chair; Teophelus was nearly a foot taller than the older priest but that didn't deter the man from asking what that needed to be asked.

"Teophelus, you have been blessed to be allowed to read Harrak's scrolls. Very few Betrovians have had such an opportunity. And because of this, you have also been chosen … just like I have been chosen … just like all Lyce-Tuereons have been chosen. Because of Harrak's diligence in writing down what Othleis revealed to him, you and I have been blessed beyond measure." The old priest's voice again became raspy, but it was as strong as it had been the entire night. "Won't you join us now? Won't you join *me*?"

CHAPTER FOURTEEN

"Othleis cries out: 'Rescue the foolish! Pull them away from danger! Bring them away from the Dark Ones!' Those doing as much seek His purity; they will be thusly rewarded."

    Teophelus' head ached as he struggled with the details of the story of Latreies and his followers, the Lyce-Tuereons. He wanted to give the old priest a positive response to his question, but was fearful in doing so. It was not that he was afraid of what might happen if anyone found out that he had become a "light-bringer." He was simply terrified of what Galena would do if she found out! And if she did find out, would she turn her back on him forever?

    Because of this conflict, and having not slept for over thirty-six hours, along with the fact that the snow on the foresters' path was still quite deep, he had some problems staying awake as he rode straight from Dridel's cabin to Lycentia. And by the evening of the next day, he had re-entered the capital city. Any opportunity for a long nap appeared to not be in his immediate future, the neophyte ascertained, but some hot food most-definitely should be. And so, he walked into the first tavern he came upon. He then breathed a sigh of relief at being able to sit on something other than the back of his horse.

A few days before leaving Noran, a letter had arrived from Lycentia. The short, hastily-scrawled note informed him that the innkeeper and his daughter were staying in a merchant's house located on the east side of the city. He pulled this letter out of his coat pocket and reviewed it as he waited patiently for his first meal in over two days. The letter, which appeared to have been written by Galena, not only included directions in how to find the merchant's house but also contained an emotional appeal that he exercise caution as he traveled to the capital city. But the part of the letter that made him smile was where Galena wrote that she could hardly wait to see him again. With that smile, however, came again the tension created by the memory of Dridel's heart-felt request.

Around mid-morning, Galena was the first to greet Teophelus when he arrived at Franck's house. Even before he had a chance to enter the dwelling under his own power, she had latched onto his hand, pulled him through the house and into the pantry.

"Now," she said after closing the door behind them. "Tell me everything that happened to you while you were gone – especially what you did once you returned to the temple in Noran."

"I ... well...," the young priest stammered. "There ... there is so much that I must tell you! Where do I start?" She playfully crossed her arms and tapped her left foot.

"Why, of course, you certainly must start at the beginning!" she chided. "And do not entertain any ideas about editing out anything you might consider dull or boring! I want to hear about *everything* ... every little detail!" Teophelus grimaced, swallowed hard, then put both hands on the table that was in the center of the room. He looked down, resisting eye contact with her, then, with uncertainty written all over his face, looked up at her.

"The temple elders told me that they are impressed with how well I have fulfilled my duties," he began. "They were so impressed that before I asked for their permission to come back here to Lycentia, they ... they gave me one more assignment."

"Oh," Galena said. "And what was that?"

"Nothing really," he responded with a whisper. "It was just one more trivial errand before they would give me their blessings to come back here." The expression on her face communicated that she wasn't a bit happy with the answer.

"What *errand*?" Galena's left toe continued to produce a sound similar to the ticking of a grandfather clock. Teophelus again swallowed hard.

"It was just one more mindless ... tedious thing to do ... something that any of the other priests could have done but chose not to. I suppose it will continue to be this way as long as I am the Noran temple priest with the least experience." A thin bead of sweat appeared on his forehead, and he quickly turned away from her to wipe it off with a towel that was on the table.

"*That* was a clean towel," Galena playfully told him as she yanked it out of his hand. "For some reason," she added, looking at the moisture that continued to form above the young priest's light-brown eyebrows. "I don't think you're being totally forth-coming with me. And I cannot understand why you are struggling to tell me *everything* about this ... errand." She then moved closer towards him, keeping her eyes directly on that line of sweat. "Maybe this errand involved talking to some pretty young lady?" she asked. Her foot started tapping again, but this time –

because she was standing directly in front of him – that left foot touched his right boot instead of the pantry's floor.

"*Pretty young lady*?! By the Creator, indeed not!" he exclaimed, this time wiping off the sweat with his right shirt sleeve. Then with both hands, he grabbed Galena's right hand and squeezed it tightly. "You certainly must know that all Netherenes – especially those wizen old bachelors – have chosen to have nothing to do with women … young or old!" Before he could finish his sentence, her left hand latched onto his hands.

"And you would *never* want to be like them, now would you, Teophelus?" she asked as she quickly pulled back both of her hands and then again laid her arms across her chest. "Of course you have no intentions of becoming a die-hard, life-long bachelor like *they* are, do you, my love?"

"Indeed not!" he replied. "Haven't I made this clear to you already? Haven't we talked about this issue more times than I can remember? It is quite unnerving how you have forgotten so quickly!" He spun around and began to peer out the window. The morning's gray clouds had melted away, and the bright rays of the mid-morning sun illuminated the small, snow-covered yard outside the pantry window.

"Teophelus! Turn around and look at me this minute!" Galena commanded. "Have you not yet deciphered when I am being serious with you … and when I am merely joking?" He obeyed, and their eyes met for the first time that morning.

"Galena, even though I have known you longer than I can remember, I still cannot fathom when … when you are serious and when you are … making fun," he whispered.

She smiled and moved slowly towards him, allowing her hips to sway back and forth with each step.

"Oh, is that right? Then this means you still have a few things to learn about me!" she said. "Why would we want to know everything about each other when we have the rest of our lives to learn it all? If we knew all there is to know at this very moment, there would be no mystery … nothing to learn … nothing to talk about in the future," she added as she caressed his left arm.

"Marry me, Galena," Teophelus suddenly blurted out. His blue eyes were as glassed over as if he had just polished off one of Franck's vintage bottles of wine. He then bent down on one knee. "Tell me that you will marry me, Galena. Say it now before allowing anything but an emphatic *Yes!* to come across your exquisite lips!" She then quickly but only momentarily covered her mouth with her right hand.

"You're … you're kneeling," she then giggled. "Is this how a Netherene should properly propose?" Teophelus shook his head but then got done on both knees and attempted to display the most-sincere, most heart-felt facial expression he had ever mustered.

"Would you *please* marry me?" he implored. "Of course, true Netherenes are supposed to be bound to celibacy, so there is no proper way – "

"Yes!" she said. "I will marry you and – "

"Oh, my sweet Galena!" he interrupted. "You don't know how much this means to me!" He stood back up and pulled her body close to his. "But there is one very important thing we now must do." With his arms still wrapped around her body, she looked up at him and smiled.

"And what would that be, my dearest one?"

"We must keep our … our impending nuptials a secret … and we especially should not allow your father to find out."

"And why not? Why *not* tell Father? He thinks so much of you and this – "

"No, we most definitely do not want to tell Patrik," he commanded. "It … it would be better that he thinks that … that I first asked for and then received his permission." Galena squealed with delight at his idea.

"Fantastic! I love it! What a superb idea! I promise to say nothing to him about it. Not a word! Not a single, solitary syllable!"

That evening, Teophelus and Galena teamed up to prepare a special meal for themselves and Patrik. Their dinner was centered around a succulent venison roast purchased just that morning from the market, and it was garnished with spiced yams and one of the innkeeper's favorites: spiced apple dumplings. As the evening was about to conclude, Galena confessed to over-stuffing herself and consequently announced that she was heading upstairs for an early bedtime. But before leaving the dining room, she dashed over to Teophelus and planted a long, lingering kiss on the young priest's mouth. Her father's response to the sudden and quite aggressive display of affection was a stern scowl. Galena covered her mouth with her hands and countered with a giggle of abject defiance. She then waved at her father and scurried up the stairs.

"I suppose her kissing you in that way implies that your relationship is once again in good stead?" Patrik asked as he thrust another chunk of the succulent dumplings into his mouth.

"Indeed, sir!" Teophelus replied. "I am quite fond of Galena. And I hope that she is just as enamored with me!"

"Good ... that is very good," Patrik said. "That kiss is convincing evidence of her fondness for you. But you must be told that I never condoned such froward behavior in either of my girls," he added.

"Of course, sir, of course. I have the utmost respect for how you have raised your girls ... and Galena especially." Patrik momentarily stared at the priest, raised his right hand as if to say something then quickly let it drop.

"What else did you want to say?"

"Never mind," Patrik whispered. "Never mind."

After cleaning up the mess which included putting away most of the cooking utensils, Teophelus asked if Patrik would like his help with anything else. The young priest's question must have come at a good time because Patrik's eyes quickly beamed with excitement.

"Why of course I do, young man! The scrolls! Might you have a few moments this evening to help me with more of Harrak's musings?"

Teophelus wanted to help Patrik decipher more spiritual insights and controversial prophecies hidden within the yellowed parchments. But he was worried that he might slip and end up telling Patrik about his encounter with Dridel; the temptation was almost more than he could bear. He believed that telling Patrik that he was even associated with the former Noran monk would put both the innkeeper and his daughter in danger. However, there was one thing he felt safe sharing.

"You ... you cannot be serious?! The scrolls? They ... they are *copies*?"

"Yes, it is true," Teophelus said somberly.

"But I do not understand!" Patrik stood up from the table and scratched his white-bearded chin. "The paper ... even the ink on the paper ... it ... they ... are so old and – "

"Even though what you found are merely copies, they are *old* copies," Teophelus interrupted. "I do not believe there are any Lyce ... oh, I mean, none of Harrak's followers are currently making copies of the scrolls. I am fairly certain of that." Patrik returned to the table and sat down.

"*Copies*," he whispered, pointing at the light-brown and crinkled sheets that were spread out on the table in front of him. "For nearly six months it has been my intention to do all that I can to protect these fragile sheets of paper ... these *documents* ... because I thought they were the only ones!" His voice got louder. "Do you have any idea of the frustration I've endured! I have been plagued with headaches, nightmares and even stomach ailments! And all because of trying to keep these ... these *copies* from being damaged?!" He stood back up and began pacing the floor and wringing his hands. "Galena! Oh, how impatient I have been towards her! Much too protective about those parchments! When I thought she was going to do something ... maybe even something drastic ... to those things! Those *copies*! How can she ever forgive me for being so ... insensitive?"

"She *will* forgive you, Patrik sir," Teophelus added. "Of this I am most-confident. Galena is one amazing young lady. She possesses a heart of pure gold, she certainly does." Patrik let out a monstrous sigh.

"Bah! And what will she think about the parchments once she learns that they are merely copies? What will she want to do to them knowing that they were not personally penned by the prophet?" Patrik stared at the young priest, as if he were expecting a logical answer.

"Patrik, sir," Teophelus replied. "Who says that she needs to learn that these documents are anything less than what you have said they are?" Patrik's eyes suddenly brightened.

"What is that? What are you saying? We ... we need not tell her? We need not tell her the truth?"

"At least not in the near-future," the young priest answered.

"Yes, indeed! That would be perfect! Oh, you have a mind like a steel trap, you do! Who *is* to say to her that they are anything but the exact ruminations penned solely by Harrak himself! Brilliant, Teophelus, simply brilliant!" Patrik threw his hands up into the air. "Thank you, Othleis! Thank you once again for blessing me with this intelligent young man! You have graced him with such wisdom! And you have shown me mercy by sending him to aid me in my mission! Thank you, thank you, thank you!" Teophelus' face turned as red as a fully-ripened Knaesin plum.

"Please, sir, you're ... you're embarrassing me," the young priest said softly.

"But there is something," Patrik interjected. "There is still something I must know about these scrolls."

"If I have the knowledge, I will gladly share it with you, sir." Patrik again scratched his bearded chin.

"If these documents are only copies – "

"Not *if*, sir," Teophelus interrupted. "They are most-definitely copies."

"Right! Fine then!" Patrik exclaimed with a smile on his face. "*Since* these are copies ... maybe even copies of copies … then … where might be the originals?" At this, Teophelus stood up from the table and walked over to the window.

"I cannot say for certain their exact location." He paused a few seconds. "But it is believed that they have been hidden someplace safe."

"*Someplace safe*," Patrik repeated in a matter-of-fact tone. There was then an uneasy silence until Teophelus broke it.

"I suppose a safe place could be somewhere here in Lycentia? Under the watchful eye of a high-ranking Netherene?" the priest proposed.

"Now I am thoroughly confused," Patrik said. "If Oliver III, the Netherene high priest, is opposed to these scrolls, why would he be complicit in allowing them to be kept safe here in Lycentia?" There was another period of silence as Teophelus' attention was suddenly drawn through the pantry window to a handful of blackbirds poking around in the snow.

"These birds … here outside the window … they are interesting," he commented without looking back at the innkeeper. "They attempt to find nourishment where it more than likely cannot be found. But they continue to try."

"What are you talking about?" Patrik asked as he walked up to the window and also began to look outside. "Birds maybe? Birds digging in the snow?"

"Yes, and their digging makes me think about what we are attempting to do with these scrolls."

"And just what are we attempting to do?"

"As I help you to understand what Harrak wrote, it is like I … like *we* … are struggling to find food … *spiritual* food so to speak … even if we think it might not be found."

"But we *are* finding it, my dear priest! We are finding that spiritual nourishment! At the very least, you are helping me find what I have been yearning for since ... since I was but a boy!" Patrik responded.

"I suppose so," Teophelus softly replied. "But I am now compelled to return to your question about the location of the originals." He stopped watching the birds and walked back to the table. "I, too, have been curious as to their location. And my curiosity was hardened when I recently learned that the originals may be hidden somewhere close by ... possibly even within the Lycentian temple itself!"

"Ha! Now wouldn't that be insanely ironic! That is exactly what that would be! Utterly and moronically ironic!" Patrik exclaimed. "How could anyone believe Harrak's original writings ... something that Oliver and Viktor have been adamantly opposed to ... might just be right under their Netherene noses!"

"Please, sir, allow me to interrupt to add yet one more thing," Teophelus said as he wiped a new line of sweat from his brow. "I believe that Oliver has no knowledge of the originals' location." Then the Noran priest peered into the innkeeper's eyes. "My source of this information, however, believes that Viktor, Oliver's prophet, more than likely knows of their exact whereabouts."

Once Patrik had gotten over the initial shock of this new information about Harrak's writings, he and Teophelus commenced once again to discuss them. As the light of the full moon painted the snow-covered streets of Lycentia with a faint, silvery glow, Teophelus translated from a section of the parchments that neither of them had yet encountered. On this particular page, Harrak wrote what Teophelus stated was a fascinating aspect of the Creator's plans:

Latreies would miraculously be returning to Betrovia. But he would not return in the same way he first arrived. This new purpose in his coming would be to not only defeat the Shadow Horde once and for all but to ultimately purify and unify all the people groups of the entire world – and not just the people of Betrovia. As Teophelus kept a finger on his place, he stopped reading and looked up at the innkeeper.

"If it wasn't for Viktor and his henchmen fervently attempting to squelch the prophecies written here about Latreies, those who want to remain true to the Netherene faith would not have to live in fear for their lives. And, more importantly, they could help to spread this wonderful news!" Patrik's forehead furrowed as he leaned back in his chair.

"Are *we* then being true to the original Netherene faith, Teophelus? As we decipher these scrolls … and talk about delivering them to the high priest? You and I … might we be hasting the day of Latreies' return?" The innkeeper looked directly into the priest's blue eyes. "Are we true Netherenes?"

"I would like to think we are, sir," Teophelus replied. "However, since you have labored so diligently to bring these scrolls to Lycentia … you have therefore demonstrated more faith than I have."

"And how might that be, young man? How have I been more important in bringing these to Oliver than you? I was simply in the right place at the right time! Any why was I there in the first place? I ran away! Escaped! Again! I ran away from those I love to that musty cave. But it was there in that cave where Othleis mercifully opened my eyes to something hidden in a small crevice in the wall." Teophelus stood up and again walked over to the window. To the young Netherene, the tiny shadows in the snow created by the moonlight and the blackbirds' scratchings resembled the markings on those controversial parchments.

"I … I should have been more diligent in helping you with these scrolls. I should have been there at the inn every night last summer translating them for you, so you could much sooner understand all of what Harrak wrote." He quickly turned around and was about to declare something else but resisted the temptation. "If I would have availed myself to you earlier, you might have already ventured to the temple and successfully delivered the scrolls. And then maybe he, the high priest of all Betrovia, would already be praying for the return of Latreies as well as the ultimate destruction of the Shadow Lords and all of their followers!"

"So are you saying that somewhere in these scrolls is the Creator's plan to bring peace and purity to all peoples of the world … even to the Muads and all the others who have aligned themselves with the Dark Lords?" Patrik asked.

"No!" Teophelus adamantly exclaimed. "I cannot believe that the Creator can redeem anyone who has aligned themselves with the Shadow Lords. I will not believe it!"

"Father?" Galena said softly as she entered the dining room, rubbing her eyes in the process.

"Galena! What are you doing up at this time of the night?" Patrik asked.

"I … I could not get to sleep. The moonlight … it is so bright, and those curtains in the bedroom … they fail to keep out the light." She released a long yawn. "And I could not keep from hearing you two." She yawned again. "So who are these *Shadow Lords*?" she then asked. Teophelus walked over to her and gently put his right arm around her shoulders.

"Dear Galena, the less you learn of the Muads and their evil allies, the better," he said sternly but softly. She responded by walking out of his half-embrace and towards her white-haired father.

"The Muads? So they are like the Shadow Lords? Why, I already know all about them! Don't I, Father? They are the ones who taught the ignorant Haarigoians how to raise sheep and to properly shear those smelly creatures and then sell the raw wool to the Lycentian merchants!" With both hands placed firmly on her hips, she continued. "And I know I heard you two talking about the Shadow Lords, not the Muads! So tell me about them and not those boring sheep-herders before I start to get angry!"

"It would not benefit you in the least to learn anything about them, Galena," Teophelus replied. "Generally speaking, think of them as merely the priesthood of the Muads ... like the Netherenes are serving as the priesthood for all Betrovians." Galena put her right index finger on her right temple and laughed.

"Oh, so now I understand," she replied as she continued to snicker. "You expect to pacify me with something banal like *they resemble the Netherenes*! What do you think I learned the last ten years living in a road-side inn? Do you think all I did was cook and clean? Ha! As I stand here, I must inform you that I know more than you think I know!" She curled her lips and took a deep breath before continuing.

"The people of the Great Forest ... they have their Netherenes. And the Rigars have their smelly cave-dwelling hermits while the Knaesins have their egotistical monks.

And of course we must not forget the Haarigoians and their incense-burning, spell-casting shamans! Now, as I come downstairs, what do my ears hear? I hear about these *Shadow Lords* ... mysterious creatures that I have heard nothing about until just now. And you, Teophelus, talk about them as if they are the ancient enemies of the Netherenes! And you have the gall to insist that I should not learn anything about them?" She then pointed that finger that had been pointed at her temple at the innkeeper. "Father, you tell Teophelus this very instant that I am not a child and demand that he tell me everything he knows about these *Misty Peoples* and ... and...." Before she could finish her sentence, she collapsed at the young priest's feet.

"Patrik sir!" Teophelus exclaimed. "What is wrong with her?"

"She has obviously fainted ... again," he replied. "Since being thrown out of the wagon and hitting her head as a result, she has lost consciousness more than a few times ... maybe as much as once a week ... since the accident."

"Haven't you taken her to a physician to have her examined?" Teophelus asked as he knelt down and put his right hand on her head. "These fainting spells must be a symptom of some kind of internal injury!"

"I do not think so," Patrik replied. "From the first time she lost consciousness until now, she's awakened and has not complained of any pain. When she was a little girl, I might add, she fell out of one of our oak trees and didn't even suffer a broken bone! Othleis has shielded – "

"Teophelus? Is ... is that you?" Galena asked as she suddenly woke up.

"The Creator be praised!" the young priest said as he leaned over and kissed her on the forehead. "Does your head hurt at all?"

"My head? I feel no pain. And what am I doing here on the floor? Oh, Father, please tell me that I did not faint again?" Patrik smiled and nodded his head. "Oh my, oh my," she muttered as she grabbed Teophelus' right hand and allowed him to help her stand back up. "What am I doing here? I ... I should be upstairs in bed. I am so very tired," she said with another huge yawn. "But I am also so very hungry. What is there to eat? Surely there is something somewhere to eat," she mumbled as she started to walk out of the room. "Oh, Father, I just remembered! Did Teophelus tell you what he did today? He asked me – "

"Food! What a wonderful idea!" Teophelus interrupted as he grabbed her by the arm and pulled her into the pantry. "Surely we can find something for you to eat in here!"

Not more than an hour later, after Teophelus had left for the night and Galena had returned to her room, Patrik opened the front door of Franck's house and looked out over the snow-covered street. The moonlight was so bright that he couldn't help but notice a large cat that was walking on the top of the stone wall across the street. The cat's attention was also drawn towards the innkeeper, and he stopped making his way across the wall. For more than a minute, the two night-owls stood there, immobile, each waiting for the other to take the next step. Patrik then smiled as he allowed a childish thought to take form in his mind. He then reached down and grabbed a handful of snow, quickly formed it into a ball, and threw it at the night-creature. The oval missile flew at least two feet above and then over the intended target. The feline watched as the snowball passed safely overhead, then nonchalantly hopped down off the wall and scampered into the shadows. Patrik let out a sigh, shivered, and closed the door.

"Yes, tomorrow will be the day," he whispered as he shivered again. "Tomorrow, Othleis, with Your help, I will take the parchments to the temple."

CHAPTER FIFTEEN

"The simple-minded finds delight in propagating his simplemindedness; he toils endlessly to spread errancy about Othleis. The Creator, however, will reward those who live justly and who fervently seek His purity."

The next morning, before the sun had come over the snow-laden peaks of the Knaesins not far to the east of Lycentia, Patrik was about to open the front door of the merchant's house again. It was not his intention to merely glance outside to see who or what might be just outside the door. However, he had been thinking about the stray cat with which he had the staring contest the night before. With the leather pouch tucked safely under his left arm and clutching one of Franck's finely-carved walking sticks with his right hand, he opened the door. As he was about to step outside, Galena bounded down the stairs.

"What are you doing, Father? And you ... you're carrying the pouch with the scrolls!" she exclaimed. "You cannot be headed for the temple now ... alone! You must wait for me to get dressed! I will accompany you!"

"No, Galena, you cannot come with me. It ... it will be too dangerous," he said. His glare was that of a mature wolf staring down one of his pack's overly-energetic but inexperienced pups.

"If you will not allow me to go with you … then … then you certainly must wait for Teophelus!" she demanded. "He would want to be there when you deliver the scrolls!" She reached for the pouch, but the innkeeper used his body to shield it from her. He also managed to step outside and close the door right as she followed behind him.

"No, no. That also would not be prudent," he replied. "I cannot allow him to be seen with me in public while I have the scrolls in my possession. He has already done enough to assist me." He looked into her light-blue eyes. "Teophelus has faithfully fulfilled his duty to the Creator … now it is…." He continued looking into her eyes as he struggled to find the best words. "It is my duty to finish the task." And with that, he waved at his younger daughter, stepped into the snow and began to walk briskly down the street. Galena went back inside the house, slamming the door behind her. But before the innkeeper had progressed ten yards, it opened again.

"Before Teophelus left last night, did he talk to you about us? About him and I?" she yelled from the doorway. Patrik stopped but remained silent; he did, however, respond by shaking his head. "That man! He *promised* he would talk to you!" she blurted just before slamming the door again.

The Lycentian streets were covered with a wet and heavy snow that was nearly a foot deep in places, and before he had made it even three blocks from Franck's house, his feet were numb from the cold. "I hope there is little chance for any more of this ridiculous stuff today," he mumbled. As he walked, his attention was drawn to the warm mist escaping from his lungs. To ignore the pain to his feet caused by the cold, he tried to focus on what he would say once he arrived at the temple. Even before leaving The Lonely Fox Inn, he had rehearsed this impending conversation. "Of course," he continued to mumble, "Oliver will want to debate about Harrak's qualifications. Ha! I do hope that the conversation will not reach that precarious point." He then looked up at the robin's egg blue sky and smiled. "Othleis, because of you sending Teophelus last night, my confidence in understanding the basics of these scrolls is as high as it ever has been! If I can but control the route of the conversation," he continued whispering as he trudged through the snow. "If I can direct the high priest to allow me to point out … to present key passages. Bah! What am I thinking? My only hope is that Oliver will merely listen to me! Othleis, can I be so bold to ask that you hinder him from asking any questions at all?"

On any normal day blessed with Lycentia's customary early-winter weather, the short trek from the traveling merchant's house to the temple complex that occupied the center of the city would have only taken half an hour at the most. But because of the depth of the freakish snow, Patrik arrived at the temple plaza's eastern gate just as the sun's morning rays ricocheted off the temple's golden spire, nearly an hour after he had left Franck's house. The gate was closed, but the temple guard stationed there perfunctorily glanced at the innkeeper, grunted incoherently, and then methodically opened it for him.

"Imagine that!" The innkeeper exclaimed. "The guard failed to ask me even a single question! Today must be the day I am supposed to be here!"

Patrik barely made it inside the plaza walls before the gate resounded with a loud *thunk*! behind him. He had walked from Franck's house to that exact gate a handful of times since arriving in Lycentia, but up until that day, he had not ventured inside the walls of the temple's inner courtyard. To commemorate the lofty event, Patrik paused to survey his surroundings. To his left stood a half-dozen nondescript two-story buildings assumed to house the covey of fledgling Netherene priests. To his right was a wide expanse of snow-covered but open ground peppered with more than a few large conifers as well as deciduous trees. Peering through that small forest, he then spied a sparkling-white, four-story structure on the other side of the stand of trees; it could only be the residence of the high priest of Betrovia.

"If I were the high priest of the Netherenes, I certainly would enjoy living in such a place," he said with a smile.

Directly in front of the innkeeper was the Lycentian temple. Its three golden spires, the center one being the tallest, were so tall that they appeared to be supporting the bright blue sky above them. After making note of the height of the spires, Patrik quietly counted the steps that led up to the temple's main doors. There were thirty-six in all with a small landing at every nine steps. On each landing were statues, dark-granite, life-sized creations representing important but long-dead Netherenes. "I wonder which one is the first Oliver?" Patrik whispered reverently.

There was one peculiar, but welcomed, aspect about this courtyard: even though the areas to his right and left were covered by the frigid white stuff, the wide path from the eastern gate all the way up to the temple doors was completely snow-free. And the most-fascinating aspect: not a single pile of snow could be seen on either side of the path.

As he reached the second level of nine steps, he was startled by a familiar voice behind him. It was Teophelus! He had just entered the gate and was running up to the first set of steps.

"And a fine good morning to you, too, my young friend!" Patrik said. "How did you know where to find me?" The innkeeper strengthened his grip on the leathery pouch in front of him as he watched the young priest scurry up the steps.

"Galena," Teophelus panted. His hands went directly to his knees in order to catch his breath. "Galena ... she ... she told me."

"Fascinating," Patrik said as he then scratched his head with his right hand. "But why did you return to the house so early this morning when you had only left but a few hours ago?"

"Patrik, sir, surely you jest," the young priest responded. "Before I left last night you told me of your plan to bring the scrolls to the temple today." Teophelus straightened up; even though the priest from Noran was a tall man, the innkeeper was a few inches taller.

"I did?" Patrik responded with a slight amount of embarrassment. "Why would I let you know that I was coming here? Haven't I expressed my concern about being seen in public with you if I am carrying the scrolls?" Teophelus took a deep breath and then exhaled. For a second, the moist, warm air coagulated into a milky-white cloud, and then it was gone.

"Why you are constantly so concerned about my safety?" he replied. "By now you should have realized that I fully intend to accompany you the entire way ... even into Oliver's inner office if the Creator deems it necessary!"

Patrik chuckled and put his right arm around the young man's shoulders.

"Othleis, why do I even try?" he cajoled, looking up into the nearly-cloudless sky. "Teophelus, more and more you remind me of my daughters," the innkeeper said. "And that is not a bad thing … not a bad thing at all." He then shifted his focus to the next flight of stairs. "Come with me then … since you are so determined to help." Teophelus responded with a huge smile. "That certainly brightened your countenance! Let us proceed then! Together!" Patrik took three steps but stopped when he noticed that Teophelus had not moved with him. "So, why are you just standing there? These parchments are not going to get inside those doors on their own!" Teophelus sat down on the tenth step.

"Patrik sir, before I proceed further, there is something I must tell you … something very important. And I must say it before I take another step." The former Noran trapper returned to the first landing and sat down next to his friend.

"So, here I am. Now what is so important that requires that I must go about freezing my posterior to this frigid stone?"

"A few days ago … as I was completing the final task assigned to me by my superiors at the Noran temple … I talked to a man who – "

"Yes, yes, my young friend, you have already told me about your conversation with the old priest in the cabin." Patrik was about to stand back up but Teophelus' right hand latched onto his left arm kept him seated.

"No, sir … I mean, yes sir, you are correct, sir, I did tell you about our conversation … but I did not disclose *everything* that we discussed." Patrik ceased trying to regain his previous posture.

"*Everything*? Now you have definitely piqued my curiosity," he said as he leaned back. He was then momentarily blinded by the sun's stark rays.

"I failed to tell you that the old priest ... Dridel is his name and – " Before he could finish his sentence, a Lycentian attired in a dark-green robe adorned with a golden sash and matching gold trim came up to them.

"Welcome to the temple of his majesty Othleis, the Giver of life and the Creator of all things," the priest said respectfully. "I hope you will not be offended by me saying that it is rather imprudent to lounge on the temple steps. If you wish to enter, please make your way up." He stuck out his hand towards Patrik as if to assist the older man to stand up. The innkeeper merely stared at the pale and bony hand as he stood up.

"Thank you for wanting to help," Patrik said. "But I am more than capable of standing under my own power." The Lycentian's right hand quickly returned inside the shimmering emerald garment. "And before you say anything else, allow me to introduce my friend and myself. This young man, a fine priest who has served the Creator from Noran, is Teophelus." Patrik waited for some kind of response from the Lycentian, but none came. So he continued. "And my name is Patrik." With that said, the stoic then replied.

"And what is your family name?" he asked as his face continued to display a polite grin.

"Now why must I disclose to you my family name?" Patrik asked. Teophelus then forced a grin.

"It is a common question among Netherene priests, Patrik sir," he said. "Take no offense by it." Patrik then merely shrugged.

"Fine then. I am Patrik ... and my family name is Vellein." Their unexpected host's expression morphed from one of detached stoicism to professional consternation.

"Patrik Vellein of Noran, Oliver III has no interest in talking to you about Harrak's scrolls at this time," the Lycentian abruptly blurted out as he turned away from them and floated quickly down the steps. He then abruptly turned back around, causing the overly-ornate robe to furl in the process. "But please allow me to encourage you to spend some time praying at the Creator's mercy seat which is conveniently located in the northern quadrant of the temple." Teophelus could only stare, awe-struck, at the Netherene in the tent-sized robe.

"But ... but I have the scrolls right here!" Patrik said slightly louder than intended. Without thinking, he then ran down the half-dozen steps that the man had already accessed, pulling a page out of the pouch as he ran. "Here! Look! I can show it to you, and then we could – "

"Pray, Patrik Vellein of Noran, go inside the temple and pray at the Creator's mercy seat," the Lycentian reiterated as he pushed the parchment away. "I cannot sacrifice my position by being seen reading those ... papers," he whispered. "You must understand that." He then glared at Teophelus. "And you, neophyte priest of the Noran temple, certainly must comprehend! The longer I stand here conversing with you, the longer I endanger my status!" He then shrouded his face by pulling over his head the golden-laced hood of the emerald garment and then scampered down the remaining steps. This commotion garnered the attention of a handful similarly-clad men who had gathered at the bottom of the steps.

"If you are not going to enter the temple to pray, then you need to leave immediately," one them offered.

"Unless, of course, it is your plan to instead leave an offering," another priest added. Teophelus stepped down to be closer to this priest and squinted intently at him. A friendly smile then appeared.

"Malthies? I thought that was you! You do remember me, do you not?" Teophelus asked. The priest didn't respond with even a slight nod of the head. "So you aren't going to respond? Perfect! Why are you asking for money? Can't we just go into the temple without someone begging for our money?" A third priest stepped in between Teophelus and the other man.

"If you are not here to pray nor to deliver alms, then just why are you here?" this one asked.

"We have something of the utmost importance to deliver to Oliver III," Teophelus answered sternly. "And it would be very prudent of you to show us the way to his chambers!"

"The high priest cannot be disturbed at this time," the priest said politely. This Netherene of the Lycentian temple wore a light-blue robe adorned with an over-abundance of silvery lace. "Once again, if you are not here to pray or to deliver offerings – "

"Thank you! Thank you for your help this morning!" Patrik interrupted. "We do appreciate your assistance and hope to meet each and everyone of you again very soon. Now ... we must bid you all a good day!" Patrik then grabbed the young priest's left arm. "Come, Teophelus. Our presence here is no longer needed," he said as he pulled him away from the temple steps.

"Why did you back down from them?" Teophelus asked. Patrik released his arm and put his right hand on the young man's shoulder. With his left hand he continued to grasp tightly the leathery pouch.

"There are only two of us," Patrik replied softly. "And I counted at least six of them. Those are not good odds. Othleis will provide another day and another time. Today's battle is over ... soon there will be another day ... and yet another battle." The innkeeper then looked back up the steps at the priests who still had not moved from the landing. "How about coming back with me to Franck's house? I am sure that we can convince Galena into preparing something special for dinner?" he then said as he looked back at his young friend "All this talking has given me a ferocious appetite!"

"No, I cannot," Teophelus replied. "I ... I need some time ... some time to think ... alone. And with Galena there in the house, there would not be much of an opportunity for much serious reflection." Before Patrik could say another word, Teophelus was walking towards the inner gate. The Noran priest smiled politely as the grumpy guard then opened the gate for him.

"Thank you, sir, for your service to the Creator. I am confident that you will be thusly rewarded," Teophelus offered sarcastically as the man slammed the gate behind him. He stopped and – for a only a moment – looked back at the closed gate. "Now where do I go?" he whispered. "Back to the hostel? Yes, I suppose that would make sense." And with that, he headed southwest around the walls of the temple grounds. He had to walk only a block before entering the markets that were south of the temple complex.

"I know what I should do," he continued whispering. "I should go back inside those walls and march right up those steps! I am a *Netherene* priest ... no different than any of those pompous Lycentians! I have as much right to seek an audience with the high priest as they do!" He stopped under the porch of a meat vendor's shop and closed his eyes. "Othleis, if it is your will, give me the courage this very moment to go back inside the temple courtyard walls and into the temple. I ask as well for your favor in going to Oliver's chambers to meet with him. And I pray that you will prepare him mentally and spiritually for my visit." He opened his eyes and took a deep breath. "There now. I feel much better. But do I feel like heading back? Let me see. I don't feel any more confident than I did a few minutes ago. Maybe if I could find something to eat first? Then might I be more receptive to receiving the courage I have prayed for? Yes, that is it! I will simply go inside this fine establishment and buy something to eat!"

After grudgingly exchanging one Lycentian silver and a few coppers for a small piece of roasted chicken and an even-smaller piece of dry black-bean bread, Teophelus returned outside. As he nibbled on his humble but over-priced meal, his attention was drawn some priests half a block away. He then walked slowly in their direction, glancing to his left and to his right hoping to not gain their attention. He got close enough without being noticed and then began eavesdropping on their conversation. They were discussing a meeting that was going to occur sometime soon between Luis, the Lycentian city administrator, and a few of the high priest's closest associates. Believing that his presence still had not been detected, he moved a few steps closer and attempted to hide his thin frame behind a gnarled wooden post. He chewed on the dry meat even faster when he heard that the meeting was to take place that very afternoon in the administrator's office. Teophelus' heart beat faster as he wished that he knew where that office was located. "I wonder ... if priests close to Oliver will today meet with Luis, might Oliver himself sometime show up there as well?" he whispered. Without weighing the consequences, he came out from behind the post and boldly approached the men.

"Pardon me, sirs, but I could not help but overhear your conversation. I too am needing to speak with the city administrator but do not know where his office is. Would you be so kind as to inform me of its location?" The priests, all clothed in light-gray smocks and long, thin overcoats, appeared to be about his age. For a few seconds, they merely stared at him. Then they went back to conversing with each other as if he wasn't even there. "I do beg your pardon," he asked, but before he could say anything else, they – in silent unison – turned from him and walked away. At that same moment, a light snow then began to fall out of what had been a cloudless late-morning sky. One large, mischievous flake landed squarely on the young priest's nose. He angrily brushed it off and shook his head.

"Lycentians," he muttered. "Their habitual rudeness never ceases to amaze me."

Teophelus, undaunted by the encounter with the rival priests, continued his trek through the market. "Now, who could I find that might know where to locate this Luis character?" he mumbled. "Surely someone in this market knows." Close to the wall that separated the southern market from the temple's courtyard was a vendor's cart overflowing with a colorful selection of late-season gourdes and melons. One of the cantaloupes was sliced in half, and Teophelus thought that a piece of that juicy melon would be a fine completion to his snack.

"Fine sir, might you cut off a small bit of that cantaloupe for me?" he asked the vendor. Teophelus displayed a copper coin which prompted the man to smile and then reach for a long knife. He cut a wedge from the melon and gave it to Teophelus.

"That will be *two* copper coins, my friend," the vendor said. Teophelus sniffed the fruit and smiled back.

"If I give you a piece of Lycentian silver instead, my fine sir, might I also purchase some information as well?"

"A silver coin, eh? Lemme see the coin first," the vendor replied. The Noran priest then set the melon slice on the edge of the vendor's cart and pulled his coin purse out of his coat pocket. Between his right index finger and his thumb, he displayed a Lycentian coin that was embossed on one side with an eagle in flight. "Ah yes, that is a fine coin, a very one fine indeed," the vendor commented. Teophelus then placed the piece of silver in the palm of the man's right hand.

"Now for the information," the young priest said. "Might you be able to tell me where the city administrator's office is located? I need to speak with him about some important city business that I am soon to be involved in." The vendor let out a guttural laugh.

"Luis' office? Is that all you wanted to know? Ha! And I thought you were going to ask me about something more juicy than that!" Teophelus returned the purse back to his coat pocket and wondered what the man could be insinuating.

"Yes, the location of his office ... that is all I would like to learn." The vendor laughed again.

"You are one strange Netherene, young man, yes, you certainly are. Nearly every other priest who ventures by my cart begs me to divulge who is sleeping with whom, who has robbed whom, and even who might want to murder whom. And all you want to find out is where our illustrious city administrator holds court!" Teophelus' upper lip stiffened, and he wiped yet another large snowflake from the bridge of his nose.

"So can you tell me – " Without any notice, a large object suddenly plummeted out of the sky into the vendor's cart, smashing gourdes and melons against the stone wall and launching them into the street.

"What was that?!" the vendor exclaimed. He quickly jumped into the cart. "A large stone! Like the ones that make up this wall! It must have fallen!" He then stood up in the cart and began to take inventory of the damage. "Oh my, my, my! There's a hole in the bottom of the cart the size of my largest melon! My cart ... my beautiful cart! It is completely destroyed! And my wonderful melons are all damaged as well!" He then looked at the Noran priest.

"But ... but a few seconds ago, young man, you were standing right there! Right where the stone hit my cart! Why, it ... it could have hit you instead of falling onto my produce!" The vendor then hopped out of the wagon and slapped Teophelus' right arm. "That stone could have slammed right onto your head! And if it had, you would have been been killed! Ha! Today must be your lucky day, young priest." Teophelus looked inside the wagon, glanced at the produce that lay haphazard on the street, and then took another bite of the cantaloupe.

"I have no faith in luck, sir," he said calmly. "My faith is in the Creator and His eternal plans for my life." He finished off the slice and threw the rind onto the disheveled cart's contents. "I have too much to do for the Creator to worry about being thwarted from proceeding now." Teophelus didn't notice that a crowd had formed around him, and they laughed at this bold, seemingly off-the-cuff pronouncement. The young priest blushed, bowed his head, and then pushed his way through the bystanders. Another short session of laughter then commenced. By the time he remembered that he had not yet discovered the location of Luis' office, he was only a block away from the hostel in which he had secured lodging. "That meeting was supposed to be held this afternoon! And I failed to learn its location! Oh, Othleis! I have failed you yet again!"

That next morning, Teophelus was out of the hostel door before sunrise and was on his way to Franck's house. He forced himself not to think about the previous day's missed opportunity and thought instead about how to tell Patrik about the adventure with the melon cart. "Yes, of course! That is it! I was supposed to be there by that vendor's cart when the stone came off the wall! It was Othleis' plan all along to show me how He has been protecting me! And yes, it wasn't his plan at all for me to meet the administrator! Yes, that is exactly how it was supposed to happen! And this is exactly how I will explain the incident to Patrik!"

The hostel was west of the traveling merchant's abode with the temple grounds situated directly between the two structures. Instead of taking the southern route around the temple courtyard wall, like he had done the day before, this morning he chose instead to traverse the northern sector. This consequently led him into Lycentia's northern market, the larger of the city's two markets. Farmers and craftsmen who lived north and west of the city brought their wares into this market while those living south and east of Lycentia tendered their goods in the southern market.

"However," he surmised aloud, "I still desire to find out where Luis' office is. And most-certainly that someone who knows its location is located in *this* market! But who might I inquire first?" As he entered this larger of the two city markets, the first person to catch his eye was a Lycentian officer. The man appeared to be on duty that morning as he stood alone dressed in full uniform. He appeared to be on the watch for anything out of the ordinary. "Why of course! A Lycentian militiaman would know the location of the city administrator's office! Who else in this city could I expect nothing less from?" With his right hand he dusted the crumbs from the hastily-prepared breakfast off the front of his coat and walked up to the officer.

"Can I do something for you, priest?" The man's voice was low and ominous. Teophelus shuddered and stepped backwards.

"Sir, might I be allowed me to ask for directions?" The officer still didn't look at him.

"Directions? Directions for what?"

"Not *for* something," Teophelus replied softly. "Directions *to* somewhere."

"What do you take me for, priest? A cartographer? What makes you think I might know of this place you are looking for?" Another shudder ran up and then back down Teophelus' spine.

"Sir, you are obviously a Lycentian officer. And therefore you must have demonstrated a great amount of knowledge and wisdom about our capital city to earn such a covetous rank," he replied. The militiaman finally looked at the Noran priest, but the expression on his face communicated anything but concern.

"Ask then!" he coarsely demanded. "I have work to do and cannot be seen wasting my time bantering with you!"

"Sir, you are much too kind," Teophelus said. "All I request is the location of the city administrator's office." The Lycentian officer stared momentarily at the priest then gave his response.

"Such a simple question," he said. "Why didn't you just come out with it sooner?" He sighed and then pointed in the general direction of Franck's house. "There. It's in that direction. Past the eastern temple gate. You can't miss it."

"Past the temple gate? Why, I was just there yesterday!" The Lycentian officer put his hands behind his back.

"Good for you. Now, move along! I have work to do!" he commanded and proceeded to do what he was doing before being so rudely interrupted.

"Thank you, sir! Thank you very much!" The officer nodded but again ventured another short glance in Teophelus' direction. Teophelus thought it best to ignore the man's callousness and chose to continue his visit to the northern market. "And to think that I walked right past Luis' office yesterday on the way to the temple. If only I had been paying closer attention! I could have saved myself that Lycentian eagle coin!"

As he walked, he quickly glanced back at the officer; the Lycentian had not moved an inch from his position on that street corner. Teophelus then turned his head back around just in time to see a cart filled with pots, pans and other metal goods moving very rapidly towards him. He leaped out its path just in time, and landed on a spot of the hard, cobblestone street that was not covered with hard-packed snow. The wagon careened into the side of another wagon which sent the contents of both in all directions. The officer ran to Teophelus and helped him back to his feet.

"Priest, you were about to become the focus of my daily report!" he announced. "And you are more than likely the most physically-skilled Netherene I've ever seen. You jumped out of the way of that runaway cart as if you had been trained to do so! If it had been any other priest, he'd be part of that mess over there!" he added, pointing in the direction of the mangled remains of the two wagons and their goods. As the officer helped Teophelus brush off the street debris, a portly gentleman wearing a leather apron came running up to them.

"I ... I am so ... very ... sorry, officer," he said in between grabbing great gulps of air. "I ... I have no idea ... how it happened ... how my wagon ... broke lose ... from its chain." The Lycentian officer held up his right hand.

"What are you saying there? That runaway cart is yours? If that is so, then you have much explaining to do! This priest was nearly killed because of your negligence!" he scolded. "Quickly now! Tell me your name! This investigation begins this very minute!"

"Sir," Teophelus interrupted. "It is not a problem, sir. As you can readily attest, I am fine ... beyond needing to discard this old coat and find a better one. It is not necessary to – "

"Don't interrupt, priest! This is my jurisdiction! And while I am in charge here, I will determine what is a problem and what is not!" The officer latched onto the back of the vendor's neck. "If you are certain that you are not injured, priest, you are dismissed," he then added as he and the stocky merchant headed for the wreckage. Teophelus removed his overcoat; a large rip below the shoulders appeared to be the extent of the damage. While he examined it, a boy of about twelve ran up to him.

"That's the second accident to occur in the markets in as many days!" he shared.

"What do you mean?" the Noran priest asked as he put on the mangled coat.

"You don't know? You haven't heard about the produce cart that was destroyed yesterday? That cart was hit by a huge stone that had somehow worked itself loose and fallen off the temple courtyard wall! And it almost killed someone!" Teophelus shuddered again, but this time it was from the cold air that had made its way past the coat and through his muslin shirt.

"Yes, I heard about that," he replied after regaining his composure. "But accidents do happen. Yes, they most-assuredly do. But I try not to clutter my mind with accidents."

CHAPTER SIXTEEN

"Othleis has promised to bless those who are contrite, who turn to Him with humility."

That evening Teophelus related to Patrik and Galena a brief and curiously-oblique account of the adventure from earlier that day. The important detail that remained hidden was the true nature of the rip in his overcoat; Galena noticed the damage the moment he entered the house. So to quickly appease her curiosity, he was compelled to create a realistic – and believable – explanation. He told them that he witnessed the crash and was even asked by the Lycentian officer to assist with the clean-up. The rip, he shared with them, occurred as he bent to pick up something out of the wreckage and a nail must have created the hole. As he finished telling that story, details about the close-encounter with the twenty-pound block of quarry-stone barreled into his mind. But he resisted allowing any of them to be spoken. "Why create more curiosity when I would only have to figure out what to reveal and what to keep hidden?" he rationalized.

"Now, dear one, you must give me that coat so it can be mended!" Galena demanded after the evening meal was finished. "We don't want you catching a cold because of a nasty hole, now do we?"

Not much later, the tear was mended, and she proudly presented her handiwork.

"There's a wonderful moon tonight! And not a cloud in the sky to conceal it! What a fantastic evening for an after-dinner stroll!" Galena said enthusiastically. "Since your coat no longer sports a hole the size of a Noran hedge-apple, won't you join me for a little evening walk around the neighborhood?" The innkeeper looked up from the over-stuffed chair and scowled.

"Don't you think it's a bit too cold to go outside? Just to take a walk?" he asked.

"Father! Why do you have to be such a worrier? It's a beautiful winter's evening!" Galena responded. "And we won't be long, now will we, Teophelus dear?" He first looked at Galena, then at the coat, and finally back at Patrik.

"I ... I think we will be going for a walk, sir." he mumbled. "And I do hope it will be a short one." Patrik stood up, groaned in the process, and shuffled towards to the two young people.

"Ha! You kids! Now, be careful out there! And definitely pay attention to the big-city traffic!" Patrik teased. "You don't want to get hit by any runaway wagons." Galena playfully pushed her father aside and grabbed Teophelus' right arm.

"Father! Please!" she exclaimed as she opened the door and pulled Teophelus out of the warm house and into the cold, moonlight-enhanced night air.

The moon was nearly full, and its silvery light was filtered by only a handful of thin, wispy clouds. As the two young people walked slowly down the snow-packed cobblestone street, Galena relinquished her grip on the young priest's arm. Then, the Noran priest cleared his throat.

"So ... why did you make me come out here? I was surrounded by this frigid air most of the day and was almost warmed up when you demanded that I join you for this *walk*," Teophelus complained. Galena stopped and looked up at him; the moonlight revealed the priest's stately chin and high but narrow cheekbones. With her right hand she gently caressed his left cheek.

"We needed a moment to talk," she replied. "In private. And going outside where my father cannot eavesdrop seemed the best place for having a private conversation." Teophelus' took her right hand into his and affectionately squeezed it.

"Othleis!" Teophelus exclaimed, looking up at the moonlit sky. "How could you allow me to become involved with a lady who is full of so much mystery and intrigue?" he prayed. She stepped back and put both hands on her hips.

"I will tell you exactly *how*!" she exclaimed. "I just happen to be the prettiest girl in all Betrovia, that is *how*!"

"And the most-clever as well!" Teophelus added.

"The most-clever? Why, that is the farthest thing from the truth!" she replied. "If I really was so smart, why would I have fallen in love with a vagabond neophyte Netherene priest from a no-account village like Noran?" Teophelus looked down and allowed his lower lip to protrude slightly.

"I am *almost* a full-fledged Netherene," he whispered. "And if it wasn't for having to wait for the high priest's blessing ... I would be a neophyte no more."

"The High Priest? Oliver III? You need Oliver's blessing? You haven't talked about this before," Galena said softly as she glanced up at the moon and then back at Teophelus.

"I have completed every task that the Noran temple has given me. The only thing that needs to happen now – "

"My word, Teophelus! It really doesn't matter, dear," Galena interrupted. "And how did we get on this utterly-boring topic in the first place? We must get back to why I wanted you to come out here!" Teophelus put his hands behind his back and waited for her to continue. "Good," she said. "I finally appear to have your undivided attention." He nodded in agreement. "So tell me: why haven't you kept your promise?" she asked as she stepped closer to him. "Why haven't you talked to Father about us? About *me* becoming your *wife*?" she asked with more than a hint of irritation in her voice. Teophelus slowly shook his head and sighed.

"Yesterday … I tried … when I caught up with him at the temple … I wanted to tell him that …." His voice trailed off as he realized that he was not being entirely truthful. "So many things were running through my mind at the time and – " Galena put up her hands, stepped away from him and began to strut up the snow-covered street.

"Wait!" Teophelus cried out. "Galena! Where are you going?" He ran up to her and grabbed her hand.

"*Walking*," she said sternly, pulling away from him. "I am simply continuing my walk."

"And I am going with you! Even if it means freezing to death!" he retorted. "You did invite me, did you not?" he asked as he again latched onto her right hand.

"And didn't *you* promise that you'd talk to Father about our engagement!" she exclaimed. "What kind of a

Netherene are you if you cannot keep a single, simple promise!"

"But," he said quickly as his mind raced to create just the right response. "But I have kept it!" he finally answered.

"How? How have you kept it? Father has not said a word to me about us getting married!" She sternly pulled her hand out of his and then thumped his chest with a stiff index finger. "You are being completely ridiculous and … and …." She stood there with the cold finger planted directly on his sternum but was at a complete loss for words.

"Galena, sweet, wonderful, *beautiful* Galena … how can … how might I help you understand?" he wisely interjected. "We … your father and I … we were standing right outside the temple door when – "

Something suddenly emerged from out of the moonlight-enhanced shadows and then barreled into the young priest and his bride-to-be, knocking both of them to the snow-covered street. Before Galena pulled herself back up, the interloper had already turned onto the first side-street.

"Teophelus! Get up! Stand up, Teophelus!" she cried out. He did not respond. She knelt down beside him and commenced to shake his body. "Teophelus! Say something! Please tell me that you are alright!" A large sigh exited the young priest's mouth and an even-larger gasp for air followed. But there were no words. Galena then put her hand behind his head but quickly retracted it. "It's warm," she whispered. "This liquid … on my hand … it is warm … it's … it is blood!" she screamed. She then with both hands shook him again. "Teophelus! Wake up! You must wake up! You *have* to wake up!"

"Ga ... Galena?" the Noran priest muttered softly. He coughed again, tried to sit up but fell back down onto the snowy cobblestones.

"Teophelus, you're alive! Thank you, Othleis, thank you!" she said.

"My head," he said. "It hurts ... it feels like it is about to explode ..."

"Bleeding," Galena added. "It is bleeding. Your head must have hit a bare spot on the street. Can you try to stand up?"

"Help me, Galena ... I will ... I will try if ... if you will help me." He put out both hands, and she grabbed them. It took a few seconds, but she was finally able to get him to his feet. Just as he was about to stumble and fall over again, she quickly propped him up by putting his left arm over her shoulder and shuffling her feet to get the best footing possible on the slick surface.

"There," she said. "Lean on me while we walk back to Uncle Franck's house. Father will know how to take care of that gash." But before they had traversed even a block, Teophelus collapsed, causing Galena to nearly fall backwards.

"Ugh," she complained as she let him down as gently as she could in the middle of the street. "Teophelus ... what just happened to us? What has happened to you?" she whispered as she leaned over and kissed him on the forehead. He was unconscious for only a few seconds before his eyes re-opened.

"Galena, it ... it is so cold ... I am so cold .... "

"Don't try to talk ... don't say anything else," she commanded. "Can you try to stand up again? Your head ... it is bleeding so badly, and we must – "

"Galena! I ... I must tell you something." This time, Teophelus stood up on his own, his body swayed once, twice and then a third time but then nearly fell backwards. Galena got behind him which prevented him from slamming again onto the street. She allowed his body to sag down. The young priest coughed another time.

"Tell me *what*, dear one?" She motioned that she wanted to pull him back up onto his feet, but he shook his head.

"That day in the forest ... Dridel ... in that abandoned cabin ... that old priest Dridel ..."

"What forest? Cabin? I have no idea what you are talking about! Try not to say anything else! We must get back to Uncle Franck's house and to Father!"

It only took a few minutes for Patrik to fall fast asleep in Franck's over-stuffed chair, and he was still there when Galena opened the front door. "You're finally back inside! Glad to see that ... Teophelus? What is this? What ... what has happened?"

"Some crazy person on a horse ... came out of nowhere and ran into us ... ran into both of us," Galena replied.

"Are you hurt?" the innkeeper asked.

"I am fine ... only a few bruises ... but Teophelus ... the back of his head." She could no longer hold back the tears. Patrik took Teophelus from his distraught daughter and guided him to the couch.

"Galena! The back of your coat! It … it is covered with …with something … it looks like … blood?!" Patrik exclaimed.

"Teophelus! It is his blood. He must have hit his head on the street. It has been bleeding the entire time," she replied through her sniffles and controlled sobs.

"My head …" Teophelus mumbled softly. "It hurts … I cannot … I need …." Galena knelt close to him.

"Don't talk. You must rest. Try to get some rest," she commanded as she wiped away some tears with her sleeve.

"Is the wound still bleeding?" Patrik asked.

"I'm not sure," she replied. Patrik then walked over to the young priest and coerced him to sit up.

"His hair is badly matted back here, but I don't think his head is bleeding now," Patrik said. "Strange, though," he continued. "This wound … and I am no expert in head wounds even after dealing with that nasty one on the back of your head … but it does not appear to have been caused by his head hitting the street. It is much too … jagged." Patrik stood back up and scratched his head. "Peculiar … very strange indeed," he added.

Galena then excused herself to change out of the blood-stained clothes while Patrik agreed to monitor the semi-conscious young priest's condition. The innkeeper was in the over-stuffed chair and had nearly fallen asleep again when she returned to the sitting room. "Has he said anything?" she asked as she knelt beside him. She then touched his forehead but quickly pulled it back. "Oh my," she whispered, "Now he is feverish."

"No, and I haven't encouraged him to say anything," Patrik yawned loudly and then replied. "He awoke only once, said the word *Dridel*, and then he was quiet again."

Patrik replied. "And that wound … it still perplexes me," he added. "So you said that a man on a horse rode up to you and – "

"Father, don't you ever pay attention to anything I say?" Galena interrupted. "The horse ran *into* us and kept going! It was like he didn't even know we were there!"

"Uhhhhh," Teophelus moaned.

"Teophelus! You're awake!" Galena exclaimed. "How do you feel?"

"My head … it still pounds with pain … and … and everything is so blurry. I can … barely see you, Galena," he muttered. Patrik stood up, yawned, stretched and then walked over to the couch.

"How many fingers do you see?" he asked as he held up three.

"Two? Three? Five? I cannot tell. Patrik, sir, my eyesight has been … quite poor as of late," he responded. "Galena, what happened? Why does my head hurt like it does?"

"Someone on a horse tried to run us over! That is what happened!" she replied. Teophelus groaned but was able to force himself to sit up.

"I … I have to … I must … tell you," he stuttered. "Yesterday … the accident … yesterday … in the market." He laid back down onto the couch before continuing. "I must confess … I was … I was not completely truthful with you … about that wagon. It nearly … the wagon nearly ran over me."

"The wagon?" Galena exclaimed. "It did what? Why didn't you tell us the truth to begin with?" She demanded. Teophelus took a deep breath, coughed and pushed himself back up.

"I didn't tell you the truth," he paused, breathed deeply again, and coughed yet again. "Because I did … did not want … I did not want you to … to worry."

"Teophelus! This is beginning to make sense now!" Patrik exclaimed. "The rip in your overcoat, the jagged gash on the back of your head – "

"And the … the stone … the stone that fell … that fell from the temple … the temple courtyard's wall," Teophelus interrupted. He then disclosed the truth concerning his adventures in both markets; he told them everything just as it had happened.

"If I could even begin to imagine it, it looks like someone could be trying to kill you," Galena announced. "No, I take that back! Someone *is* trying to kill you! This is horrible, simply horrible! You have to leave! You must leave Lycentia! Immediately! You are in danger here! You must leave now! Oh, Teophelus, what have you done? What could you have done?" She whimpered and tears began to fall again as she knelt beside him. "Why would anyone want *you* dead?" she whispered.

"Leaving Lycentia," the priest said almost too softly, "Running away from the capital city … is exactly what the Lycentian Netherenes want me to do. Yesterday at the temple … they told us to leave … they said that Oliver … that he wants to have nothing to do with Harrak's scrolls." He then said, looking at the innkeeper, "Patrik sir, if the Netherenes … if they are trying to get rid of me … then your life … it must be in danger as well." Patrik thrust his hands into the air and laughed.

"My life? In danger? I cannot believe a word of it! I also refuse to believe that the Netherenes are trying to do you harm. It must be someone else … someone you offended or insulted or ...." The innkeeper's voice trailed off as he returned to his favorite chair and plopped down into it. "I must take time to ponder this," he mumbled. Galena stared at her father as he rubbed his white-haired covered chin. Then she looked back at the young man on the couch.

"Teophelus has never offended or harmed anyone! Nor has he ever even attempted to do so! Have you, dear?" she asked, glaring at him. "Well, have you?" she repeated with irritation in her voice.

"From the day I began ... I began my training to become a priest, I was aware that the Creator ... has protected me," Teophelus said. "He protected me years ago that day when a terrible fever ... when that fever brought me right up to death's door. And then ... then yesterday in the southern market ... and this morning in the northern market. Even though my head is throbbing ... it is throbbing so badly that I can barely think, I ... I am still alive." He took in another deep breath. "Othleis the Creator of all there is ... He is my protector and my shield. He has appointed me to ...." He coughed and laid back down. "The Creator has told me ... he has assigned me to stay the course to help Patrik ... to assist him to deliver the scrolls." The Noran neophyte priest then collapsed before he could finish his sentence.

"Father! Are you hearing this nonsense! It's those ridiculous scrolls! It is their fault! This would not have happened if it wasn't for them!" she screamed. "Destroy them! Take them outside and burn them! Destroy them this very instant!" She frantically searched the room as if she hoped to find them sitting out in the open. "Where is that pouch? Where are those stupid parchments!"

"No, Galena, no!" Teophelus commanded from the couch. "The scrolls ... they are not the ... the problem. They are the solution! Patrik sir, you must tell her ... please explain to her."

"The scrolls will not be burned. They will not be destroyed," Patrik replied. "Galena, you have to understand! What Harrak wrote ... those scrolls ... they are anointed by the Creator. They are certainly not the problem. Those stubborn and *dogmatic* Netherenes that rule from their golden tower here in Lycentia ... *they* are the problem and – "

"Galena, come here!" Teophelus interrupted. "Would you ... come over here ... now?"

"What? Teophelus! Oh, yes, yes, I am here! I am here!" she exclaimed as she once again ran and knelt at his side.

"You burning the scrolls ... destroying Harrak's prophecies ... would be a ... a monstrous act ... an act very much out of character for my ... my bride-to-be."

"Teophelus! You ... you said it! You remembered! Oh, Father! He remembered! Did you hear it? Did you hear what he said?" she asked as she bent over and wrapped her arms around the groggy priest. Teophelus reciprocated, putting his arms around her and squeezing her tightly. Then his eyes fluttered, his arms fell, and he faded away.

"Yes, Galena, yes," Patrik said. "I heard it. And I am not at all surprised that he asked you to marry him," he said."More than a year ago, the young man and I talked in detail about his plans ... his plans for you and him," he then added. The innkeeper then walked over to the couch and put his right hand on his younger daughter's strawberry-blond head and softly began to pray.

"Where have you been?" Kristof asked as Dalten suddenly entered the dark cabin. "You said you were going to the village to buy us something to eat. And that was hours ago!" Dalten took off his coat, stomped his boots to remove the remainder of the snow from them, and sat down at the small table.

"I went to the city," he replied, staring at the floor. "I went back to Lycentia."

"Back to the city? Why? And how? In this weather? You could not have walked to Lycentia – "

"I stole a horse from the stable," Dalten interrupted. "And with that horse I rode to that old merchant's house. And then I waited."

"What?!" Kristof exclaimed, throwing his hands into the air. "We didn't talk about going back into the city! *It is too dangerous*, you said just this morning! *We must be very careful from now on*, you specifically told me! We tried twice to make it look like an accident! Two times in the last two days! And just this morning you said – " Dalten jumped out of the chair and pointed at the former stable-hand.

"Don't you start in on me, Kristof! He would have already been dead! Dead, I tell you! Our mission would have been accomplished by that rock splitting his asinine skull if you had pushed it the moment I told you!"

"No, No! If it had fallen when *you* wanted it to, it would have landed on that vendor instead! Why are you trying to blame me again for that?" Dalten shook his head.

"There is no point in arguing about that now, Kristof," he said. "It matters not what happened in the south city market yesterday," he said as he sat back down. "Nor does it matter that this morning Teophelus somehow dodged that wagon in the north market. What matters now …." Dalten paused and looked at Kristof. "What matters now is that he is dead." Dalten glared at the slightly-taller but thinner former militiaman.

"What did you do? How did you kill him?!" Kristof shouted.

"It was quite simple, actually," he calmly replied. "I merely rode up to them and then hit him across the back of the head."

"You hit him … wait … you said *them*. What do you mean by *them*?" he asked.

"She … she was with him … *Galena*," Dalten nearly whispered.

"Dalten! Are you insane?!" Kristof was livid. "Now we definitely are in serious trouble! What has gotten into your sick, deluded – "

"Shut up!" Dalten commanded. "Just shut up! I knew exactly how I wanted to do this, and it happened exactly how I had planned it!" He then walked over to his coat and pulled out of it a thin but sturdy iron bar. He grasped the bar like a club and then explained how, from out of the shadows, he swiftly rode up to them and then smacked Teophelus on the back of the head with the bar. He then said that he simultaneously guided the horse into Galena to knock her to the street to keep her from seeing what had happened to Teophelus.

"Is she alright? Tell me that you did not kill her, too!" Kristof demanded.

"By now you must know that I lack nothing when it comes to riding a horse!" Dalten replied as he pointed the bar at Kristof like it was a saber.

"But it was a horse that you stole! A horse that you have never ridden! I cannot believe that you – "

"You must believe that it happened just as I have explained it," Dalten interrupted. "And you will believe it! Allow me to clarify: I tied the horse up to a tree not far from where they fell onto the street. I then secretly watched as Galena helped him get up and take him back to the merchant's house." Kristof laughed again, but this time it was a dry, unsettling guffaw.

"So, the priest is certainly dead, is he?" he mocked. "You hit the priest hard enough to kill him, you did? So how did Galena – a girl nearly a foot shorter and as much as fifty pounds lighter – take him back to the house? Don't tell me! I know how! She screamed for help, and you stepped out of the darkness to help her! You became her hero for the night, didn't you?! That is how!" Dalten again pointed the bar at Kristof and this time slowly waved it back and forth.

"By now, that priest is *dead*! By now he must be!" Dalten responded. "Like I told you, I hit him *hard* with this bar! It is not possible that his brain could recuperate from such a mighty blow! It is definitely not possible!" Kristof suddenly lurched forward and latched onto the other end of the rod, consequently pulling it out of Dalten's hand.

"Yes, this does feel like it could be used to harm someone … to hit someone over the head … to knock someone senseless … maybe even to kill someone!"

"Give that back to me, Kristof!" Dalten demanded. "Don't think about doing anything with that except putting it right back into my hand!"

"This piece of iron ... this crude weapon ... it has been used to completely ruin my life! I am now better off dead than alive! Teophelus was supposed to die! He was supposed to be the only one killed in Lycentia! Oh yes, that is why we are here! That is why we are in this filthy hut and not in a warm and comfortable hostel somewhere in the city! Oh yes, we are no longer assassins! No, not in the least! We are now nothing but common street thugs! Common murderers!" Kristof then pointed the iron rod at Dalten. "No, I retract that. You! *You* are the murderer! That's right, Dalten! You heard me! A murderer! And I call you *murderer* for plotting to kill not one but two people! Your trial is now underway! And I am your judge! Oh yes, it is true, Dalten Molic of Noran, you are on trial! And guess what? Your trial has now come to an end! Have you heard the verdict yet? Here is the verdict! Guilty! Guilty, I say! You have been judged guilty! And do you know the punishment for your crime?" Dalten shook his head.

"Kristof, put down the iron bar and listen to me," he said softly but sternly.

"I am your judge! And I command you to say nothing more! Your trial has ended! Your life is now mine to do what I choose with it! And I now choose to pronounce your sentence! And might you even be able to guess what your sentence might be? Why, it is death! Ha! What a perfect sentence for such a senseless crime! I sentence you to death. Dalten Molic! Death!" Kristof proclaimed.

He then swung the bar at Dalten's head, and he nearly hit it. But the young man adroitly stuck up his left arm and deflected the blow. "Kristof! You cannot be serious! Put that thing down and listen to reason!" Dalten commanded as he swerved to miss another wild swing.

"No! *You* listen to *me*, Dalten Molic! This was supposed to look like an accident! An accident, I tell you! And what do you do? You take off into the night! You were not truthful with me about your plans! You decided to take matters into your own hands and look at what happened!" Kristof exclaimed as the bar again careened off Dalten's arm when it was aimed once again at his head. "You destroyed the mission! You completely destroyed my life! Argh!" Kristof took another swing. This time he was successful. The iron bar connected satisfactorily with his partner's skull. Dalten howled in pain, grabbed his head with both hands and then somehow managed to open the cabin door and stumble outside into the frosty, moonlit night.

Kristof stood at the door and watched as his former partner and the sole heir of the Molic fortune ran down the snow-covered road. He then held up the bar and glared at it.

"Blood," he whispered. "There's fresh blood on this thing. Good. Fresh blood is good. It is a very good thing."

INTERACT WITH
THE LAND OF BETROVIA!

Keep up with and even "like" *The Land of Betrovia* trilogy on Facebook!
    Betrovia – book one (published Fall 2011)
    Lycentia: Harrak's Scrolls – book two (the one you are reading right now!)
    Ahnak: Edelin's Revelation – book three (early Summer 2013)

It would be great if you would post a review of Lycentia: Harrak's Scrolls on Amazon, Goodreads, Shelfari, etc.!

Please send your comments, questions and even suggestions about *The Land of Betrovia* to
dave@betrovia.com

Made in the USA
Charleston, SC
23 August 2012